The Solitary Envoy

"LIFE BRINGS MANY CHANGES, BOTH ON THE PERSONAL LEVEL AND TO CHARACTERS IN THE PAGES OF NOVELS WE HAVE READ. I AM EXCITED TO SEE DAVIS AND ISABELLA'S CLOSE PARTNERSHIP NOW EXTEND INTO CRAFTING THE SOLITARY ENVOY. THEY HAVE MOVED THE ACADIAN SAGA FORWARD A GENERATION TO CONTINUE THE FASCINATING STORY OF A NEW NATION BEING FORMED AND NEW RELATIONSHIPS FORGED."

—JANETTE OKE

HEIRS OF ACADIA

-ONE-

T. DAVIS BUNN
&
ISABELLA BUNN

The Solitary Envoy

BETHANY HOUSE
Minneapolis, Minnesota

The Solitary Envoy
Copyright © 2004
T. Davis Bunn and Isabella Bunn

Cover photograph by Claudia Kunin

Published by Bethany House Publishers
11400 Hampshire Avenue South
Bloomington, Minnesota 55438
www.bethanyhouse.com

Bethany House Publishers is a Division of
Baker Book House Company, Grand Rapids, Michigan.

Printed in the United States of America

ISBN 0-7642-2857-9 (Trade Paper)
ISBN 0-7642-2862-5 (Hardcover)
ISBN 0-7642-2861-7 (Large Print)
ISBN 0-7642-2863-3 (Audio)

Library of Congress Cataloging-in-Publication Data

Bunn, T. Davis, 1952-
   The solitary envoy / by T. Davis Bunn & Isabella Bunn.
      p.   cm. — (Heirs of Acadia ; 1)
   ISBN 0-7642-2862-5 (alk. paper) — ISBN 0-7642-2857-9 (pbk.)   1. United States—History—War of 1812—Fiction.   2. Women—Washington (D.C.)—Fiction.
3. Americans—England—Fiction.   4. Washington (D.C.)—Fiction.   5. Acadians—Fiction.   I. Bunn, Isabella.   II. Title.   III. Series: Bunn, T. Davis, 1952-   . Heirs of Acadia ; 1.

   PS3552.U4718S65   2004
   813'.54—dc22   2003021806

FOR JANETTE AND EDWARD OKE

We join countless readers and students
in gratitude for affirming our faith and
inspiring our imaginations.

T. DAVIS BUNN is an award-winning author whose growing list of novels demonstrates the scope and diversity of his writing talent.

ISABELLA BUNN has been a vital part of his writing success; her research and attention to detail have left their imprint on nearly every story. Their life abroad has provided much inspiration and information for plots and settings. They live near Oxford, England.

By T. Davis Bunn

*with Janette Oke   †with Isabella Bunn

PART
ONE

Chapter 1

As with every morning, Erica was the first to enter her father's office. Her mother insisted upon calling it the library, but library was too fancy a word in Erica's mind. Not that the room wasn't lovely. Just entering it gave her a little thrill. She walked down the long line of high windows, sweeping back the heavy drapes. Sounds of the exhilarating world outside entered with the brilliant May sunshine. Erica paused by the last window, the one whose light spilled onto her father's desk, and felt a rush of delight. She never tired of this view. But that was not all that made her happy on this day.

The Langston home occupied the highest hill in the village of Georgetown, which was also the closest point to the new government structures rising further along the Potomac River. Erica could just make out the armory and the Capitol in the distance. The president's official residence was finished. The Continental Congress had been renamed the United States Congress and had its own new building. Even so, further north there was still some argument over whether this new city of Washington should be called the nation's capital. The critics asserted the capital should be located in a city with more history. Some said New York, others Philadelphia, and the loudest of all declared it must be Boston. Erica's family came from the Massachusetts colony; she had as much right as any to disagree. The truth was, all those northern towns had *foreign* history.

They were founded back when America was still a collection of British colonies. But here in this year of our Lord 1812, America was its own nation. And America needed its own capital. Anyone who stood at this wall of windows and watched the town awaken to another glorious day could see that Washington was the heart of this great new country.

The office's other three walls were covered in paneling and lined with glass-fronted shelves. The floor was mahogany planking, brought up from Brazil on one of her father's ships. Whale-oil lamps gleamed from the walls and hung from the ceiling. Above the shelves were paintings her father had commissioned, four in all, one of each of the merchant ships his company operated. And soon there would be a fifth ship, the first her family would own outright. All the others were owned with other investors. Ships were frightfully expensive things, as Erica well knew. But her father said it was time for them to strike out on their own. And Forrest Langston was never wrong.

There was a space on the wall ready to receive the new painting. The previous week, her mother had removed the portrait of her own father to make room for the new vessel. This fifth ship was one of the new clipper designs. Her hull had been laid in New Haven the previous summer. She was to be called the *Erica,* and Father said she would make their fortune. But not even that accounted for Erica's excitement this morning.

She moved to her father's desk. It was made of imported African stinkwood and was gigantic, larger than Erica's bed. Father called it the only ship he would ever captain. Erica and Carter, her father's chief clerk, were the only two people permitted to touch it.

Carter was older even than her father and had been with the family forever, as far as Erica knew. He had a steel trap of a mind and was Father's right hand, loyal to the core and entrusted with every detail of the company's affairs. But at the moment Carter was away with her father, so the task now rested in Erica's hands. It was a responsibility of which she was particularly proud.

Erica placed the ledgers front and center on the desk. Beside them was the correspondence she had already separated into two careful piles. The larger was from the interior, as everything west of Washington was known. The second pile was correspondence from their partners and clients in other nations, arriving on the ships calling at Annapolis or Baltimore or Norfolk or even New York and brought down by coach. This second pile was quite small for representing almost a month's mail, which was worrisome indeed.

Even more alarming was the collection of newspapers and pamphlets stacked upon the desk's right-hand corner. Erica tried hard not to look in that direction. But despite her best efforts, her eye was caught by the top broadsheet, a London paper dated six weeks earlier. The news was far from good.

"Erica?"

She started as though she had been caught doing wrong. "Yes, Mama?"

"Child, I do hope you are dressed."

"Of course I am, Mama."

"Come and let me have a look at you."

Erica was already crossing the carpeted expanse. Beyond the doorway to her father's office was Carter's office. Beyond that was a parlor used for business meetings. A tiny table was nestled up close to the parlor's only window. Erica felt another thrill of joy pass through her when she saw it. Then her gaze darted away, for her mother was standing just inside the parlor and was watching her closely. Erica dropped a curtsy. "Good morning, Mama."

But she could tell that her mother had caught the look and was now frowning over its cause. There had been numerous discussions between Erica's mother and father over that little table and what it represented. Thankfully, Erica's mother was apparently choosing not to say anything just then.

"Child, why are you not wearing your lovely new frock?"

"This is Father's favorite dress."

Mildred Harrow Goodwind Langston was a woman of rather stern bearing. Her parents, Nicole and Gordon Goodwind, had held a large estate in Western Massachusetts, and she had received a considerable inheritance when they had gone to their eternal reward. Mildred's great uncle, Charles Harrow, was a titled landowner in England until his death. Erica thought her mother tended to place far more importance on wealth and position than her actual heritage warranted, but she did not speak her mind. What little Erica knew about England left her unsettled. England had gone to war with her beloved America to keep it a colony. England now barred America from trading directly with France and Spain, with whom England was still in conflict. England's blockades delayed her father's ships and charged ridiculous tariffs to cross the high seas. Erica had many reasons to dislike England.

But Erica's mother set great store by her connection to this Harrow family. No matter that Grandmother Nicole had died when Erica had been only five, nor that she had never met Great Aunt Anne. Her mother loved to mention oh-so-casually to her guests that she was fourth in line to some fortune that did not even exist anymore. Erica loved her mother very much. But she was her father's daughter. Everyone said so.

"Child, your father is not due back until this afternoon at the earliest." She regarded her only daughter with a worried expression. "You really mustn't let yourself be disappointed if he is delayed. You know—"

"What time are we expected to join Mrs. Simmons?"

"Eleven o'clock, as you well know. And please don't interrupt." Despite having birthed four children, two of whom were lost in infancy, Mildred Langston was still a most attractive woman. She held herself erect, dressed well, and was known far and wide as a hostess of considerable standing. Politicians and merchants alike vied for the chance to be a part of her social set. "Your father will do everything in his power to be here for your birthday celebration. But times being what they are, you must understand if he is delayed."

Erica lifted her chin, as she had often seen her mother do when confronted with something she did not care to accept. But the act did not help. Erica could not bear the thought of Father not being home, today of all days. She tried but could not completely erase the tremor from her voice. "But he *promised.*"

"He promised to *try.*"

"But he's been gone almost a month!"

"As I know all too well." A trace of her mother's own apparent worry showed through. "I have not heard from him in eight days now. And you know it is his custom to write me three times a week."

"Surely nothing—"

"No, everything is fine. While at tea yesterday at the Mooreheads', I met a banker from Philadelphia. He traveled on the same coach as your father five days ago and said he was in fine fettle. No, it is just . . ."

"Just what?" Erica encouraged.

Mildred crossed her arms. "Just that we must wait and see. Now please turn around."

Erica sighed and did as she was told.

"Who did your hair?"

Erica reached up to the collection of decorative hairpins, fearing that something had come undone. Her hair was dark and so thick she could hardly run a comb through it. Others called it luxurious, but Erica considered it a bother and kept it long only because her mother insisted. It was always threatening to tumble down, no matter how carefully she pinned it. But today everything felt in its proper place. "I did, Mama."

"It is quite . . . remarkable."

"It's called the French weave. I saw it in one of the journals from Paris." She turned back around and caught sight of her mother's face. "Whatever is the matter?"

Her mother's normal reserve seemed shaken. "You are growing up."

"I'm seventeen, Mama." That very day, in fact.

"Of course you are. But saying the words and accepting the fact with my own eyes are two entirely different matters." She smiled then. Mildred Langston's smiles were rare events, which was a great pity. They were luminous, transforming her features and making her look more like an older sister than a mother. "You are every bit as lovely as they say, daughter."

"As who says?"

"Never you mind. I won't have your head swollen with coffeehouse chatter. Now give your aging mother a hug."

Erica let herself be enveloped by her mother's arms. For some reason the closeness left her feeling sad, perhaps even a little frightened. "You're not old, Mama."

"If I am to have a daughter finishing her seventeenth year and every inch an adult, I most certainly am that. Possibly even ancient. But enough of that. Have you had your breakfast?"

"Not yet. I was just on my way down."

"Well, you'd best hurry along then. We can't be late—" Mildred was interrupted by a great thumping sound that became louder with each passing moment. "What on earth is that?"

Erica followed her mother back through Carter's office and into her father's chamber. The rear entrance, the one that led down the passage to the main warehouse, was shoved open. In came her brother and a warehouse worker, carrying something heavy between them.

"Top of the morning to you both!" Reginald Langston was tall for his age of fifteen and a half, with his father's build and personality both. Reggie greeted the entire world with one great smile. "Where do we drop this?"

Erica saw what it was they carried, and her hand flew up to her mouth. She could not speak.

"Quick now, else I'll just heave it through the window!"

Erica forced herself forward. The light played across the

16

surface of her brother's burden like oil upon gold. "It's the most beautiful thing I've ever seen."

Reggie laughed heartily. "Brazilian rosewood. Father ordered it up special. Been sitting down in the warehouse for months, stowed back behind a pile of jute where not even my nosy sister could spy it."

"Father had this built for me?"

"Fashioned by the finest cabinetmaker in all Washington. He called it his signature piece, whatever that means. Quick now, my grip is slipping."

"Let's see . . . how about over there, by the far window." Turning around meant seeing her mother's disapproval. Erica was only too well aware that Mildred was not at peace with this particular development. But her father had prevailed, and Erica hoped the discussions were behind them. Seeing her mother now, with a frown creasing her forehead, she steeled herself for more objections.

But her mother only turned and said, "Five minutes, Erica. No more. Then I want you downstairs in the kitchen with a bowl of hot porridge."

"Yes, Mama."

"We can't be late. Especially not today." She turned and left the room.

Reggie said nothing more until the two had deposited the desk beneath the tall window. "Sorry. I didn't know she was here."

Erica ran her hand over the surface as the warehouse worker turned and left. "It is most exquisite."

"It's called a secretary. French in design. A woman's writing desk." Reggie took a rag out of his rear pocket and gave it a quick rub. "Father made me promise to bring it up personally if he wasn't back in time."

Erica hugged him tightly but could not take her eyes off the desk. "You are the best brother in the whole world."

"Certainly, but you're the odd one. Never knew anybody could be so excited over a place to work."

17

"I'm thrilled, Reggie, as you well know."

"Yes, I do know." Reggie was far from being a lazy young man. When not in school he worked long hours in the family warehouses. "And I am glad of it. You know I've no head for this kind of thing."

"Neither does Father. But he does well enough."

"Aye, but I don't have to, do I?" He gave her a friendly push. "I've got you to do it all for me."

"No, you don't. You have to learn all this yourself. How else . . ." Then she caught his smile and knew he was jesting. She turned back to the desk. "Isn't it the most glorious thing you've ever seen?"

"It's just a desk, sister. But I'm glad you're pleased." He hugged her. "Happy birthday."

But Reggie was wrong. It wasn't just a desk. It was a future. "Thank you, Reggie. Thank you so very much."

"Erica!"

"Coming, Mother!" She hurried downstairs to the kitchen.

Mildred Langston considered Erica's fascination with business an unfitting preoccupation for a young lady and put up with it only at her husband's insistence. Erica knew this and did her best to be a proper young lady in polite society—which today meant having a boring old tea with boring old Mrs. Simmons. And on her birthday, of all days.

But today she would sit through it and smile politely and pretend to be interested in the latest gossip. Because starting that very week, she was moving from the tiny table in the upstairs parlor to her own desk in her father's office, where she would watch and learn and be involved.

Father had to be home for her birthday banquet that evening. He *had* to.

Chapter 2

Every time Erica passed the fireplace, she paused to look at the ticking mantel clock. The sun had just set and the lamp-lighters were making their rounds. Her father said traveling at night was a recipe for disaster and forbade his wife to go anywhere without one of the housemen traveling ahead and another riding upon the carriage's rear station. Sometimes his natural caution was exasperating.

"Miss Erica, I have searched for you everywhere."

She fastened on her most winning smile, but not for the young man. She knew her mother was watching. Horace Cutter came from one of Washington's finest families. His father was a merchant and a builder; his mother vied with Mildred for the premier ranks of Washington society. The Cutters were also landowners, with an estate just east of Harpers Ferry.

"Horace, what a strange thing for you to say. I have been glued to this very spot all evening."

Mildred Langston liked the idea of having Horace within her family. But she took her Christian morals very seriously, and not even the prospect of such an advantageous match would make her lie. And the truth was, Horace was a man uncomfortable within his own skin. Mildred described him as "a man of uneven countenance."

Now Horace blushed under the power of Erica's smile. He pulled at his collar and tugged at one earlobe . . . and there was quite a lot of ear to tug upon. He had reddish hair and a freckled complexion, and though he was twenty-two, he looked sixteen.

And he was hopelessly in love with Erica Langston.

Not even the most fashionably cut evening wear could hide the way his larynx protruded. "I was hoping to ask you to dance," he said.

Erica's peal of laughter drew smiles from most of those within the parlor. Only her mother did not share in the gaiety, and she frowned her daughter a warning. Which was why Erica allowed her hand to rest upon Horace's arm, as though they shared a delicious jest. "You dear sweet man, we are here to dine and not to dance."

"But it is your birthday. Surely you will have music."

"Music, of course. But it will be Miss Adelaide singing while I accompany her on the pianoforte."

Horace looked so disappointed at the news she had no choice but to add, "Had there been dancing, I assure you I would have looked forward most eagerly to our moment upon the floor."

While Horace stammered over his reply, Erica glanced out the parlor's front window. The street remained dark and empty. Had she been alone, she would have stamped her foot in vexation. As it was, the only sign of her distress was the loss of her smile.

With the room's light behind her, Erica's reflection in the window was almost as clear as it would have been in a mirror. Her height was accented by the graceful posture she had inherited from her mother. In fact, almost everything about her physical form was her mother's. Her long brown hair was just one shade off black. Her eyes were also dark and somewhat slanted at the edges. "Frenchified" was how one male admirer described them, to Erica's secret delight.

She still wore the dress she had donned that morning, the one her father had imported from Paris. It was canary yellow, fashioned from Chinese silk, with ivory trim and tiny whalebone buttons that ran all the way from hem to neckline. In the flickering light they glowed like the pearls wound about her neck. The French had designed an entire wardrobe based on the idea that modern ladies were far too busy to change between afternoon tea and evening dinner parties. "Modern daywear" was how the illustrated journals described such outfits. Her mother called the concept utter nonsense. For Erica, something both French and modern suited her wonderfully.

"I fear I have lost you yet again, Miss Erica."

She forced her attention away from the window. "Forgive me, Master Horace. I was just hoping my father would still arrive in time to join us."

"It is well known that Mr. Langston doesn't travel at night."

"But it is my birthday!" Erica turned her back so that she did not have to endure her mother's frown. "I know that sounds petty. But I so wished to have him here."

"You two are very close," Horace said. "It is an admirable quality, I suppose. Yet my father—" He hesitated.

"No, go on."

"I do not mean to be indiscreet."

"What you have started you must complete." It was one of Father's favorite expressions.

Horace blushed again. "My father merely expressed concern over how much you are involved in your family's affairs."

"Your father wishes I were more ladylike, is that it?"

"He did not say that."

"No, but that is what he meant." Erica remained standing with her back to the room and the other guests. "Ever since your father's heart began troubling him, you have shouldered much of the family business. How old were you at the time?"

"Nineteen. But I am a man, Miss Erica."

"Yes, I am well aware of that convenience." Disappointment over her father's absence caused her to speak more plainly than before. "For three years now I have kept the family ledgers."

"You?"

"None other. My handwriting is the most precise in Washington. Those are Father's very words. I can do sums more swiftly than Carter, who has been in my father's service for centuries, or so it seems. What is more, I do them in my head. We walk through the warehouses together, my father and I, and I keep track of the figures as we go and give them back to my father whenever he wishes."

Horace clearly had no measuring point against which to gauge this news. "But, Miss Erica—"

"Permit me to finish. For my birthday, he has given me my very own writing desk in his private office. I am to help Carter with Father's correspondence and aid in preparing manifests. That is all we have spoken of with my mother, who is already opposed to this venture. What she does not know is that my father wants me in his office because he is preparing me. I am to observe him at work, in private and in meetings. Do you understand what I am saying, Horace? He is giving me the chance to arrange shipments of my own."

Giving voice to the thoughts and desires she had carried so long in her heart left her unable to remain still. Erica reached out a hand a second time, only now it was in entreaty. "Horace Cutter, do you truly wish to pay suit to me?"

He looked down at the hand gripping his arm. "More than anything in this world."

"Then offer me my heart's longing. Accept that I wish to become a woman of affairs. Agree to let me be a merchant in my own right. The manager of—"

"Master Cutter, you must please forgive me."

"Mother!" Erica dropped her hand in alarm, frightened at her mother's unseen approach. "I was just—"

"I fear Master Cutter has forgotten there are other guests who would wish to offer their birthday greetings." Her mother's icy tone was nothing compared to the steel in her gaze. "You must please excuse us if I take my daughter away momentarily."

Horace gave a short bow. "Of course, Mrs. Langston."

"Come, daughter."

Erica swallowed hard and slipped in docilely behind her mother. She should never have spoken as openly as she had. A single glance at her mother's face was enough to be certain she had heard. Oh yes. Mildred Langston had heard far too much.

At that moment the front door boomed open, and the most wonderful voice Erica knew called out, "Where is my darling lass?"

"Father!"

"Where is my special girl?"

"You came!" In her haste, Erica almost knocked over a slender-legged side table. Thankfully a guest managed to catch the crystal lamp before it spilled oil all over the carpet.

Erica flew out of the parlor and down the hallway to her father, who stood by the open door with arms outstretched. "I was so afraid you would not arrive in time!"

"Heaven and earth could not stand between me and my daughter's very own birthday banquet!" He enveloped her in his strength and the smell she loved most in all the world, cigar smoke and horses and the spicy bay rum he used upon his face. "Happy birthday, my sweet."

"Thank you, Father. Oh, thank you."

Forrest Langston was a burly man with a wide chest and so tall his daughter scarcely reached his shoulder. He wore fashionable muttonchop sideburns, which only accentuated the breadth of his features. "Where is your brother?"

"Reggie's gone to escort Mrs. Burke home. Her husband has been taken ill."

"That's a good lad." He beamed at his daughter, then turned his affection to his wife, who stood quietly to one side. "And here is my other darling. Hello, my dear."

"You came after all." Mildred Langston offered her husband a cheek to peck. "I will instruct Cook to set another place at the table."

Forrest Langston showed genuine disappointment. "Your husband returns from a month of dusty roads and hard work, and this is all the greeting he receives?"

Mildred spoke demurely. "We have guests, Forrest."

"Indeed we do. And this is a gala occasion. Even so, I

would expect a bit more warmth at my homecoming."

The hard glint in Mildred's gaze and voice did not abate. "Your daughter was just relating to young Master Cutter plans I had not been party to."

"Ah." Forrest gave a slow nod. "Things are now becoming clear."

"Things to which I would most certainly never give my approval." Only the presence of guests in the next room kept her voice from rising. "Things that I most heartily dislike. Now if you will both excuse me, I have guests to whom I must attend."

Erica did not release her breath until her mother vanished into the parlor. "I'm so sorry, Father."

"Aye, well, it had to come out sooner or later." He did his best to offer up a warm smile. "I might have preferred a different timing, is all."

There came a light tap on the open door behind them. "Begging your pardon, Mr. Langston."

"What is it, Carter?"

"Evening, Miss Langston. And a very happy birthday, I'm sure."

"Thank you, Carter. How was your journey?"

"Long, miss. Very long indeed." And the old man did look most weary. "Sorry, sir. But Mr. Bartholomew, the gentleman who shared our carriage, is most persistent."

"Is he?"

"Indeed so, sir. Mr. Bartholomew insists upon having a final word."

"One word is all he'll have."

Erica detected the change in her father's tone. "What is it, Father?"

"Never you mind, my dear." But his hidden strength was revealed, that and the chilling severity he rarely showed. Forrest Langston was generally a good-natured man. But he was also one of Washington's most successful merchants. Any man in such a position must from time to time display a harder resolve.

A figure climbed the bottom stair leading to their front

portico. To Erica's eye, it seemed as though he was drawn from the night's very shadows. The house's light pushed the gloom aside just enough to reveal a sharply angular face. His eyes were green and very cold, like the iron-hard surface of a frozen lake.

"You failed to give me your answer, Mr. Langston."

"I gave you all the answer you deserve."

"I fear we must disagree upon that point, sir. You have elected—"

"I elected to place a substantial sum of money in your bank's coffers. To date, I have failed to see anything in return."

"The war affects us all, sir."

"The war." Forrest Langston fairly spat the words. "There has been war between you and the French for centuries. You would think by now you'd have managed to sort things out!"

Erica's breath drew in sharply. Mr. Bartholomew was British. She knew her father did business with British merchants. There was no alternative. The British navy ruled the high seas. The merchants' charters under which her father and so many others chafed forced them to use British ports or pay onerous duties. But from the sounds of things, her father was also using a British banker. This was shocking news. Her father had always spoken of the British merchant banks with vast distrust.

From down the hallway, Erica's mother called, "Forrest, our guests are waiting to greet you."

Erica's father did not look around. "A moment."

But Mildred was not so easily dismissed. "In case you had not realized, our house is quite crowded with people."

Forrest turned then and gave his wife a sample of the same tone with which she had greeted him. Only his contained an additional edge, one Erica had scarcely ever heard, and never within the confines of their home. "You *shall* grant me the time required to conclude this matter."

He returned his attention to the banker standing on the bottom stair. "I see no alternative but to withdraw my funds from your establishment."

This was clearly not what Mr. Bartholomew wished to

hear. "I have acted in good faith—"

"On the contrary, good faith is what I have seen the least of in my dealings with your bank. You promised me two shipments, one of coffee from South America, one of spices from the Orient. As you requested, I paid in full, in advance. Half was in gold."

"Sir, if you will only—"

"You will hear me out!" Forrest's thunder was loud enough to silence the guests in his own parlor. "Neither of these shipments has been delivered on time. In fact, only yesterday I heard a rumor that one of your leased vessels was spied at anchor in Martinique with her holds utterly bare!"

"Vicious rumors, borne by scandalmongers seeking to do us grave injustices."

"Then where, pray tell, are my goods?"

"Scarce moments away from arriving, I assure you. There is simply the matter of the additional funds we require."

Forrest gaped at the banker. "You dare stand here before me and ask for more?"

"The war, good sir. It has laid unexpected burdens upon all of us."

"The war against Napoleon is as good as over! How could this affect transport from the Orient or the southern Americas?"

A flicker of a smile traced its way across the banker's features. Or perhaps it was merely a play of the light; Erica could not be certain. "It is not that war of which I speak."

"Enough of that," Forrest barked. "Now if you will excuse me, I have guests."

The banker tipped his hat. "I shall await your good sir on the morrow, then."

But as the banker stepped into the waiting carriage, Forrest Langston did not turn away. Instead he mused, "I am missing something here. Something of grave importance."

Erica spoke. "What did he mean of a different war, Father?"

Forrest neither seemed to hear his daughter nor in truth even realize that she stood beside him. He murmured to the night, "Now what was it I did not fathom?"

Erica hesitated. She had ventured to speak her mind once before this night and received the sharp edge of her mother's tongue as recompense. Dare she do so again?

Her mother spoke from behind them. "Forrest, please."

He remained as he was. "A moment."

Erica could not merely stand there in silence. She ventured, "The banker was too assured."

"Indeed." Her father stroked his chin as he mused. "Too assured by half."

"He spoke as though you had no choice but to do as he wished."

Forrest Langston swiveled slowly. "What did you say?"

"You gave him the advance he insisted upon. He hasn't delivered the goods. The first ship is two months late, the second almost three weeks overdue. You threatened to withdraw your gold. Yet he did not seem the least bit worried. Instead, he asked for more."

Her father's gaze sharpened. "What does that tell you?"

Erica felt a thrill so great she could not quite hide the tremor that ran through her frame. Her father had never before asked her opinion. "Mr. Bartholomew knows something you do not."

Forrest frowned mightily as another carriage rumbled past their open doorway. "My thoughts exactly. But what, I wonder."

"We need to discover what war it is he mentioned."

"Perhaps. As I said, I am missing something. Which is not a good thing." He turned toward the interior of their home and attempted to regain his original good cheer. "Never you mind. This is your night, not theirs."

Erica wanted to say more, but she saw how her mother was studying the two of them. As though they were two strangers standing in Mildred Langston's front hallway.

"Come, my dears," Forrest said, offering mother and daughter his arms. "Allow me to escort you."

Chapter 3

By midmorning, Forrest Langston's office was awash in aromas. Erica loved the flavors trapped inside the air. Her father smoked a pipe of good Virginia leaf on occasion, particularly at night when seated with his wife and family in the front parlor. During the day he favored slender hand-rolled cigars imported from the Spanish island colony of Cuba. He permitted himself one with his morning coffee and one at midafternoon. More than that he claimed would be an improper indulgence, particularly now, when ships from the Spanish colonies were forced to run the English blockades.

When the house was originally designed, Forrest struggled with the best way to keep his goods and his work close at hand yet establish a clear barrier between his work life and his home life. So he built his fine foursquare brick home, and twenty paces away he erected his main warehouse. The warehouse's broad second floor was one large open room with Forrest's office occupying the northeast corner and nine clerks, who kept track of all the Langston activities, occupying the remainder of the room.

But during a particularly frigid winter when he had gone down with grippe, he lay abed, frustrated by his body's unwillingness to rise up and return to work. He came upon the idea of building a broad covered walkway running from the house to the warehouse. But her father was a man who dared to dream big. As he developed his plan, it grew, and no longer was he content with merely a covered walk. So the simple walk became a two-story edifice, the second floor providing new office space for Forrest and his master clerk.

As he congratulated himself on his plan, it occurred to him that the street that ran in front of their house was becoming a major thoroughfare. Why not take advantage of the passing traffic? After much deliberation over what form the downstairs should take, he finally decided that rather than a simple walkway, the lower level could be made into a coffeehouse. He didn't know of any others in Washington, but such establishments were quite in vogue further south. Forrest and his architect designed two parlors, one for gentlemen and another for ladies, with paneled dividers between that could be opened to form one large chamber.

All the coffeehouse's furnishings were for sale, including the tables and silver coffee service, wall hangings and paintings, chandeliers and carpets. All these were either drawn from what Forrest imported or others left there on consignment. Once a month there was a proper auction. On those days the crowds spilled out into the streets, and people vied for seats in the main salon. The Langston name was now known from New York to Charleston because of these highbrow auctions.

Erica knew better than to trouble her father first thing in the morning. She waited as he worked through the manifest of a newly arrived ship. She observed how he and Carter ground and brewed a sample of new coffee beans and discussed the flavor. She tasted a cup herself but did not offer an opinion. Her father was very strict about such matters. First she was to learn. She was to study and grow and wait until her father deemed her ready.

Reginald Langston would never be able to abide such a lack of activity. To Reggie, an hour in his father's office was punishment. He loved to shout and sing and roll up his sleeves and dive headlong into whatever task lay ahead of him. He knew every inch of their warehouses and was known to every captain on every ship that transported Langston wares. He could cover the distance from the warehouses to the Potomac harbors faster than a racing horse, darting over fences and through gardens and making a path where none existed. He could set his hand to any task where skill and strength were required. He helped serve in the coffeehouse, he sorted the incoming beans, he stoked the cooking fires, he rolled hogsheads and stacked goods and even acted as an auctioneer on occasion. Reggie could do anything, so long as he was not asked to stand still.

Which was why it was Erica's desk, and not her brother's, now sitting by the corner window in Father's long upstairs office. Erica loved her brother dearly, but in spite of there being only sixteen months between them, she sometimes felt a full generation older.

"Forrest? Might I disturb you a moment?"

Erica jumped at the unexpected sound of her mother's voice. Why did she always feel she'd been caught in a misdeed when Mildred Langston came into the room? But the fact that she was seated for the first time in Father's big office was enough to have her every nerve highly tuned. She leaped to her feet, almost overturning the inkpot. "G-good morning, Mother."

Mildred was dressed for going out. She wore a high-necked dress of burgundy velvet, with matching feathers adorning her dark tresses. She gave her daughter a long look.

Erica swallowed hard. She could see the storm gathering within her mother's gaze.

Forrest greeted his wife. "Ah, Mildred. Excellent. I was just going to send Carter for you. Come in, come in."

"I was wondering if I might have a word with you."

"And I the same. All right, Carter, tell them the entire batch is acceptable and I will sign for payment."

"Very good, sir. Good morning, madam."

"And a good morning to you, Carter. Forrest, I wish to discuss—"

"No, don't sit down quite yet. Come over here, please. I want you to have a look at this."

Mildred allowed her husband to take her by the elbow. "Is something the matter?"

"Quite a lot, actually. But nothing that cannot wait a moment."

Forrest Langston was known within the business community as a man of considerable power and a personality to back it up. Within his own family, however, Mildred Langston ran things much the way she wished. Or so it normally was. Today, however, the jovial acceptance Forrest usually showed his wife was gone. He neither smiled nor commented on how attractive she looked, which was uncommonly strange indeed.

A bit tentatively Mildred said, "Child, await me in the parlor."

"Yes, Mama."

"No, Erica. Remain exactly where you are."

"Forrest, what I wish to say to you—"

"Pertains to our daughter, does it not?" He led his wife over to where Erica stood by her desk. "Erica, show your mother what you have been working on."

Hesitantly Erica swiveled the sheet of parchment around.

"Tell me what you see, Mildred."

"Forrest, I fail to understand—"

"Attend me a moment, I beg you."

"Oh, very well. I see a letter."

"Precisely. Examine it, if you would."

The name at the top of the sheet finally registered. "She is writing to the vice-president?"

"None other. But that is not what I wished you to see. Notice the quality of the script. Notice also that she has no notes from which she is working. Our daughter, my dear, is able to take my words as I speak them and script them in a hand so fair most recipients think she has taken all day to prepare it." He slid the letter to one side and pointed to the open ledger. "Erica, explain to your mother what is on this page."

"Costings from a bill of lading, Father."

"When was this made up?"

"The shipment arrived in November of last year. The cost of each product along with the accrued price of transport is in the first column." She disliked the way her finger shook slightly as she pointed, but there was nothing she could do about it. "Here in the second column is the agreed strike price, if the item is due for auction. Beside that is the price at which it finally sold. Here in this column is our profit from the transaction. These two paintings remained unsold. The vice-president saw one when he visited the coffeehouse last week."

"Fine. Now add for me the figures in the profit column."

"Forrest, please—"

"Just a moment longer, my dear. Go ahead, Erica."

"Four hundred ninety-seven pounds and thirteen shillings."

"Do you see, Mildred? Without need for pen or paper, without batting an eye, your daughter can work out all our figures. What's more, she carries them about in her head. Erica, tell your mother the total charges outstanding against us from the two ships now overdue."

"That will not be necessary." Mildred attempted to gather herself up. "Forrest, you force me to speak plainly. I did not raise our daughter to become a glorified clerk. Do you hear me? She is a Langston, and I expect her to act like one!"

"Listen to yourself, my dear. She is a Langston. And a clerk she will not remain. She is learning the business. Learning all I can teach her, and more." He swept a hand above the work spread across Erica's new desk. "Would you have Reginald do this work?"

Her mother faltered. "Perhaps in time . . ."

"In time, yes, if I forced him. And do you know what would happen? He would do it. Just as Erica would follow you into the salons of Washington. Because they are both good children who love and honor their parents. But they would be miserable, my dear. Would you consign both our children to lives of melancholy?"

Erica grasped her hands in front of her. It was the only way to keep the tremors in check. Her mother chose that moment to glance over, and Erica knew with sickening realization that she was going to order Erica downstairs. Down to sit through another round of boring teas with women twice her age, who had nothing better to do than gossip about their children and neighbors and discuss the matrimonial prospects of a young woman who wished to remain precisely where she was, doing exactly what she was doing.

Before Mildred could speak, the rear door that led to the warehouse flew open and Reggie cried out, "Everything's ready, Erica!"

"Not now," Erica said, her voice so weak she scarcely recognized it as her own.

"Good morning, Father. 'Morning, Mother! Isn't it wonderful?"

"Isn't what wonderful, child?"

"Erica's idea, of course. An absolute topper!"

Both parents looked at her, puzzled, and Mildred demanded frostily, "Precisely what idea is this?"

"Nothing, really."

"Don't say that, Erica!" Reggie bounded across the room. "I can't believe you haven't told them yet."

"I was going to. But things . . ."

Reggie tugged on his father's sleeve. "It's been right there in front of my eyes for weeks, Father. Longer. Then Erica comes in looking for me, and she sees it, and Bob's your uncle!"

Erica blushed more deeply than Horace Cutter had the previous evening. Her brother's enthusiasm was touching, but his timing couldn't have been worse. "It really isn't anything, Father."

"You say the pair of you have something to show me?"

Reggie said, "I've laid it out just the way Erica asked."

"Very well." He offered Mildred the crook of his arm. "Coming, my dear?"

Her mother began to protest but found herself swept along. "I am not finished with our discussion, Forrest."

"Of course not. But let us attend to the children. Come, Erica."

Reluctantly she followed the others out the office's rear door. What she had spent excited hours planning and sleepless nights envisioning now seemed like a child's idle fancy. If only she could turn the clock back and make the whole thing disappear.

The clerks' room was almost as large as her father's office. The family proceeded down the central hall as the clerks stood or sat upon high stools and worked the ledgers opened on their tall slanted desks. They wore armbands to keep their sleeves from dipping into their inkwells, but the tips of their fingers were stained a permanent black by the India dye. Erica saw how her mother stared at the clerks' fingers as each man greeted the employer and his family. She saw the delicate shudder that shook her mother's frame and realized that Mildred was imagining this as her daughter's fate. Erica hung her head. It was only a matter of time before she would be banished from the work she loved.

The rear door of the clerks' office opened onto a broad balcony. This was another of her father's designs. To her right stood a clerk's slanted desk, this one empty. Her father called this his foredeck, and no one could remain here except upon his express invitation. From this high perch Forrest was able to view his entire operation. The empty desk was there to hold a ledger, should Father desire it.

The warehouse was a vast affair. As they started down the stairs Erica spied four workers erecting a set of portable walls, something her father had seen done in the holds of a ship and decided to use here. Once in place, the walls formed a solid barrier. The space could be used for woodworking or loom spinning or anything else that might create dust and noise. Or a netting could be thrown over the top and the space used to house valuable items. Yet Forrest Langston could look down and still see all the activity going on within his empire.

Normally such matters brought Erica a sense of swelling pride. Just as she loved the mingled aromas of spices and roasting coffee and dried leaf, she loved to see the evidence of her father's ingenuity. Today, however, she dreaded displaying her idea before him. If only she had not spoken about it to Reggie. If only he had not been so enthusiastic. If only . . .

"Over here, Father!" Reggie led them into one such temporary alcove. From the spicy fragrance, Erica knew the piled-up sacks contained peppercorns.

Beyond them, an older man in tattered overalls stood nervously by a little table. His skin was so black it looked almost purple, and his yellowed eyes darted nervously from one figure to the next.

Reggie turned to him and struggled to shape the simple French words, "This is my family!"

The old man might not have understood. More likely, he was too nervous to make much of a response. He continued to bob his head at no one in particular and fumble with the brim of his tattered straw hat.

"I know this man." Forrest's brow furrowed in concentration.

"His name is François, Father." Reggie's eyes danced in anticipation. "Do go on, Erica!"

"Yes, daughter," Mildred agreed. "Do tell us why we are here."

Erica forced herself to take a step forward, wishing a hole would open at her feet and she could disappear into it forever. "I—I, well, this is François."

"As I've already said," Reggie inserted.

"He is one of the new men hired for warehouse duties, do I recall that correctly?" asked Forrest.

Forrest Langston had no slaves. He was a staunch abolitionist, the name given to those who felt the American constitution was intended to serve all men, of all races. But the president owned slaves, and so did many within his cabinet. Forrest Langston and his fellow abolitionists knew theirs was a struggle that would take many years to realize.

"Yes, Father. But François does not speak much English." Erica forced herself to stop fumbling with the sweep of her skirt. "He is from Martinique. Well, he was born and raised in Cuba. Then he was an indentured servant in Martinique for twelve years. He worked his passage to America, and he's been here in our employ for almost three months."

"Forgive me, husband, but I have far more pressing matters than this discussion of a new employee's personal history."

"Abide with me a moment longer, my dear. Go on, Erica."

"Yes, Father." She turned to the man and said in French, "Would you please begin?"

"The mademoiselle wishes for me to do as we discussed?"

"Yes, please."

François continued to fumble with his hat brim. "I did not mean to steal, mademoiselle. All the workers, they take leaf scrapings to smoke."

The man's accent was quite thick, what the proper French called a patois. For once Erica was glad for all the lessons her mother had forced her to endure in learning this most difficult tongue. "We are not here to make trouble. I told you that."

Forrest inquired, "What is he saying?"

"He is frightened that he will lose his job for using our tobacco."

"All my workers may take a pipeful now and then. Tell him that."

"I already have, Father."

"Well, then." He pulled the pocket watch from his vest and clicked it open. "Please proceed."

"Yes, Father." She said to Francois, "You are please to show them what I saw. Now."

"Very well, mademoiselle." Anxiously the old man lowered

himself to the stool by the table. He opened the sack at his feet and pulled out several leaves.

Forrest's frown deepened. "Is that my Virginia leaf?"

"No, Father."

"I thought not. The color is far too yellow." He leaned forward as the old man selected one leaf, the broadest of the lot, and flattened it upon a sheet of damp muslin on the table. "Is this Cuban?"

"It is Carolina golden leaf."

"It looks Cuban."

"Yes, Father, I know."

"Where did it come from?"

Reggie spoke up. "I brought it from the Cutters, Father. They have a plantation down near New Bern."

"Did you now. And why, might I ask, are we purchasing Cutter tobacco when our larders are full of good Virginia leaf?"

Erica felt so miserable she wondered if perhaps she was coming down with a fever. "François says this is better, Father."

Her mother demanded, "Better for what? Wasting everyone's valuable time?"

"I must say I agree with your mother—" Forrest was cut off by the old man's actions.

Despite François's evident nervousness, his hands moved with remarkable swiftness. He took a broom that was lying on the floor by his feet, selected a twig, and broke it off.

"He is using a leaf that has been dried slowly," Erica explained. "This keeps it flexible. Most Virginia leaf crumbles. He has wet down the muslin, and he lets the leaf sit on it for a moment before he begins to roll."

They watched the man place the twig at one end and form an elaborate fold in the tobacco leaf. Then he began to roll, carefully and deliberately flattening the leaf with his thumbs before snapping the roll forward.

"He cannot press down on the tobacco, because that would stop the draw," she continued. "At least, I think that's the word. His speech is very hard to understand sometimes, and I don't know the proper word in English."

"Draw is correct," said Forrest. "Do go on."

"Now he has finished rolling. He will wrap it in the muslin for a moment, like that, and roll it a few times more. He says that in truth anyone can roll a cigar; the secret is in knowing how to select a leaf."

Reggie blurted out, "It's not true, though. I tried and tried. When I finished I pulled so hard I turned blue, but I couldn't draw enough air through even to light the end. It's jolly difficult, Father."

"Now he pulls out the twig, very slowly. Then he trims away any spare leaf and gives it one final roll. And now he uses the press."

The wooden implement was the size of a cutting board and carved with eight grooves, four on either side of a set of hinges. François settled the cigar into one of the grooves, then clamped the two sides together, sealing the cigar inside. He pressed down very hard, holding it for several moments. Then he opened the press and offered Erica the cigar.

"Father?"

Forrest accepted the cigar, inspected it a moment, then said, "Ask the man if I might use his knife." He clipped the edges, then waited while Reggie lit a taper and handed it over. Forrest rolled the cigar to get it burning well. He then puffed hard enough to make the end glow brilliantly and released a long plume of smoke toward the ceiling. He did the same thing a second time. And a third.

Mildred protested, "Forrest, we really must be returning to the matters at hand."

"Not quite yet." Her father's eyes held a very different light now as he returned his attention to Erica and asked, "Is this all?"

"No, Father."

"I thought not. Proceed."

She detected the difference in her father's voice. She was almost afraid to believe it, but she had been around him enough to know the tone. So, apparently, did her mother, for Mildred's further protest died before it reached her mouth. Erica felt a faint flutter of something deep in her being, but it took a long moment to realize it was excitement.

She said to François, "Please do the other one now."

"But of course, mademoiselle."

His hands were more nimble now, his movements almost blindingly fast. Erica found herself speaking almost as swiftly. "This is what I saw him doing the first time. He can make this one from scrapings off the floor, because it's so much smaller. These miniature cigars are what the poorer folk use in the islands."

Forrest accepted the second item, which was scarcely larger than his little finger. "Have him make another."

When François had done so, Forrest asked of his son, "Do you smoke, my boy?"

"No, Father."

"Quite right, too. Filthy habit. Put this out for me . . . there's a good lad." Forrest handed him the cigar and used the taper to light the smaller cigar. He took a few puffs, then said, "I'm listening."

"The English blockade of the Spanish colonies has made it both difficult and expensive to import cigars from Cuba. We always thought it was impossible to make them here, and it is if we use Virginia leaf. But according to François, this Carolina leaf is ideally suited."

"Quite remarkable, Erica. I am very impressed."

"Forrest, really. There's no need to encourage the girl."

"I am merely stating the truth, my dear. What she has done here is nothing short of genius."

Erica fought down the burning lump in her throat. "Father, if I may continue . . . I was thinking . . ." She swallowed hard. There was no way forward but straight ahead. She said in a rush, "We keep the roasted beans for the coffeehouse in a room by the street. We could move the coffee roasting back here into the warehouse and put in another window and turn it into a tobacconist. We could put François in the window and show him rolling our cigars and put up a sign that says, 'Langston's. Home of good American leaf.'"

Her words were greeted by total silence. Finally her father said, "Slow down from your gallop, lass, and let me hear that once more."

When Erica was done, Forrest regarded her for a long moment. Then he turned to his wife and said, "I believe we have concluded the matter, my dear."

"Really, Forrest, I must object." But everyone knew the argument had already been won.

"Must you? Must you really? After what we have just seen? Knowing the difficulties this family faces, with all we have to endure, and hearing your daughter come up with such a remarkable proposal, still you feel you must object?" His tone did not harden, yet there was the sense of his bearing down. "I would urge you to think long and most carefully before you insist upon discussing this further."

"I . . ." Mildred pursed her lips. "Very well. I shall do as you suggest."

"I could ask no more of anyone, most especially of you, my dear." Forrest bowed his gratitude to his wife. He then said to Erica, "You will please thank François for his demonstration and say he will be well recompensed for this display of skill."

"Yes, Father."

Erica was glad that her parents left swiftly then. For she would not have wished to have her mother see her collapse as she did upon a sack of peppercorns and accept a cloth from François to wipe the perspiration from her brow.

Chapter 4

Erica sat in the carriage next to her mother. Fifteen days had passed since her birthday, but she did not count from that happy event. Rather, it was two weeks since the incident in the warehouse. Already Father had removed the coffee roasters, installed a street-front window, and stocked his new tobacco shop. Or rather, Erica had supervised most of this under his instruction. Only her mother did not share in the general excitement surrounding the new venture. In fact, things had been quite frosty about the house since that morning in the warehouse. And there seemed to be nothing Erica could do about it.

This afternoon's excursion was a perfect example. The family had gathered for their midday meal, as always. When her mother announced that she was attending a tea given by Senator Burrell's wife, Erica's father had not responded at all. He had lost much of his joviality since returning from his northern journeys. He spent most of his time locked inside a preoccupied air, seeing and hearing nothing that went on about him.

When he did not respond, Mildred demanded, "I do so wish you would attend me."

Forrest shook himself awake. "Forgive me, my dear. My thoughts were wandering."

"You have not heard a word I have spoken!"

"Did we not have that splendid discussion regarding

Reggie's further tuitions this very morning?"

"That was the day before yesterday." She set down her nap-kin. "Really, Forrest, is what I have to say so insignificant you do not need to listen to me any longer?"

"Not at all, my dear. Not in the slightest. It is just, well . . ." He fumbled with his pocket watch, then rose from his chair. "You must forgive me. I have pressing matters to attend to."

"You do nothing but sit upstairs in your office and stare at the wall. Look at your plate; you haven't touched a thing!"

"I fear I have no appetite." He bowed to the table but seemed to see no one. "Please excuse me."

In the ensuing silence, Erica quietly offered, "I would love to attend the tea with you, Mother."

She could see that her mother was tempted to refuse. But when she spoke, it was to say, "I suppose you might wear the blue frock."

Erica started to say that what she had on was perfectly ade-quate for an afternoon gathering, but she swallowed her pro-test. "I'll just go change, then."

"You had best hurry. I have already asked for the carriage to be brought around."

When Erica left the room, her mother was still watching the doorway through which Forrest had departed.

Once underway, Mildred Langston sat in silence and stared out the side window. Erica accepted it with a dull ache in her heart. Things were most certainly not right in her world. The day might be balmy and the June sunshine brilliant, but the chilly atmosphere within the carriage permeated her very spirit.

Finally she could bear it no longer. "I do wish you wouldn't treat me so, Mama."

Her mother addressed her words out the window. "How would you like me to treat you, then?"

"As your daughter." Speaking those words brought such a lump to her throat Erica could scarcely breathe. *I will not cry,* she told herself. *I will not.* "Nothing has changed."

"On the contrary, I am under the distinct impression that quite a lot has been altered. To my dismay I find my child has elected to become a shopkeeper."

"Mama, I am not a shopkeeper! I am a merchant."

Mildred waved the correction aside.

"Do you not want me to be happy, Mama?"

"Child, it is high time you realize the world does not revolve about your every whim. There are certain demands that society places upon a woman. A proper lady does not delve too deeply into the affairs of men. She disposes herself in polite company. She attends to her elders. She learns the proper graces."

"Do I not attend you? Am I not going to tea with you this afternoon?" Erica struggled to keep the entreaty from turning into tears. "Is it not possible to do both?"

Only when the carriage halted before an imposing manor of brick and whitewashed pillars did Mildred turn to regard her daughter directly. "No," she replied firmly, "it is not."

Once inside the manor, Erica was quickly separated from her mother by the crush of ladies. Even so, she could feel Mildred's gaze tracking her about the room. She held her head high and greeted each of the ladies in turn. She spoke when she was addressed and listened avidly to the latest gossip. Yet she could not dismiss the leaden weight that enveloped her heart, and inwardly she continued the discussion begun in the carriage. Why was it not possible to be both a proper lady and a woman of affairs? Why could she not assist her father in running their business and be a lady in her mother's eyes as well?

"You have not heard a single word I have spoken to you."

Erica started as though shaken awake. The same words her mother had said to her father, now addressed to her. "Forgive me."

"Your mind was wandering, Miss Langston."

"Yes, ma'am." She curtsied to Abigail Cutter, Horace's mother. "I beg your pardon, Mrs. Cutter."

"I take it you have no interest in how London fashion has

taken to peacock feathers this season."

"It is lovely, I'm sure."

The older woman smiled. "Come over here by the window, my dear."

The parlor was elegant, with two sets of bay windows framed by long velvet drapes. In the relative privacy of sunlight and crimson, Mrs. Cutter steered Erica about so that her back was to the room. "You look troubled, Erica."

"Everything is splendid, I'm sure."

"Look at me. Have I not known you since you were crawling about my front parlor? Do I not hear my son go on about you endlessly?" She grimaced. "I should not have said that. Horace would be mortified to learn I was so open about his affections."

"I did not hear a word, Mrs. Cutter."

"Please call me Abigail. Now tell me what is the matter. No, allow me to guess. Your mother is distressed by your venturing into your father's business dealings."

Erica could not hide her concern. "I wish I knew what to do."

"Shall I tell you what is swirling about this fine chamber today? It is how a young lady in this company spied a sweeper at her father's warehouse, borrowed some leaf from our own company, and from these modest beginnings has put together an idea so remarkable every merchant in town is speaking of nothing else. There are many among us who envy you, my dear."

"Why would any of these ladies envy me?"

"It is the Age of Enlightenment, have you not heard? We watch the overthrow of the French aristocracy, we observe the rise of our own nation, we fight for the abolition of slavery. Whyever should the right of women to choose their own course through life not be part and parcel of this? That is, some of us speak thus, and more think the same yet are afraid to speak out. Others, however, decry all of this as utter nonsense, and they condemn you for representing what for them is an absurd new trend."

Abigail Cutter was as spare a person as her son, tall and angular and not particularly attractive. Yet she possessed a certain vivacity and sharpness of wit that overcame her physical shortcomings. Particularly when the fire was in her voice and she revealed a passion that defied the polite confines of this chamber. "You spoke to my son about a desire to enter into the business world alongside your mate."

Erica found herself very glad she faced the window and the day, so as to hide the blush that rose upon her features. "I might have mentioned something to that effect."

"Shall I tell you what I said to my son?"

"Y-yes, I suppose, that is . . ."

"I said that he should grab onto this woman with all his might. He should seek her as he would the highest treasure." She smiled and the years dropped away. "Of course, my husband was livid."

"He was? At me?"

"Assuredly. He objects most strenuously to women seeking any place outside the home. And then to have a woman create such a business coup with his very own Carolina leaf . . . Oh my, be glad you were not around when he learned that."

"I am sorry to hear this, Mrs. Cutter. I hold your husband in the highest esteem."

"Did I not tell you to call me Abigail? And don't worry about Horace Senior. I for one was delighted to see the male hierarchy taken aback by a lovely young lady. It does them a world of good, if you ask me." She smiled a greeting to someone Erica could not see. "Now, then. Is there anything else troubling you this fine day?"

"No, ma'am. Well, that is . . ."

"A word of advice, my dear. Learn to identify allies. No matter how smart you may be, no matter how strong, you will always need those you can trust and to whom you can turn in times of hardship. Which come to all of us, I am sorry to say."

"There is something." Erica paused, but her hesitation was not due to the subject. It was because this was the first time she had ever spoken to an older woman as she would an equal. "My father is most distressed by the rumors of war."

"As are many of the merchants among us."

"We have heard nothing of any definite nature. Can you tell me, is there anything new developing that we should know about?"

Abigail Cutter set her cup down on a nearby sideboard. "You know that my son-in-law, Samuel Aldridge, is quite well connected within this administration."

"Yes, ma'am."

"What I am about to tell you is in the strictest confidence, my dear."

The sudden tension caused Erica's voice to tremble. "Of course, ma'am."

"Word arrived yesterday of another incident at sea. A group of British vessels surrounded an American merchant ship. They press-ganged more than half the men."

"That's dreadful!"

"Softly, my dear. Softly. I agree. What is more important, so do our leaders. This is the third such incident in as many months. The British government continues to harass our traders at every turn. Now there is discussion of doubling the tariffs they charge vessels flying our flag."

"We can scarcely pay what they demand now!"

"Precisely." Her voice held a tension as taut as a ship's cable. "The president has convened a special meeting of his cabinet for this evening. Tomorrow he addresses Congress. He spoke this very morning with Senator Fulton, who is one of his key allies, to warn him of their intentions." Abigail Cutter leaned in closer still. "You must prepare yourself for a shock."

As gently as possible, Erica inserted herself into the group at the room's other end. She tapped her mother on the shoulder.

"Ah, Erica, there you are. You remember Mrs. Lawrence."

"Good afternoon, ma'am. Mother, please excuse me. I am unwell."

"My dear?"

"It has come on me all of a sudden." She gripped her mother's arm with fierce intent. "I really must be leaving."

Mildred's face tightened with alarm. "But of course."

"Shall I have my man attend you, Mildred?" asked Mrs. Lawrence.

"No!" Erica knew she spoke too loudly. But she also knew she was no longer able to hide behind her polite mask. "No. Really. Thank you. Mother, we must leave at once."

Rushing in the long skirts with their multitude of petticoats was such a bother. She almost tripped over her own hem upon the broad front stairs, which only heightened Mildred's alarm.

"Erica, what on earth is the matter?"

"Wait until we are underway." Erica cried to the footman, "Where is our carriage?"

"I sent the boy to fetch it, miss."

Mildred added her voice to that of her daughter's. "Well, send another! Can't you see my daughter is unwell?"

"Of course, madam. Miss, would you care to sit down?"

"Yes, do take his chair, Erica."

"No, I'm— There it is now!"

Erica was bundled into the carriage with the footman on one arm and her mother on the other. Mildred called up, "Make all haste for home!"

"Yes, madam." The driver cracked his whip, and the horses leaped forward.

"Do you need a blanket, child?"

"No. Can't he go any faster?"

"There is traffic to all sides. You look all flushed. Are you sure—"

"My ailment is not physical, Mother. I have heard news." Erica twisted her parasol handle so hard it snapped. "Oh, please tell him to hurry!"

"Driver!"

"Yes, madam?"

"There is an emergency here. Do what you must, but fly!"

"Fly it is, madam. Heyah!"

"All right, Erica. Now, will you tell me what is transpiring!"

"It has to do with business, Mother. You have always preferred not to hear of such things."

"Don't argue with me, child!"

She looked at her mother clearly and saw a woman distraught. She also knew there were threads that had to be woven together for the situation to make sense. "You know how upset Father was the day of his return?"

"Of course. I was there beside you when he spoke with that gentleman."

"Mr. Bartholomew is a British banker. Nine months ago, he approached Father with an offer. I have only learned about this in the past few weeks. Father treated it as highly confidential. From what I gather that was part of the arrangement." She straightened a fold in her dress to give her hands something to do. "By then the blockade had made it nigh on impossible to obtain either tobacco from the islands or coffee and cocoa from the southern Spanish colonies."

Just thinking of the situation they had endured for almost a year now made Erica's blood rise. The British claimed it was not a blockade at all, for did they not permit all ships finally to pass? But any vessel bound from New Spain or New Portugal, as their colonies south of the United States were known, had to first travel to a British port and be inspected by British customs officers. The same was true for vessels bound to or from the island colonies. The British said it was perfectly reasonable. They had been at war with France for twenty years and with Spain for almost five. Of course they had to inspect all goods headed to and from their enemies' lands to ensure there was no contraband.

But this meant that a vessel traveling from Cuba to

Washington, a voyage of some two weeks, was required to travel first to Portsmouth. The journey to and from England could take four months. Not only was the cost staggering, but these vessels were minutely searched. For weeks. During the process, goods vanished, as did a number of their men. So many sailors had been press-ganged from some vessels that their skippers were forced to scour the byways of England for farmers, men without any sea experience at all, just to return home.

But there was no need to explain all this to her mother. "We had just lost a blockade runner, filled to the gunwales with coffee. The British navy requisitioned the entire supply."

"I remember that day. I had thought your father's heart was ailing him. But what does that have to do—"

"The British banker offered Father two ships, one of coffee and one of spices. One was at anchor in Martinique, a vessel taken under the Spanish flag and thus a spoil of war. The other would be granted letters of marque and thus permitted to pass through the British naval blockade of our waters."

In an instant of astonishing clarity, Erica looked at her mother and saw not her parent but a distressed and confused woman. Mildred disliked becoming involved in the affairs of men. She felt that her role was to provide an island of safety and calm in the tumult of Washington politics and business. She had given her life over to anchoring her family within the rough-and-tumble Washington society and had raised her children as best she could. She set a fine table. She was a perfect hostess. She lived by the rules of her day. Erica saw all these things and found herself flooded by a love so intense she was silenced.

"Don't stop now, child!"

"I do wish you would stop calling me that, Mother." For some reason, the love was so intense, the vision so clear, she could say the words with utter calm. "I mean no disrespect. But the time for calling me a child is past."

Their eyes met. Erica saw a refocusing within her mother's gaze, then a light of realization as clear as her own.

"Go on with your story," Mildred urged.

"One of the most difficult matters we have faced is costing our product. How do you price something when half of what you pay for never arrives and the shipping costs and customs duties have skyrocketed?"

"So this is why," Mildred offered, "I see the prices of coffee and cocoa rising so ridiculously fast."

"Doubled and doubled again, just in the past eight months," Erica confirmed.

"And why has tea not risen so sharply?"

"Because, Mother, tea comes from British colonies. The British ships do not pay such tariffs. Nor are they harassed by their navy. So long as we buy our cloth from British mills, and drink tea instead of coffee, and use British wool, then we are fine."

Erica glanced out the window. They had been forced to a crawl by a wagon filled to the brim with uncut logs. Erica leaned farther out the window. There was no chance of over-taking the wagon. Traffic flowed by in a steady stream. Had it been permitted, she would have leaped to the ground and run on her own two legs. "Oh, why is it taking so long?"

"Erica, look at me." Mildred was catching her daughter's distress as she watched Erica bunching and releasing fistfuls of her dress. "Tell me the rest."

"The banker offered Father such an astonishing price it would mean recouping all we had lost on the earlier ship. And Father claims that Bartholomew's bank is most reputable."

"There was a catch. I can see it in your face."

"You heard it yourself, Mama. They insisted upon payment in advance. Father agreed, but not with a direct payment. This was very shrewd of him. He established an account in their bank. He deposited payment in gold, as they insisted. He gave them a letter stating that only when we received the goods, *all* the goods, would the funds be theirs."

"I-I don't understand. The goods have not arrived, have they?"

"No. You heard Father complain about that, just as I did."

"So the bankers cannot have taken our money?"

"No. At least I don't think so. Not yet." She forced her voice to hold to a false calm. But the inner tumult left her feeling as though she were listening to another person speak the words. Someone far more composed then she ever could be. "But Mr. Bartholomew was so confident, did you see?"

"And if Bartholomew's bank did somehow manage to get hold of Forrest's funds, what then?"

The sick dread rose in her. "We would be ruined."

"You are not exaggerating?"

"No, Mama. It has been a calamitous year. Between the loss of a vessel and the cost of building another . . . Everything has become so expensive, as you well know. Money has been pouring out and too little coming in."

"Your father said the banker knew something he did not. Is this what you have learned today? Was it from Abigail Cutter?"

"Please don't tell Father you saw us talking. Please. I promised her I would not tell anyone."

"What . . ." Mildred stopped as the carriage rounded the final corner and halted in front of their home.

Erica did not even wait for the footman to help her alight, but her mother stayed her with a question.

"Daughter, do you recognize that carriage?"

Standing in front of theirs was a black coach pulled by a four-in-hand. "The ships' merchant Arimond," Erica identified immediately. "Out of Baltimore."

"Come with me." Instead of heading straight upstairs, Mildred led her daughter into the front parlor. She moved to the mirror and removed the long pin that kept her hat in place.

"Really, Mother, shouldn't we—"

"Follow my lead here, Erica," she replied firmly. "Do you think your father would wish our affairs to be known to all?"

Instantly she saw the wisdom of her mother's words. "No, Mama."

"We must set the proper pattern in front of guests. Now let me inspect you. Fasten up that button upon your neck." She tucked a wayward strand of her daughter's hair behind her ear. "Now smile for me."

Erica did her best to follow her mother's instructions.

"Head up. That's right. We are merely paying respects to your father." She patted her daughter's cheek. "You are a Langston. Never forget that."

"I won't, Mama."

"Very good. Let us proceed."

How her legs supported her up the stairs, Erica did not know. She drew strength from her mother's easy tread and proceeded slowly.

Mildred found the chief clerk seated in his outer office, head bent over a vast ledger. "A very good afternoon to you, I'm sure, Master Carter."

"Mrs. Langston." Carter rose to his feet. "Forgive me, madam. I did not hear your approach. Good afternoon, Miss Erica."

"Is my husband in?"

"He has visitors, ma'am."

"Would you tell him that I require a moment of his time?"

"He, ah, that is . . ."

"Now, if you please, Mr. Carter."

"Of course, madam. Excuse me."

Mildred turned from Carter's office and positioned herself in the middle of the upstairs parlor, seemingly content to wait in utter stillness all afternoon. Erica marveled at her mother's poise, her absolute composure. She wanted to rush into her father's office and blurt out their news, but she followed her mother's example and waited patiently for what seemed like days.

Finally the office door opened in a billowing cloud of tobacco smoke. Forrest came lumbering through his clerk's office and said, "You wished to see me, my dear?"

"Ask Mr. Carter to take your guests on a tour of the warehouse, please."

"I . . ." Forrest blinked slowly. "My dear, we are in the midst of rather important matters."

Mildred kept her tone light. "I am sure they would relish seeing your man roll his special cigars, husband."

Erica added a tremulous "Father, please. Do as she says."

He examined his two ladies, then turned and went back to his office. An agonizing moment later, he returned. "What is it?"

"Your daughter has something of dire import to tell you."

"Erica?"

"You recall the night of your return. The banker said something—"

"I remember vividly. What of it?"

"Bartholomew spoke of war."

"It is an excuse as old as the hills. Whenever the British wish to renegotiate, they bring out the conflict against France." It was a measure of Forrest's internal distress that he permitted his impatience to show. "Really, Erica, this is nothing new."

"He was not speaking of the war with the French, Father."

He froze. "What?"

"Tomorrow Congress will vote on a new measure. They are declaring war against Britain."

Forrest Langston took the news as he would a blow to his heart. He staggered back against the rear wall. "This cannot be true."

"It is, Father. I can't tell you how I know, so please don't ask. But it is true!" Hot tears spilled down her cheeks. "What if the British banker suspected this would happen all along? What if they had no intention of ever delivering the goods? Would war not grant them the perfect excuse to claim the ships were casualties of the new conflict?"

Forrest Langston's face had turned a waxen gray. "They intend to destroy us."

Erica's worst fears had now been spoken aloud. "If Langston's goes under, could they not go before a British court and claim the gold as their own, recompense for goods that were lost to the war?"

"That will not happen." He gathered himself with great effort. "You are certain this news is correct?"

"Yes, Father."

"Absolutely certain? Our very lives depend upon this, Erica."

"The news came from the president himself."

"Then there is no time to lose." A trace of the vibrant Forrest of old returned. His eyes held a frantic light, but the lethargy was now cast aside. "Come, Erica. We have matters to attend to."

Chapter 5

They could never have managed it without Reggie.

It was not the work, although there was more of that than ever before. But the work did them all a world of good, keeping them too busy to worry. Even so, they all felt the strain. Erica moved through the hectic days with the hand of fear squeezed tightly about her heart.

But not Reggie. Erica found her brother's attitude completely baffling . . . and most welcome. He threw himself into whatever task came his way and sang the latest music hall ditties as he labored. He was always ready to do anyone's bidding, race to the market for his mother, or act as escort for his sister. Erica's father was sending her on an increasing number of errands, trusting her to be his eyes and ears.

In the eleventh week after Congress declared war, the two siblings were off for yet another visit to the office that prepared provisions for conflict. Forrest sought to obtain contracts from the quartermaster general. The carriage clip-clopped down streets dressed in autumnal finery. The wind through the open window was fresh but lovely. Reginald sat across from his sister, dressed in his formal day garb of dark frock coat, top hat, frilled shirt, vest, and tight black breeches. He hummed a jaunty tune.

"You certainly do look like a dandy," she observed. "I thought you hated dressing up."

"Father said it was important, this meeting, so I thought I

should look my best." He gave her the lopsided grin that split his features with merriment. "It seems we're all doing things we'd rather not these days."

"However can you be like this?"

He didn't ask what she meant. "Would it do any good if I worried?"

"No more than it does me. But I can't stop."

"Ah, but you're smart enough that your worrying just might lead you to think of something good. Me, I'd come up with a right corker and burn the place down around our ears."

"Don't talk like that, Reggie. You're not slow-witted."

"I know exactly what I am, dear sister. I am a pair of strong arms and a willing heart. I have enough sense to know I'll never be as smart as you. And you know what? It doesn't bother me a whit. Why should it, when I have you to worry for the both of us?"

She stared at him. "If you weren't my brother, I do believe I would have to marry you."

"No chance of that, I'm afraid. Besides, I shall never marry."

"Don't talk nonsense. Of course you shall."

"Marriage is a lot of bother, if you ask me. I can tip my hat to all the ladies now and whistle up the wind. Once a female has her hooks in me, I'll be obliged to behave. You know how I hate to behave, Erica."

When they pulled up in front of the War Office, Erica alighted from the carriage with a smile on her face. "Do you remember what to say?"

"Don't worry, sister. I have all of Father's proper words written down and stowed in my pocket. You want to see?"

"You shouldn't make a joke of everything."

"And why not? You frown enough for the whole family."

"I do no such thing."

"Erica, you are the queen of frowns. You frown from your hair to your fingertips. Like this." He pulled his features into a ridiculous scowl.

"Don't make such terrible faces." She allowed him to take her elbow and escort her up the front stairs. "Else I shall have to tell Father you made an utter mess of everything."

"So? Just watch me."

She was forced to regain her composure as they entered the long office. A battery of desks was arrayed at the far end, behind a waist-high partition. A sentry stood duty at the passage through the barrier, with a clerk standing alongside taking names. The room was filled with somber gentlemen smoking and talking in grave tones.

Even Reggie was brought up short by the atmosphere. "What do I do now?" he whispered.

She whispered back, "Give your name to the clerk and say you are here to receive word on our tender."

"Right. Of course." He straightened his frock coat. "Leave it to me."

Erica was the only woman in the room, which happened often and yet always left her ill at ease. She felt every eye upon her as she stood and waited by the exit. Then a familiar face emerged from the waiting throng, and Horace Cutter bowed with more grace than she would have thought possible from his angular frame.

"Miss Erica, what a delightful surprise."

"A very good morning, I'm sure, Master Cutter." She smiled with genuine relief. "How do you happen to be here today?"

"I am drawn by the same reason as you, I suspect."

"I am merely accompanying my brother, as you see."

Horace might have been an awkward young man whose social graces were somewhat lacking, but he was his father's son when it came to business, and he observed Erica with a very shrewd eye. "More likely it is the other way around."

She did not dispute that. Instead, she snapped open her fan and waved it before her face. "A pity they all feel obliged to smoke. The air is quite close."

"I have noticed a number of them puffing upon your own little invention."

"I invented nothing, and you know it."

"My mother thinks you are quite the most remarkable woman."

"How is your mother?"

"She is well, and I am sure she would have sent you her fondest regards had she known of this meeting."

"Please remember me to her." Erica chose her words carefully. "Tell her I shall remain ever in her debt."

"Indeed I shall." He nodded to the murmuring throng behind him. "The world is awash with rumors this day."

She had to struggle to hide the sudden tension. "Tell me what they are saying."

"Most of it is stuff and nonsense, as you well know. Idle men making idle chatter."

"Horace, please, I beg of you. For once treat me as an equal and not an addlepated woman." The strain of holding to a polite whisper caused her voice to tremble. "Those men would never speak to me, but I desperately need to know what they are saying. Is that not why you came? To listen and to observe?"

Horace examined her long and hard. "They speak of war."

"But of course they do. What are they saying specifically?"

"That it will be fought upon the seas. That America's navy is not well equipped. That we do not possess enough ships, nor are the ships we own of the fastest sort."

An idea came to her in a flash. She hid her sudden thrill behind a fluttering fan and a delicate cough. "What else?"

"The British broadsheets have made no mention of our declaration of war."

This time she could not hide her astonishment. "That's impossible."

Her tone drew stares. Erica flipped her fan as fast as a butterfly's wing and turned to observe down the hall. Her brother now stood before one of the desks. "How can that be true?"

"I assure you it is. All Europe's attention is focused upon the battles with Napoleon. More than half a million men stand to arms, from Siberia to Salamanca."

"But surely they must consider us a threat."

"A threat to trade. Not as foes in war. I have read the broadsheets myself, Miss Erica. Everything they speak of has to do with trade. How our embargo against British goods will soon cause workers in their mill towns to starve. How we must be brought to pay for our aggression. But also how this must wait."

She saw the flicker in his gaze. "You are not telling me something."

"My father . . ."

"Go on."

"My father would be most displeased to see us speaking in such a manner."

"Then speak to me as would please your mother. I implore you, Horace."

He sighed. "My father says all the English papers are controlled by allies to the Crown. That if we want to learn what the people are thinking, we must read the pamphlets."

Erica was well aware of the power of pamphleteers. They printed small booklets and sold them for a halfpenny apiece. Pamphlets were written on every subject under the sun, from medicinal cures to frontier tales. "And what do the British pamphlets say?"

"That we are justified in our cause. That if only the British Crown were to accept our independence and court our favor, we would become strong allies. That they have missed a great opportunity."

Their conversation was halted by Reggie's excited approach. "We have it!"

"What?" For an instant Erica could not recall what he was speaking of.

"The tender! Our tender offer has been accepted!"

The entire chamber ceased its banter. Horace said, "This

will mean a great deal of new business for Langston's. My congratulations to you and your family."

"Hello there, Horace." Reggie cast his easy grin, utterly unfazed by all the attention. "You are well?"

"Other than a bit envious of your good fortune this day, I am most well." He cast his gaze back to Erica. "I trust the rumors I hear of Langston's current difficulties are untrue?"

She refused to lie to this young man, especially after he had spoken to her with such candor. "We face the perils of everyone doing business in such uncertain times. But we will survive."

"I am glad to hear it." He opened the door and bowed them through. "Washington would be a far poorer place without Langston's good name."

Forrest Langston heard out his daughter's report in silence. When she finished recounting what she had heard, he continued staring out the window. His face had aged considerably over the past few weeks. Erica noticed new creases in his forehead and grayer tints to his hair.

"What does it all mean, Father?"

"That we have more time for our preparations, so long as these rumors are true."

They had been frantically purchasing supplies that would be difficult to obtain if the British blockade tightened. The warehouse was now full to the brim and their funds almost depleted.

Forrest continued speaking to the sunlight. "I have heard other rumors, however. That Britain has been preparing an army in Canada. They intend to empty the northern provinces of troops so as to catch us unawares."

Her father had begun to speak to her thus, examining unfinished ideas in her company, weighing options. Had the circumstances been better, she would be reveling in this new level of trust. As it was, however, Erica would have given anything to return to earlier days. They seemed so carefree now from where she sat.

Carter stood quietly to the side. One glance was enough to show her that the loyal old man did not understand the situation any better than she did. "What does this mean?"

"Nothing, unless or until we discover where these troops will attack. If they exist at all."

Reggie piped up, "But this War Office contract is wonderful news, isn't it, Father?"

As always, his son's presence was enough to bring a hint of cheer to Forrest's features. "You have done well, my boy."

Reggie beamed with pleasure. "If you're finished with me here, I'll change and return to the warehouse. There are a hundred tasks awaiting me."

"Go on then. Off with you." But the light in Forrest's face dimmed as the door shut behind his son. He stared at the tender offer on his desk and murmured, "How on earth shall we pay for this new tender? Our credit with the banks is taken right up to the limit. And the government only compensates upon delivery."

"I have an idea, Father."

Forrest Langston could not hide his skepticism. "Out with it, then."

Erica took a very hard breath. "The American navy is seeking fast ships. We could sell them our new vessel."

The idea pushed her father back in his seat. "Sell my *Erica*?"

"Think of it, Father. Sailing in these wartime conditions would be doubly dangerous, would it not? All the shipbuilders are frantically busy, but new vessels take time. We have one that is almost complete."

The idea even brought a smile to Carter's face, which merely rearranged the hard edges of his angular visage. With an approving glance at Erica he said, "I must say, sir, this is quite a brilliant concept."

"The idea pains me deeply," Forrest protested.

"The government would pay a fancy premium for a clipper almost ready for sea, sir."

Forrest could not argue with that, much as he wanted. He sighed long and hard. "Very well. I will speak to the authorities this very afternoon." He examined his daughter. "You have done well, lass."

"Thank you, Father."

"Very well indeed. I am proud of you." He formed two fists, planted them on his desk, and pushed himself to his feet. "And I give you my word that I will lay the keel for a new *Erica* as soon as these troubles are behind us."

Chapter 6

Erica pulled back the drapes in her father's study, letting in the fresh light of a new day. She pried open the central window and breathed deeply. The air was laden with the fragrances of summer. From an oak across the way, a cardinal burst into song.

"It's over," she murmured, scarcely able to believe it herself.

"What's that, daughter?"

She turned to watch her father shuffle into his office. "The hardship is truly behind us."

He moved over to stand beside her and scratched at his face. Erica needed to look no farther than her beloved father to see just how long and harsh these months had been. Forrest Langston had always been fastidious in his dress. It was as much a part of who he was as his great booming laugh. But there had been little cause for merriment in these days. As Erica stood and felt the sun's warmth upon her cheek, she tried to recall the last time she had heard her father laugh.

"Why do you regard me so?"

She started as though coming awake. "I was just thinking . . . that word should come today about the latest peace efforts."

"Aye, that it should." Her father's traditional good humor had been replaced by mounting ire. That and numerous bouts of ill health had aged him. He had taken to rubbing his chest above his heart and complained of vague pains that moved out from his ribs to his left arm, sometimes all the way down to his fingers. His once ruddy cheeks now sagged. He ate without tasting anything and stared into space for long periods of time.

"You instructed our agents to send word as soon as possible?"

Erica had to clear her throat before she could speak. Sorrow still cracked every word. "Yes, Father."

But Forrest did not notice his daughter's state. "I should be ever so glad to have this war behind us. Then we shall take aim, and—"

"And do what, Forrest? Do what, precisely?" Mildred Langston appeared in the doorway to her husband's office. "Whatever could be of such vital importance that you would appear in public in your dressing gown?"

"Have I done that?" Forrest Langston glanced down at his own form. "Have I indeed?"

"Forrest, my dear husband, you are worrying me." Mildred crossed the room to take her husband's hand. "Do you not see how this anger of yours is consuming you?"

Erica could not stifle her sob. She was filled with such a mixture of emotions. Distress over her father, relief that her mother had finally expressed her own worries.

Forrest drew himself fully upright. "Do I not have cause for anger? Am I not justified in wanting to identify those who seek to destroy us?"

"Listen to me, my husband. You have lost sight of everything else. You are afflicted in the very core of your being."

"In case you had not noticed, we were almost destroyed by this matter. The English bankers came within a hairbreadth of doing us in."

"But we *have* survived, Forrest. Langston's is still a solid name."

Their family concern had indeed survived, but it had been a very close-run affair. The government's purchasing order had been enormous, far greater than anything they had ever attempted before. Only because they had managed to sell their almost-finished vessel at an extremely good rate could they fulfill the order at all. But they had been forced to borrow money at usurious rates in order to fulfill the military's demands for goods. Then there had been delay after delay over payment, with the interest charged by the banks eating into the profit.

Finally they had managed to sell all the merchandise stockpiled in their warehouse. Then, just that week, the government had paid them in full. Reluctantly, grudgingly, four endless months late, but they had paid. And Langston's had survived. The banks were repaid. They had money in their accounts. Their credit and good name were restored. They could restock the warehouse and accept the new purchasing order being offered to them by the government.

Forrest protested, "Yet the Bartholomew Merchant Bank still holds our gold in London, and we now know there was indeed a conspiracy. I will retrieve our wealth, and I will destroy them all!"

The last words were a great thunderclap of rage that left Forrest visibly trembling. From her place by the window, Erica could hear her father's strained breathing, see the flushed patches on his unshaven cheeks.

To her credit, Mildred's demeanor did not change. She continued to stand in her strong erect manner and addressed him in a tone both stern and loving. "Husband, I know how you pace during the night. I see how you have struggled to bring this house through this dark period. But we have survived! Can you not see this is what is most important? We have each other, our children are with us, the house is strong—"

"You would have us ignore what they have done to us?"

"I would have my husband alive and well and standing by my side. If that means turning away from all this, then yes, I would ignore it. Better a husband whose laughter rings through our home as it once did than all the gold in the world."

Erica studied her mother. The previous winter, Mildred Langston had taken to attending a new church. Their Sundays were still spent in the grand stone structure that dominated Washington, but several evenings a week Mildred visited with friends in a much plainer chapel not far from their home. These were called Bible and Social Hours and were open to women only. On several occasions she had invited Erica to join her, but the last thing Erica wanted was something more to occupy her time. Mildred had not insisted. Yet Erica had noticed a marked change in her mother during that long, hard winter. Gradually she had lost much of her cold demeanor. In its stead had grown a calm that emanated from her, even in the most trying of moments.

Forrest's outburst left him so weak that he could not pull his hand free of his wife's grip. He cried petulantly, "Release me!"

"I will do no such thing. Not ever." She pulled him forward. "Now come, Forrest. I shall draw you a bath, and then you will have a nice bowl of hot porridge and cream."

"But word is expected any moment from—"

"You have awaited their word for over a week now. Have they not told you repeatedly you will hear just as soon as you possibly can?"

Reluctantly he permitted himself to be led across the chamber. "I mustn't wait a moment to begin the proceedings just as soon as relations are restored."

"As you have been saying for months. Now come."

"Erica, you will find me as soon as news arrives?"

Her eyes were brimming over so that she had trouble seeing more than the vague outline of two forms passing through the doorway. "The very instant, Father."

Then she heard it. Or perhaps she had perceived a trace of the sound before. But her attention had been so tightly focused upon her parents that she had not identified it. Now she wiped her eyes and stepped back to the open window. Yes. There was no question.

"Father!"

"Do you see our man?"

"Forrest, please . . ."

Her father rushed over to stand alongside her. "Where is he?"

"Listen, Father."

But her father continued to lean out the open window and peer at the empty street below. "I don't see him. Are you certain—"

"Father, please!" She gripped his robe and shook his arm. "Listen to that noise!"

Mildred moved up behind her daughter. "Whatever is the matter?"

"I don't—" Then she heard it. Closer still now. "There it is again!"

Erica heard screams drifting in the gentle wind.

Then a second sound joined in, so distant at first she thought it was thunder. Only the sky was deepest blue, and the day fresh and lovely. Except for the rising sound of wails in the distance, and now this new echo.

Drumbeats. Stomping feet. The rumble of heavy wagon wheels over cobblestones.

But the noise made no sense. Of course she knew the sound of soldiers. This was, after all, the capital. Washington was full of military and uniforms. There were parades several times a year. But they almost always took place down toward the House of Congress and the armory, Washington's two largest structures.

"Forrest?"

Her father waved for silence. His entire frame seemed caught by the need to hear and identify.

The noise was definitely growing in volume. Erica could make out the clatter of shod horses dancing upon cobblestones, the clank of metal, the tromping of many boots. And the shouts of men.

Angry men.

Then the first bevy of people streaked past their home. A dozen or more women and children, running as fast as they could, shrieking as they went.

Erica could catch only one word.

British.

The door to the warehouse crashed open, and Reggie appeared. "Soldiers! There are soldiers coming down the street! British soldiers!"

They all looked instinctively at the head of the household.

For an instant, Forrest Langston faltered. Erica had never seen that look before, not even in the midst of the past dark and awful winter, when every day was a struggle. Her father had aged, he had suffered bouts of ill health, he had become gripped by a feverish ire against those who had sought to bring them down. But never had she seen what she saw now.

Forrest Langston leaned out the window and listened to the heavy tromp of leather-shod feet marching in unison. He heard with the others the cry of officers and the jangle of military steel.

And he was afraid.

He drew himself upright with great effort. "Downstairs, everyone. Reggie, come with me. We must gather the workers and prepare."

"Forrest, what is happening?"

Once again he was his former self, strong and determined and knowing what was required. "My dear, you must gather the house servants. Take everything of value and stow it in the cellar strong room."

"But—"

"Go, my dear. Make great haste." He raised his voice. "Carter!"

The head clerk tottered in from the warehouse. "Sir, Master Forrest, there are—"

"Gather all the ledgers and our bills of lading. All the account records. Everything of note. Take them into the cellar strong room. Reggie, go and help him."

"Yes, Father!"

"There's a good lad." He turned to his daughter. "Erica—"

She never heard what her father wished for her to do. For at that moment there came a bellow of rage from a street beyond her line of vision. Then a harsh command.

And then a volley of gunfire.

The shrieks came louder then.

"Forrest! What is happening?"

"Go and do as I say!" Her father ran for the warehouse door, his dressing gown flapping behind him.

Erica raced to keep up.

From the upstairs balcony, the empty warehouse looked huge. The absence of wares accentuated the vast space. In the far corner a cluster of workers had risen from where they were sewing jute into sacks. Others spilled from the coffeehouse and the tobacco bay. The workers stood in fearful indecision as Erica hurried down the stairs after her father.

"Lock the doors and windows!" Her father's words galvanized them into action. "You four, shutter all the windows to the coffeehouse and bar the door! You three, do the same for the tobacconist!"

Then Erica detected faint tendrils of smoke. "Father!"

Forrest Langston must have smelled it as well, for he halted and peered about him.

She was certain now. Smoke. But where . . .

"Fire! There, in the corner! The warehouse is on fire!"

Her father's voice rose to a bellow. "Form a fire line!"

Instantly the workers leaped into action. Her father raced for the main entrance. "Unbar the door and make for the troughs!"

Already workers were racing forward with buckets sloshing from both hands. Fire was a constant worry, what with the tobacco drying sheds and the coffee kilns and all the flammable merchandise. Only now the warehouse was almost empty.

But the fire had been set by the corner where the last bales of tobacco were kept. Already the flames were eating around the edges of the bales nearest the walls. The wooden partitions went up in a great whoosh of flames. Fire began licking at the overhead beams.

Forrest picked up a brace of buckets himself and raced outside.

And ran straight into the marching soldiers.

"Here, you! Get back!"

"My warehouse is on fire!"

"And I'm telling you to step aside!" The lead redcoat was a burly sergeant with a great walrus moustache, a high bearskin hat, and a scowl as fierce as the steel glinting from one hand. The sergeant roared to the men behind him, "Stay in line!"

But Forrest was not so easily halted. "The troughs! The troughs are across the street and—"

"Here, you!" The red-faced sergeant shoved her father back over the curb. Forrest stumbled and would have gone down had not Erica caught him. "Out of our way!"

"But I must save my business!"

When Forrest stepped forward, another soldier swiveled his musket about and clapped a massive blow upon his forehead.

"Father!"

Erica could not keep him from spilling to the ground. His eyelids fluttered and his limbs twitched. *"Father!"*

Then he seemed to be gripped by a massive unseen hand, one that shook him so violently he was almost flung from her embrace. His eyes shot open, and both hands rose to grip his chest.

Then he was still.

Erica knelt in the gutter, her father's lifeless form in her lap, the red imprint of a rifle butt upon his brow. The soldiers continued to troop by. She felt strong hands try to pry her away.

"No!"

"Hold hard, there!" An officer slid from his saddle. He stomped over on boots that gleamed as sharp as the steel at his side. "Release the lady!"

"But, sir, the wagons need the whole road."

"Can't you see she's in distress?" He lowered himself so that his face became visible. He was sweating beneath the visor of his officer's cap. "Who struck this man?"

None of his soldiers cared to respond.

"Miss, forgive me, I am most sorry. But we must clear this way."

Was that her voice that replied? It seemed some other person spoke for her, in tones low and dark with sorrow and rage. "Your men have fired my home and killed my father, and this is all you can say?"

"Fire? I gave no orders . . ." The officer straightened and caught sight of smoke billowing from the doorway. He saw also how men with buckets hovered anxiously, desperate to reach the troughs on the roadway's opposite side. "Let these men through!"

"But sir—"

"Did you not hear me? I gave explicit orders. Only government buildings are to be set ablaze! None but their soldiers are to be fired upon!" He pointed at the men hovering in the warehouse's doorway. "Move!"

They leaped forward. The British officer turned to his man-at-arms. "Stay here and ensure that these men have access to the water. Our wagons and men will work around them."

"Yes, Major Powers."

He lowered himself to the level of Erica's face. "Listen to me now." He had a natural leader's ability to demand her full attention.

"My father," she moaned.

"He is gone, and there is nothing you or I can do about it. Your warehouse is lost as well, by the looks of things. Is that your house connected to it? And a shop I see? Langston, is that your name?"

His soft but pressing queries drew her through the fog of pain and sorrow and back into clarity. "Erica Langston."

"I offer you my deepest sympathy, Miss Langston. This terrible deed should never have happened. But your men need direction now, and your father is gone. Someone must guide the hands of your workers if you are to save your house. Do you hear me? Rise up now. My man will help move your father. He will rest easy until this work is done. Release him . . . that's it. Your responsibility lies with the living."

Only when he was certain she understood did he let go of her arm. "Again I must ask your forgiveness, Miss Langston. And now I must move on. The tides of war wait for no man."

Chapter 7

Erica sat at her little desk. Sunlight spilled through the windows of yet another August morning . . . only this time the sunlight was tinted a harsh copper color. A number of the windowpanes were cracked. The two windows closest to where the warehouse had stood were streaked almost black. Forrest Langston's empty desk was shrouded in darkness. The chamber stank of cold smoke and ashes. Erica had cleaned and scrubbed and oiled and worked through much of the night, as she had the day before that, and the night before that . . . all the six endless days since the British had attacked their city.

The previous evening she had not gone to bed at all, merely worked until she could work no more, then curled up on the settee in the office parlor and, for the first time since the attack, cried herself to sleep. Now she knew it was time to get back to business. There were a hundred tasks that needed doing, but Erica had no idea what they were.

Twice her mother came in to speak to her, but Erica could not even make out her words. Mildred walked over and hugged her very hard, but she did not respond. She was too busy fighting back more tears. She was afraid of how she had cried the night before. The sobs had been so fierce, her sorrow so deep, she felt as though she had stood at the edge of a dark abyss. No, she did not want to permit any more tears. Her mother left.

The mantel clock ticked very loudly in the quiet. The

street outside her window was strangely empty. Bells tolled, then stopped, then tolled again. Now there was silence, save for the dreaded count of time. The door opened behind her, but Erica could not manage to turn her head. She heard a heavier tread cross the carpeted floor. A voice spoke her name. Her brother.

Reggie pulled over a chair, seated himself beside her, and took her hand. "Look at me, Erica."

He succeeded where her mother had not. She drew her brother and the world and the morning into focus.

"It's almost time."

She winced, not from the words, but from the fact that she now remembered. Today was the day. That was why the bells had been ringing throughout the city and why the streets were so still. Today the city mourned its loss.

"You must bathe and dress. Mother wants you to eat."

"I can't."

"You ate nothing yesterday. You must."

Each word held the leaden quality of an intolerable burden. "I can't go."

"You must," he repeated. "For Father. And for me. How could I possibly do this without you? And we can't force Mother to endure this alone."

But he had not understood. How could he? Her sentence had not been complete. She forced herself to say what she felt in her bones. "I can't go on."

Again she had not managed to complete the thought. She filled her chest with air and ashes. "I can't go on without Father." Sorrow's heat flamed in her heart, her throat, behind her eyes. She felt the tears come. She blinked them away, and others came. The hardest thing in her world was to halt the sobs before they rose.

"But you will, Erica. You will go on, and you will know exactly what needs to be done."

The matter-of-fact way Reggie spoke acted like a great calming force, and her words came more easily now. "You don't know what you're saying."

"Don't I just? Who's been keeping all of us sane and focused through the worst week of our lives? Who told me how to pull up my own bootstraps? Who got me directing our workers to scrub down the coffeehouse and air out the furnishings? Who suggested we salvage the wood and timbers from what's left of the warehouse and shore up the scorched rear walls?"

She shook her head. "I can't recall a thing."

"There, you see? Even when you're addled, you're working."

Erica examined her brother's face and saw his own pain. The center of his eyes looked hollow, as though his gaze had been bored through with a great merciless awl. But there he sat, giving her comfort, helping her rise out of her own dark place. "You're the strong one."

"Aye, I've got a good set of shoulders on me." He stretched his face in a parody of his former smile. "Pity I don't have your head to set there on top."

The mantel clock struck the hour. Erica felt each musical chime like a fist beating her into a future she had no wish to enter. "If I had the strength, I would smash every clock in this city."

Reggie did not understand—she saw that in his face. But he did not ask her meaning, which she found touching. He trusted her. She could see that in his weary wounded eyes, in the way he sat there waiting for her to rise up and move forward. "Thank you, brother."

"Are we ready now?"

"No. But we don't have any choice, do we?" She forced herself to her feet. "When does the service begin?"

"In three hours."

"Is it safe?"

Reggie rose with her. "There's been no sign of the British for three days."

The redcoats had caught Washington totally by surprise, overwhelming the small local garrison and entering the city at a gallop. They fought a running battle to the city's heart, where they burned the Capitol and the armory and a number of other structures. Then, just as troops from the Virginia and Maryland garrisons marched on Washington, the British vanished. They made no attempt to hold the city. Munitions in the armory were still exploding two days after they had departed.

Now there were rumors from every quarter. The redcoats had taken New York, Richmond, Charleston, Boston—the stories of dire deeds swirled like the ashes. In truth, no one knew where the British were or even how strong were their numbers. All that could be said for certain was that the nation had been caught unawares. It would not happen again.

So now the hour of mourning had arrived. Churches all over the city were holding services for those lost to the invasion force.

Erica permitted her brother to take her arm. "Do you know, I'm glad it won't be just for Father. Does that sound selfish?"

"No, Erica. It sounds like you. Maximum efficiency, minimum of fuss and bother."

She could not tell if he was jesting. "This way I think I shall be able to hold on to myself. If we were alone and all attention were upon us . . ."

He gripped her arm tighter as the shudder passed through her frame. "You would still hold on. I know you would."

"I wish I shared your confidence."

"You would do it because you have to." He held open the door leading into their home. "How else are we to survive?"

Major Gareth Powers sat amidships, surrounded by a group of junior officers. The day smelled of fresh sea air. The steady following wind carried with it the prospect of a swift start to their voyage home. Gareth was not sorry to leave the Americas behind. In his opinion, his superiors were wrong to have ever let this conflict arise. Almost half of his men had relatives in the former colonies. He had been forced to constantly keep watch for deserters or, even worse, mutiny from men he cared for and trusted with his life. No, this entire war was wrong. America was a nation in and of itself. It may have begun as a group of British colonies, but they were independent now. One look was enough to make him certain there was no going back. What was more, these former colonials were kindred spirits. They should have been counted among the Crown's staunchest allies. And the British had never needed friends as much as they did now, fighting for their very survival against a real foe—the upstart Frenchman, Napoleon.

The freshening wind sent a dark squall line scuttling toward their ship, and Gareth raised the collar of his greatcoat against the pelting rain. But not even the cold wash of rain could erase the odor he had carried for almost a month now. Woodsmoke mingled with burning roof tar and billowing plumes of fine tobacco. Overlaid upon this was the more acrid flavor of gunpowder. Though the real fighting had not started until much later that day, in his memories Gareth could not separate the burning private warehouse from the subsequent battle for Washington.

Nor could he erase a certain lovely face from his mind, one streaked in tears as the young woman cradled her father in her arms and watched her family business go up in flames. Officers were trained never to allow such moments of war to bother them. But try as he might, Gareth could not protect himself from this memory. He even found himself repeating the young lady's name in his sleep. The lovely Miss Langston.

He turned to the burly sergeant leaning against the nearby gunwale. "I was thinking of Washington."

"A miserable affair, if you don't mind my saying so, sir." Daniel was a veteran of countless skirmishes, a hard-edged giant with eyes constantly on the alert for danger. "March in, fight a scuffle we had no business starting, fire the town, march away."

"We didn't have sufficient strength to hold their capital."

"Never should have gone there in the first place if you ask

me, which you didn't, so excuse me for speaking as I shouldn't."

Gareth would not have accepted such an attitude from any other noncommissioned officer. But Daniel was his most trusted ally and friend. "There was some trouble early in the day."

"Trouble from start to finish," Daniel grumbled softly. His voice was now pitched low enough for Gareth to pretend the words were meant for no one but Daniel himself if he chose. "Nine deserters that morning. Nine from three hundred. Just slipped away into the night, men refusing to fire upon them what might be kin."

"I remember."

"Set me in a terrible state," Daniel continued softly. "First desertions in my whole time with the brigade. Had to post sentries facing inward like we were guarding prisoners. This with the enemy all around us. Or them we called enemy. Only they weren't. Leastwise, they never should—"

But Gareth was too much the king's officer to allow him to continue. "The scuffle that morning as we entered George-town."

"Sir?"

"A warehouse was fired."

"I remember. Terrible, it was."

"Who struck the old man?"

"Nary an idea, sir. I suppose I could ask about."

"See what you can learn." It was a fruitless gesture, Gareth knew. Nothing he did could restore the young lady's loss. Or grant him what he truly wanted, which was to behold those lovely eyes once more.

He turned his face upward, hoping the rain would wash away the tumult in his mind and heart. But the wet and cold only beat down harder, as though seeking to cry tears for him and for the stranger he would never glimpse again.

PART
TWO

Chapter 8

Erica opened the drapes in what had once been her father's office. It was a very different room now, and she was a very different woman. In the two years since the British invasion, her entire world had canted sharply upon its axis, not once, but numerous times.

The chamber was now her bedroom. She had fitted it as best she could, for in truth it was more like a bed-sitting-room, her own living chamber. At twenty-one years of age, she was now referred to as a spinster. The unmarried and increasingly unweddable Erica Langston. Her suitors were older men, widowers seeking a mother for children from previous marriages. Her own mother had ceased referring to them as unsuitable. In fact, she scarcely seemed to notice them at all, which was fine as far as Erica was concerned. One positive outcome of these two long and dreadful years was that those families with whom her mother had aspired a connection now avoided them. Erica was no longer being pressured to form a proper match. She was glad for this small taste of good fortune.

The issue of social standing did not occupy Mildred Langston these days. She now lived for the church. The family no longer attended the huge stone edifice in central Washington, but rather gave its Sundays over to the simple Georgetown chapel where her mother also spent many evenings. At first, Erica had assumed all these changes were merely her mother's way of coping, but increasingly she had come to accept this as a genuine fundamental change. How Erica felt about this, she honestly could not say.

She heard her mother stirring in the next room, previously Carter's office. Carter's will to live had vanished with the man he had served for almost half a century, and he had passed on the summer after her father had. By rights Erica's mother should have taken her husband's former office as her own chamber, for it was by far the nicest of the upstairs rooms where they now lived. But Mildred still disliked entering this room, although now for very different reasons.

Reggie occupied what had formerly been the clerks' quarters. The moneys were simply not there to rebuild the warehouse after the fire. Instead, they had used the salvaged wood to repair their home and erect a much smaller structure. The coffeehouse still occupied much of the downstairs, along with the tobacconist, where François still rolled his miniature cigars and served patrons from as far away as Boston. The extended downstairs housed a tobacco storage room and a space for roasting and grinding coffee. There was also a cramped storeroom for articles coming up for auction.

A narrow hallway ran the length of the upstairs against the wall opposite the windows, so that the family could move about without entering one another's private space. The upstairs parlor was now their sitting room. What had once been the formal upstairs vestibule was now walled off and sectioned into three chambers—a kitchen, a dining room that scarcely seated three, and a bath. Their former home was rented out to a senator from New York.

Washington had changed much in the past two years. Leading up to the British invasion, rumors had swirled that the capital was to be moved yet again. Richmond and Philadelphia had been the two most likely choices. But by burning the city's major structures, the British had not wounded the American spirit as they had intended. Instead, they had unified public sentiment. The next congress had convened in a midtown church and unanimously voted that all the structures be rebuilt. The capital remained exactly where it had been. Washington's future had been solidified by the war.

The two communities that rose to Washington's either side also prospered. Alexandria was the older village, full of prosperous shops and fine homes. Georgetown remained a port city, bustling and crowded and noisy. The Potomac harbors had been expanded greatly during the war, so that the Georgetown port now provided almost all the materials required for Washington's rebuilding, as well as supplying most of the military's needs. Washington's own military garrison was also the nation's largest, used both to protect the capital from a second attack and to maintain a close connection between the generals and the elected politicians.

Erica heard a tap on her door. "Yes?"

Reggie opened the door. "Good morning, sister."

"Is Mrs. Cutter here?"

"Seated in the first alcove downstairs, just as you requested."

Erica rose from her desk and stepped in front of the tall oval mirror. There was no indication of the worries she carried over this coming day or of the burdens she had taken on since the British invaded Washington. She still had her mother's proud carriage. Her hair was a rich mélange of black and brown. Her eyes were clear, her lips full, and her chin had a slight cleft just like her father's. The dress she wore was her finest, frayed somewhat from too many washings, but never worn like the others when working the coffeehouse auctions or tending the ledgers. She studied her features and was pleased with her resolute expression.

"I am ready," she said to her reflection and wished it were so.

She took the staircase by her brother's room so as not to risk having her mother call her in. Mildred Langston was extremely perceptive. She would recognize what Erica managed to hide from the rest of the world. Erica had no intention of concealing her plans from the family, but she could not speak of them now. Not even Reggie had any idea why he had been enlisted to help. For the moment, Erica needed to focus exclusively upon the task at hand.

But what if Abigail Cutter refused to help her? Erica was a merchant's daughter. Merchants succeeded because they never placed their hope in just one venture. They spread out their resources and their risk. If one project failed, another was there to keep them afloat. Erica hated the fact that she had no second option. Her family's future rode upon this coming conversation.

The coffeehouse's rear wall had been scorched by the British fire. In rebuilding, Reggie had suggested they include three small alcoves. These were shaped like glass-fronted rotundas, with rich velvet curtains that could be drawn for privacy. A number of politicians continued to take their afternoon coffee at Langston's, enjoying the private elegance, even on days when the next auction was far off and there were few wares on display.

Erica swept open the red drapes of one of these alcoves and could not quite hold back a gasp of surprise. She knew that some merchant families, including the Cutters, had prospered greatly as her own had fallen. It was not something she dwelt on, for that only led to bitter regret. But even so, she was startled to see Abigail Cutter dressed in the height of fashion. Her dress was of layered silk in shades of cream and ivory, with black onyx buttons and black laces across her bodice that were tipped with what appeared to be tiny gemstones. Her hair was piled high and held in place with tortoiseshell pins. Around her neck dangled a ruby pendant the size of a quail's egg.

"My dear Erica, what a delight it is to see you again! You cannot imagine what a pleasure it was to receive your note."

"I am very grateful that you would come, Mrs. Cutter."

"I asked you years ago to call me Abigail. Why on earth have you waited so long to contact me?"

Erica's tone sounded stiff and forced to her own ears. "I

assumed your interest in my family had dimmed. Especially after Horace became engaged to the Wilkins girl."

"That was neither Horace's doing nor my desire. My dear husband and I had quite a tiff over it, I don't mind telling you."

Erica seated herself facing Abigail. "Would you take coffee? Or hot cocoa, perhaps?"

"Your dear brother has already been by twice offering everything under the sun. I shall have nothing, thank you. And you must excuse how I am fitted out, but I am due to meet my husband for a luncheon with visiting French dignitaries. He insisted I dress for the occasion."

"Then I shall not keep you a moment longer than necessary."

"Erica, look at me. This is Abigail Cutter. Do you remember what we spoke of at the last tea party we both attended?"

"It seems like another lifetime."

"That it does. But some things do not change with time. At least they should not. I offered to be your friend. Do you remember that?"

Erica wanted to respond with a shred of pride. *Vaguely, yes, I remember something to that effect,* she wanted to say. But she could not. Too much depended upon this woman and this conversation. She stared down at her hands. They were stained now, the India ink so deeply imbedded she wondered if she would ever manage to clear it from around her nails. And her dress. Upstairs it had seemed adequate. But here in the sunlit alcove, seated next to this elegantly clad woman, she felt shabby and faded.

"You do remember, don't you?" When Erica said nothing, Abigail continued. "I wrote you three times, asking that you permit me to call upon you. I invited you on countless occasions to our home. Never once did you accept."

Erica forced herself to raise her head. "How could I?"

"What on earth do you mean?"

"You know perfectly well . . ." She stopped. No bitter tirades, Erica reminded herself.

But it was Abigail who melted. "Forgive me. Of course. Erica Langston, daughter of one of the finest merchants in all America, a young woman of such pride and determination, brought to her knees. How could I have expected her to enter into our haughty society and endure the stares and comments? No. I knew you would not come. But I hoped. And now we are together again, and I see you strong and able and still very determined. Of course you did not accept." Abigail fished in her purse and drew out an embroidered hankie. She dabbed at her eyes. "I am very proud of you, my dear."

"Proud of me?"

"A weaker woman would have folded in upon herself and disappeared into the waiting gloom. She would have fed upon bitterness and gall. She would have accepted the offer of marriage from an unsuitable gentleman and given herself over to a life of regret."

"I have been tempted." Merely saying the words brought such a burning to Erica's throat and eyes that she could not entirely keep it from her voice. "It would have been so easy to give in."

"But you did not. You are a credit to your father." Abigail bundled up her hankie and reached for Erica's hand. "Now you will tell me what it is that you require."

The barriers were broken now, but the need was so great it threatened to overwhelm her. "I am so desperate I am almost afraid to speak."

"Then I shall save you the trouble of further worry. I shall tell you yes now. There. Do you feel better? I have already agreed to whatever you wish to ask."

Erica gave a little laugh. "How can you be so good to me? I have been a stranger for almost two years, and yet you respond so generously."

"You are a fine woman who shall not be kept down, of that I am certain. One day very soon we shall look back upon this day's meeting, and you know what we shall say?"

"I cannot possibly look that far forward."

"We shall say that this was the day we became true friends." Abigail squeezed her hand tighter. "Now tell me what you require."

Erica took a breath. "I have heard that trade between America and Britain is finally to be reestablished."

"How could you possibly know that? The news is not made public."

"We have any number of visitors here."

"Of course. And you are always one to know the value of being first with vital information." Abigail beamed with such pride she might as well have invented Erica herself. "I am happy to confirm that your information is true. The president will announce this tomorrow. Although it is hardly a triumph in any true sense of the word. We should never have entered into this tiresome conflict that neither side could hope to win."

"But trade," Erica pressed, wanting to make sure her information had been correct. "And political ties?"

Abigail studied her anew. "You can't possibly have heard that as well."

"Then it's true? John Quincy Adams is to become the new ambassador to the Court of St. James? And your son-in-law is to be his deputy minister plenipotentiary?"

"Tell me what this is all about, Erica."

She took another breath, the hardest of all. Then she launched in. Not as she had planned, however. She had intended to take a roundabout course, but she sensed there was nothing to be gained by subterfuge. So she told Abigail everything. About Bartholomew Merchant Bank and the two ships that had never arrived. About the gold in the account, still sitting there in London in her father's name. Of course it was, since the ships had never arrived and the papers expressly forbade the bankers to touch one gold coin until the goods had been received and the bills of lading initialed. Erica had all the documents upstairs, everything signed by her father and the bankers. Everything properly witnessed.

She concluded, "I have spoken to several lawyers here.

There is no hope of doing anything from this end, especially since we have neither the money nor the time to press the case."

"It is becoming clear to me now."

"I need to travel to England as an envoy for my family. I will carry these documents and demand what is rightfully ours."

Abigail had long since removed her hand from Erica's. She sat and listened with an intensity that had her eyes glittering like the ruby dangling about her neck. "I can well understand why my husband does not like you," she said. "You would make a most formidable adversary."

Erica wanted to know what she meant, especially now, when the Langston house was on its knees. "But Mother would never permit me to make such a journey unless someone of proper standing were willing to act as my host."

"I shall speak with my son-in-law, Samuel Aldridge, this very day."

"But your husband—"

"Did I not already agree to whatever it was you required of me? Did I not claim you as my friend?"

This time Erica could not hold back the tears. She never cried these days, which meant she had not brought a handkerchief with her.

Abigail pressed her own hankie into Erica's hands. "Here, my dear."

"Please excuse me."

"There is nothing for you to apologize over. I cannot imagine the strain you have endured."

"No." Erica forced herself to straighten once more. She pressed the hankie to the corner of each eye. "You cannot."

"So, that is done. All I can say is I am glad that what you require is within my reach to give."

"What if they refuse? I have never even met Horace's sister." Lavinia Aldridge, Abigail's daughter, was ten years older than her brother. She had married the son of a senior New York merchant.

"They will not refuse." Abigail revealed a very different side, one of steely resolve. "In that you may have utter confidence."

"I do. Have confidence." Erica looked around her. The unseen weight had been lifted from her heart so suddenly she could scarcely believe it was gone. The sunlight through the lead-pane windows was far brighter now. The hedge marking the rear of their property shimmered with an emerald glow. "I don't know how I can ever thank you for this."

"You will take advice if offered?"

"From you? Always."

Abigail leaned forward. "You are a strong woman, Erica Langston. One of the strongest and finest it has ever been my pleasure to know. And though you cannot see it yet, these years of trial and testing have served you well."

"I cannot possibly see how these days have served any good purpose whatsoever."

"In time, you shall. Now hear me out. One of the great risks of strength like yours is thinking that you can proceed on your own. It has taken a moment of dire need for you to seek me out. This should not have happened."

"I was wrong."

"No, child. You were proud. You saw coming to me as a humiliation. Were we not friends, it would have been so. But I offered you my alliance. I demonstrated this by granting you highly confidential information. You should have accepted me at my word and come to me."

"Again, I can only apologize, Mrs. . . . Abigail."

"I am not after your apologies, my dear young lady. I am speaking here of things to come. Never see yourself as too strong to need help. None of us is. Find allies you can trust. Do not let pride or your own strength stand in the way of this. Develop friends, and offer to them the same gift that I have offered you."

Chapter 9

Erica's conversation with her mother was as great a surprise as her meeting with Abigail. When she returned to their apartment, Erica found Mildred seated in the upstairs parlor, the one formerly used by Forrest and his business guests. Now it contained a number of their most treasured belongings. Every surface held pictures and mementos. Upon the walls hung paintings of her father, her grandmother, and a ship now sailing under a different name. The room overwhelmed Erica with memories.

"Erica, there you are. Where have you been?"

"Downstairs, Mama." She watched her mother set aside the prayer missal she had been studying. "Did you rest well?"

"What an odd question to ask at midday. What were you doing in the coffeehouse?"

"Visiting with Abigail Cutter."

"Abigail was here? Why was I not invited to join you?"

"I needed to speak with her alone."

"Did you, now." Her mother indicated the place beside her. "Am I permitted to ask what this was all about?"

"Us. The family." Erica had worked and reworked the way she wanted this discussion to go. But the effects of her conversation with Abigail still lingered.

"You are wearing the most extraordinary expression."

The silence spanned several ticks of the clock. Mildred

spoke again. "I did not realize you two were in contact."

"I have not spoken to her in almost two years. She wants to be my friend."

"Well. I suppose it is good to renew such connections." Then her mother waited, an aura of deep calm emanating from her.

Actually, calm was not precisely the word Erica sought. Her mother sat with the same formal posture as always. She displayed no bitterness or anger over their situation. Instead, she observed her daughter from a haven of peace that Erica most certainly did not share.

Although Erica had faithfully accompanied Mildred to Sunday services, she had no inclination to join her the many other evenings her mother spent at church. She felt grateful that her mother was not just sitting upstairs in her cramped little parlor, surrounded by relics of a bygone era and dusty reminders of a man now in his grave.

"I invited her to come," Erica now said. "I needed to ask a favor." She had not intended to come into this so directly. But so little of this world came about as she wanted. "Mother, I must travel to London."

"I beg your pardon?"

"And soon. Time is not our ally here."

"Daughter, be sensible. London is . . ."

Erica actually observed the change. Her mother had started to respond that London was out of the question. And she was going to revert to the haughty tone of command Erica had heard all through her childhood. "Yes, Mother? London is what?"

But the sharp edge was gone from her mother's voice. Instead, Mildred Langston's attention seemed at least partly held by something Erica could not see. "Perhaps it would be better if you told me what this is about."

Erica laid it all out, not attempting to gloss over anything. At one point she went back into her bedroom and returned with the ledgers. "Our existence remains poised upon a knife's edge of debt and expenses. We have no hope of ever rising above our current station unless I go to London and recover these funds."

"Please, daughter, close the books. I trust you and your calculations. I also know you could tell me anything you like about the figures written there, and I would have no choice but to accept your words."

"I am sorry, Mother."

"For what? For managing our affairs so that we have a roof over our heads and food on the table? I know how hard you and Reggie are working."

"I do the best I can."

"I know. It defines your very nature. Now I want you to do something for me."

The words rocked her. They were almost exactly what she had heard from Abigail downstairs. "Yes?"

"I want you to treat *me* as a friend as well. I am sorry that I have become someone to whom you cannot come first. That you must turn to a virtual stranger before you approach your own mother."

"You have often viewed my work suspiciously, Mother."

"Well do I know it. And no better than this moment, when I see you sitting there prepared for yet another quarrel."

"Mama, I . . . I don't know what to say."

"No. And that is also most distressing." Mildred sat very precisely, poised and erect as always. But the sunlight coming through the streetside window formed a gentle crown upon her graying hair, one that matched the soft light in her eyes. Erica realized for the first time just how much her mother had aged in the past two years. Mildred went on, "Let us begin by assuming you will be departing for London."

Nothing that her mother might have said could have shocked her more than this. Erica felt the strength drain from her. "What—I mean how—?"

"I must trust your reason," she continued. "I trust you every day to do what would have made your father very proud." Only a faint trembling of Mildred's cheeks revealed the strain these words caused. "Now explain to me why this trip to London is so vital, and tell me more about it. When do you hope to depart? With whom will you travel? Where will you lodge when you reach England?"

Erica answered her mother's questions, although she remained numb throughout. Of all the ways this conversation might have gone, this was the most astonishing. She talked of the bankers. She talked of trade. She talked of the newly appointed emissary from America to London. She talked of her hopes and her plans. And not once did her mother object or interrupt or demand that she put aside these ridiculous notions. Erica paused several times in the telling, not because she expected these protests, but because she was confounded by their absence.

Mildred sat and watched and did not speak. What was more, she *listened*.

Erica did not stop so much as drift into silence.

At that moment, the clock chimed the noon hour. Twelve long strokes. The bell's music resounded through the still air.

When the ticking resumed, Mildred said, "That was very clear, my dear. Thank you."

"Mama, I don't know what to say."

"Nor do I." She grasped her daughter's hands. "So let us join together in prayer and ask for God's wisdom in finding both the right words and our way through all that lies ahead."

Over the ensuing days Erica found the idea of her journey gradually growing and taking root. She would start awake in the night, scarcely able to breathe. There were so many emotions tied to the very idea of traveling. She yearned for this trip fiercely and yet feared it with almost equal intensity.

She found herself pondering her conversations with Abigail

and her mother through the long, dark hours. The two women were so different and yet tied so intimately together. Abigail's words became a reflection of her own inner state. The last two years had taught Erica a great deal about loneliness. Shunned by those she had once counted as friends, at least close acquaintances, Erica had neither the time nor the interest to develop new connections. Most of the time, she remained too busy to care. In these hours of reflection, however, she could not escape how desperately lonely she felt. How she yearned for someone in whom she could truly confide!

Her mother's words seemed connected to such feelings, raised to the surface by Abigail's discussion. Time and again Erica found herself thinking about the astonishing change in Mildred Langston. She could discount the transformation no longer, for it affected everything about her own future and her plans. When they were together during the day, Erica often observed her mother discreetly. Her mother's calm agreement seemed to challenge her in some subtle way.

Erica could not explain precisely why she felt this way nor why she often watched and waited for the storm. Yet it was this new calm that came to her most often in the night hours, when she would lie awake and find herself forced to accept that her mother had grown from this tragic period. She had changed in ways that were utterly lost on her daughter.

Two weeks to the day after her meeting with Abigail, Erica's mother called her into the upstairs parlor. "Might I have a word?"

"Of course, Mama."

"Don't hover, child. Come sit down beside me." She indicated a sealed envelope resting upon the corner table. "I have prepared a letter to your great aunt. At least we have thought of her as part of the Harrow family since she was raised by my grandparents as their own. You, of course, recall my speaking of her in the past. It is Anne Crowley's son who became the adopted heir to the lost Harrow estates and titles."

"I remember you telling about this when I was younger."

But, in truth, Erica's mind was held by what the letter represented. If her mother was writing distant relatives about the journey, it meant that she was most definitely going.

"Anne's husband was a lawyer turned vicar. They lived in Nova Scotia for a time, but her husband was called back to take over a church in Manchester. That is a city north of London. I wish I could be more pleased with this family connection in England and what it might mean for you. But recently I learned that her husband is in the last stages of a serious illness and is not expected to survive. Anne is apparently quite devastated." Mildred sighed. "But I suppose it can't hurt to write of your journey."

"No, Mama." Erica felt a hidden knot of tension begin to unravel. She was going to London.

Mildred studied her daughter. "You once asked me not to address you any longer as a child. Do you recall that?"

"Vividly."

She took her daughter's hand and spent a long moment inspecting it. "You will accept an old woman's advice?"

"You are not old, Mother."

"I will take that as an affirmative. Listen carefully, my dear. Do not make the same mistake as your father."

Erica jerked her hand free. "Father was the finest businessman I have ever known. This matter with the London bankers was—"

"I am not referring to his business. I am speaking of how he was affected by the setback."

"I–I don't understand."

"You say you are going to London to speak with lawyers and seek to obtain what is rightfully ours. I fear that is not all that drives your mission."

Erica did not respond.

"I am concerned that you are also going for revenge. You must set this aside, my dear. It will eat away at you from within. Heed my words. It will consume you."

"Mama—"

"Oh, I am well aware how you and Reggie view the time I spend with the church community. It fills an old woman's hours. And that is true, as far as it goes. But it has also kept me from falling into the same trap that caused your father such anguish during his final months. Do you recall the anger and the sleepless nights and his overwhelming urge to wreak vengeance upon those who had wronged him?"

Mildred continued to face her daughter, but her eyes stared back through time, and what they saw aged her features by decades. "He became a man possessed by the furies. He saw none of life's goodness. Revenge was all he could see, all he wanted, all he had room for in his life. He was blinded. He was turned into a man unhappy within his own soul, one who could never be satisfied. Even if he had received what he had wanted, he would have remained unquenched."

Mildred blinked slowly, drawing Erica back into focus. "You are your father's daughter. Go to London if you feel you must. But do not seek vengeance. Instead, seek what was good in your father. Seek what is good in yourself. Go with lofty purpose, and pray God will guide your every step. As shall I, my dear young lady. As shall I."

Chapter 10

Three and a half months passed before Abigail Cutter delivered the longed-for invitation from her daughter and son-in-law in London. The acting ambassador's family was occupying the embassy's upper two floors while better accommodations were being sought, but they would most certainly make room for Miss Langston.

Another two and a half months passed before companions were located for the journey, as Erica, of course, could not travel alone. A suitable family was found. The head of the family was the son of old acquaintances. He was a silversmith taking over a family concern in the Prussian capital of Berlin, stopping off for six months' work in London.

All this delay was in truth not without its benefits. Winter had passed in the meantime, one of the most ferocious on record, and as Erica visited the port offices she heard tales of what a winter voyage could mean. One ship arrived with the loss of eighteen souls, half of them children. She trod home through the snow and ached for the families fated to start life in the New World bearing such terrible woes.

With the new year came word that Britain had finally conquered the emperor Napoleon. England had warred against France for a quarter of a century. The English broadsheets were full of the great victory. Erica stocked the coffeehouse with three such British papers, supposedly for the patrons but in truth so she could study this unknown terrain. What the British victory meant for her own undertaking, she did not know.

Then suddenly the months of waiting turned into days of frantic activity, counting down to the moment of departure. There were still a thousand things to do, and Erica knew she could never finish it all.

That morning, Erica stood over a desk piled high with articles still to be packed and complained to her brother, "Why did I ever think this was a wise course to take?"

"Because it is." Reggie held up a final bundle of documents held together with ribbon and wax. "Where do you want these?"

"In the case with the other papers."

"If I put even so much as a hairpin in there, the case will explode and we will be back where we started, only your precious papers will be spread out all over the floor."

"That can't be possible."

"Have a look if you don't believe me."

Erica glanced into the trunk. "What is all this?"

Reggie laughed out loud. "If you don't know, Erica, we are all in great and serious trouble."

She looked at him, the wide beaming mouth that was so much like her father's, the light that never dimmed in his eyes, the shock of hair that fell so charmingly over his forehead.

"Remind me why I started down this road, would you? I've completely forgotten."

"Because you must. Because there is no one else who can do this." Reggie beamed. "Because you trust me to do a perfect job of running everything until your return."

"That last statement is true," she replied. "You are the best brother any woman has ever had in all the world."

"If there were time I would make you write that down and seal it with a royal warrant," Reggie asserted. Then he caught sight of someone over Erica's shoulder and said, "Mother, did you hear? I am the finest man on the face of the earth."

"I did not say that."

Mildred approached with a rustle of skirts. "Are you ready, daughter?"

"I suppose. . . . Mother, am I making a terrible mistake?"

Erica froze in that instant, wishing there were some way to pull back the words. Why had she given her mother such an opening? But the words were out there, and it meant that Mildred might now say what had remained unsaid for the past five months. Erica should put this foolishness behind her. Her role was to accept her place in this world and be a proper young lady, one who did not seek to stray far from home.

But instead, Mildred showed the same equanimity that had possessed her all the winter long. "Reggie, the carriage is downstairs. Be a dear and take down these trunks."

"Of course, Mother."

"If the coffeehouse can look after itself for a bit, I want you to accompany your sister to the docks."

"You are not coming?"

"No. Erica and I will say our farewells here." She indicated that Erica should join her in the parlor.

Mildred waited until Erica was seated. "You will forgive me if I do not accompany you to the ship? I do not feel up to the journey."

"You are unwell, Mama?"

"I am fine. But seeing my daughter off to strange lands, in the hands of strange people . . ." Her eyes were overly bright, her tone somewhat brisk. "I think I shall be more able to handle our farewells if they take place here."

"Of course."

"I see you do not understand. My child . . . Forgive me, but in this moment I cannot call you anything else. My darling child, you are embarking on a voyage I could not contemplate making. It pains me greatly, but I recognize that you are doing what you must, and I will not stand in your way."

"No, Mama. I appreciate your words. Truly I do." Here was her mother's place. Here was where she felt most comfortable, where she could maintain her semblance of a proper order in a chaotic world.

In that instant, Erica saw a great deal more. Only at the very last minute, when the barriers she had kept up for so long were not required, did she see her mother in a new light. Mildred Langston was a woman raised to expect a certain pattern to life, and it had been ripped away from her. But she was trying as hard as possible to hold on to what she saw as correct for a woman of her station—her dignity, her poise, her family, her home. Erica felt such a sudden deluge of love for her mother she could scarcely draw breath, much less frame the words, "Reggie will do a splendid job of seeing me off."

"Of that I have no doubt." Mildred settled her hands into her lap. "My child, I would ask that you do something for me."

"Anything."

The swiftness of Erica's response caught them both unawares. Mildred's eyes misted over momentarily. "You and I are different in so many ways."

"I'm sorry, Mama, I—"

"Shush, my child, I did not mean that as a criticism. You are your father's daughter, and I should have been willing to accept that far sooner than I did."

"I am your daughter too."

"Of course you are." Mildred reached over with both her hands. "A lovely, wonderful young lady who has done so much to make us all proud. And will do so much more. Of that I am most certain."

She wanted to thank her mother, but the words would not come.

"Which is why I want to ask a very special favor of you. Actually, I am hoping to exact a promise. Consider it a parting gift to your mother."

Erica was forced to make do with a nod.

"I want you to promise me that you will pray each and every day."

Erica swallowed down the sorrow and worked hard at making sense of the words.

Mildred sat and studied her and said nothing more.

"Mama . . ."

"Yes?"

It was very hard to say what she thought; perhaps it would be better to say nothing at all. Their lives had been spent keeping so much from one another, particularly these past months. The daughter had been busy making arrangements for a journey her mother would have never dreamed of taking. The mother had studiously avoided expressing any concerns she might have regarding the entire affair. But now, on the verge of so many endings and even more beginnings, Erica wanted nothing but truth between them.

She said, in a voice so soft she did not recognize it as her own, "I am not certain that I believe in God at all."

To her great surprise, her mother seemed pleased with that response. "But if you are willing to pray, you will at least give our Lord a chance to speak."

"Why would He want to speak with me?"

Mildred Langston gave her daughter a very rare smile. "Because He sees in you the same wondrous talents I find myself."

"Oh, Mama."

"Now, I have three volumes I want you to find room for in your valise." Mildred became brisk again, no doubt so that she would not give in to the tears Erica found burning in her own eyes. "One is the church prayer missal. If you are unable to find words to speak, this may help guide your thoughts. Another is the Bible; do try and read a few words of this each day. And finally, a copy of *Pilgrim's Progress*. You are, after all, a pilgrim of sorts. Perhaps you will find solace in this tale."

"Oh, Mama, I shall miss you so."

But her mother refused to give in to the sorrow. She maintained her cheery tone as she said, "Now perhaps you would do me the kindness of bowing your head and letting me say a few words to our God in heaven before you go."

The high seas were not at all what Erica had expected. She had never dreamed people could be so crowded. The hold where she and the family she traveled with slept was home to 91 souls yet was smaller than her family's cramped apartment. The ship's crew ran to 118, yet the common sailors slept in a room half the size of their own. It was only possible because they lived in watches, two sleeping while the third worked. And yet surrounding them on all sides was the greatest emptiness Erica had ever known. She sat for hours staring out over the rail. Not because she loved the sea. She was terrified of it, the great impersonal power that swept by with nary a care for who she was or why she traveled. Yet she continued to look because it was the only way she could be alone, just for a moment, in the midst of all these people.

They journeyed through a universe of water, yet there was never enough of it aboard the ship. Her personal washing was done in a cramped little closet with a sponge and a pail of seawater. Clothes had to be washed on deck, sluiced with water drawn by buckets over the side. Her skin cracked and flaked from the salt. Her clothes rustled with every movement and scratched her roughly. By the fourth week she was always thirsty. She and all the below-decks passengers, those in the common hold, were limited to three cups of water each day. It was not enough. Her lips became blistered with the salt and thirst that were her constant companions.

The wind blew every day, yet it came from the wrong direction, straight out of the east. This meant the ship had to travel far to the north, then turn and go far south, back and forth, each leg of the voyage taking a week and more. This north-and-south travel was called tacking. First-timers like Erica learned the vernacular from those who had voyaged before, though why people who knew of the seafaring life would ever agree to make another trip was a mystery to her. They tacked until the wind blew bitter and hard as winter knives, and Erica joined the others in wearing every stitch of clothing she had brought, even in her narrow bunk. Then the ship would turn and tack south until the days grew steamy and she perspired away her precious water and was wracked by thirst. All this travel, day after day of endless sweeping waves . . . yet their forward progress seemed to be measured in inches, not leagues.

The ship held to a very rigid caste system. At the top was the captain. Directly below him were all the ship's officers and the richest passengers. These fortunate few secured not just a private cabin but also the right to share the captain's table. Erica heard tales of how these folk ate, while below decks they fared upon gruel with thin strips of salt beef twice daily. By the fourth week her teeth ached constantly, and her joints felt swollen. Even the children moved like old folks, and Erica knew she was doing the same.

But what caused her the most bewilderment was how she could travel on while her thoughts remained far behind. Here she was, setting off upon her first adventure. She had obtained exactly what she wanted. Yet her mind remained fastened upon what her mother had said, both the day they spoke in the parlor and during their farewells. Despite Abigail Cutter's assurances, Erica had felt it necessary to have something in hand before setting out, a written confirmation that she had a place to stay and people to aid her. In truth, part of her insistence was framed around knowing what her mother would want. She hoped that by showing this prudence she would halt any objections she might otherwise make.

But Mildred had never opposed the journey. She had remained calm throughout the weeks of preparation; in fact, she had rarely spoken of it at all. She had observed carefully and listened as Erica and Reggie discussed matters over meals. She had asked the occasional question. But not once had she said that her daughter should not go. Erica had found her presence to be a surprising comfort.

Now she stood by the windward rail and watched yet another sunset dust the waves with gold. Hour by hour they plied their way farther from home and closer to England. Yet her mother's voice echoed louder than the wind, louder than the drumming ropes and the snapping sails and the barked command of a nearby officer. She nodded to something spoken by one of her fellow travelers, yet her mother's words were far clearer.

The ship's bell clanged the hour for the day's second meal, and together with the others Erica made her way across the deck. Yet her mother's presence seemed to accompany her, even down into the hold and into the line of passengers awaiting their food. As Erica accepted her bowl of gruel and salt beef, it came to her. A thought so illogical that she questioned how it had occurred to her at all.

Perhaps her mother was praying for her.

Erica ate the gruel without tasting it, for her mind and heart remained occupied with this new marvel. Could the hardships of a journey of weeks and countless sea miles be overcome by such a simple act? Were they joined by ties that defied her own mind and strength and determination? Was this what prayer was truly all about?

Chapter 11

The ship was not scheduled to stop in Portsmouth at all. But the wind gradually shifted at their approach until it was blowing hard out of the north, and a reach up the narrow English Channel would have meant another week of tacking and fighting for each mile. Water was growing desperately short, almost as short as the passengers' tempers. So the captain elected to first berth in Portsmouth before rounding the Dover Strait and beating upwind.

Virtually all the passengers, including the silversmith's family, chose to alight there and take the two-day coach north to London. Erica elected to remain on board. Her papers promised that she would be delivered to the London docks, and there she would go. Why should she pay twice for the same journey?

The next day, after taking on barrels of water and fresh produce, the ship raised anchor and sailed up the narrow channel. For the first time since leaving America, the winds turned in their favor. Yet now Erica would have preferred to see the ship flail into the storm's teeth and delay her arrival by another few days, a week, or even forever. Because no matter how hard she tried to ignore her worries, she faced them constantly. What if she failed at her mission? How could she return home and tell her family? What hope could she find for her life if she was not successful? What hope did any of them have of returning to life as it once had been?

She paced the empty deck and watched the shoreline race by. The wind was south by southeast and balmy, the summer heat kept at bay only by the sea's constant chill. She heard a sailor's cheery tune drift down from the bowsprits overhead. Why should they not be happy? The sun was shining and they were drawing ever closer to home.

On the third dawn after leaving Portsmouth, the skipper steered his vessel past the Southend fort and entered the Thames estuary. A cannonade boomed from the fortress walls, and the ship responded with a noisy salute of its own. The colors were dipped at the main mast, signal flags were raised and lowered, and the ship sped on toward its final destination. Erica heard one of the few remaining passengers observe that England's defenses must still be holding to a military footing.

The sun's warmth was stronger now that they had left behind the ocean's briskness. Erica raised her face to the light, shut her eyes, and wished she believed in God enough to ask for help.

She had held to the promise she had made her mother. Every morning she read a few lines of Scripture, then opened the prayer missal and silently said the day's entreaty. But they were little more than words, read because she had said she would. In fact, the very act seemed to drive her even farther away from whatever shred of belief she might still hold. Questions would arise, things she could not answer. How could a benevolent God have permitted her father to die in such a brutal fashion? Where were the mercy and the reasons for thanksgiving in such a senseless act? She would then close the missal and go about her day, untouched by anything save regret. So many things she had once held dear had been stripped away. Childlike faith in an unseen Protector was merely one more entry in that sad ledger of loss. Yet she found herself unable to keep the words from rising within her. *Oh, God, if you do indeed exist, help me now.*

Erica opened her eyes to an unchanged vista. She felt vaguely ashamed, as though she had slighted her principles by begging for help in this manner. She straightened her shoulders and peered into the future. If only she did not feel so very alone.

All the pictures and all the books in all the world could not have prepared Erica for London.

Where the estuary narrowed and became a true river, a flotilla of small boats waited. Clusters of men stood by their oars and watched them pass with neither a word nor a gesture. Among the passengers still on board were two men who had made this journey before. They explained how when winds or tides made travel impossible under sail, these oarsmen would row the vessels upriver for a price.

The pastures and bleating animals and carefully tended farms of Essex had gradually given way to thicker clusters of buildings. Up ahead the blue sky was blanched by a hovering fog, one so thick that not even the southern wind could push it away. The buildings grew denser and larger. Canals powering great wooden wheels pulled away from the river itself. Smokestacks rose higher than any structure she had ever seen and belched great clouds into the air.

Then they rounded a bend and Erica stared open-mouthed at a scene unlike anything she could have imagined. A manor stood proudly upon the hill, its granite facade shining brightly in contrast to the red-brick houses that clambered up the slopes below. The river broadened and formed a semicircle about the hill's base. Huddled there were perhaps two dozen ships, all arrayed in perfect symmetry. A whistle piped upon one deck, the sound drifting in the wind. Erica mused, "I never thought London would be this grand."

One of the more experienced travelers guffawed. "This is

naught but the village called Greenwich, lass."

The village, as he called it, contained more people than Georgetown and Washington and Alexandria combined. Of that she was certain. "But surely that is a palace?"

He must have noticed her wonder, for he gentled his tone. "What you see upon yon hillock is the Naval Observatory. They study odd things there—maps and stars and time and such."

She wanted to sound more sophisticated, but her desire to understand what she observed was not to be denied. "And the ships resting at anchor?"

"The Greenwich flotilla. There to protect the approach to London. Part of Nelson's fleet. What Napoleon left afloat, that is."

The other passengers became caught up in a discussion of Napoleon and the recently concluded wars. Every meal on board their ship since leaving Portsmouth had triggered further discussion of these events. Every step of the conflicts had been fought anew. Erica stepped away from the others. She would be pleased never to hear of war and battle again.

She studied the village and the convoy and struggled to accept what this meant. She counted twenty-seven ships of the line. Surely these could not be just "part" of anyone's navy. She knew for a fact that the entire American fleet consisted of thirty-three ships. This casual display of gathered naval might left her weak.

"You all right there, lass?"

"Fine, thank you, sir."

"You've gone all pale."

"I can scarcely believe the voyage is almost at an end."

It was just one bank, not the whole British Empire, that Erica had to face, yet she was struck anew with the realization that she was one lone woman from a backwater capital, without power or connections. How could she have ever imagined herself capable of taking on any such adversary and winning?

Gareth Powers, former major with the British fusiliers, found himself unable to remain still. He craned his neck out the carriage window and called up instructions. When the jostling throng halted his carriage's progress yet again, he sprang out and climbed nimbly up to the driver's bench, where he demanded, "Can't we make swifter progress?"

"We might." Daniel had remained his closest ally from the military days. "If a certain major would see fit to leave me to the task at hand."

"No chance of that." Gareth had asked Daniel countless times to stop referring to him as the officer he no longer was, but at this moment he chose to ignore the reference. He studied the crowd milling about on all sides. "I smell danger."

"Rumors are all of strife and woe," Daniel agreed. He was a huge man and held the long carriage whip as he would a child's toy. "Pity your aunt's vessel is docking on such a day as this."

"Can't be helped." Gareth indicated the carefully prepared bales stacked upon the luggage bay. "Besides which, these really must get off with the next boat for France."

Gareth had always seen himself remaining with the fusiliers his entire life. His father had been a colonel with the House Guards, his grandfather had served two kings, his great-grandfather had been granted a dukedom for his supremacy in combat. And so it should have been with him. Even now, when he felt himself blessed in almost every way, he missed his regiment and his friends and the ordered way of military life.

He had returned from the American conflict certain they had made a grave error in going there at all. Thankfully their foray onto American soil had been very swift. His regiment had been called home after only a few short weeks because Napoleon was a far greater threat. Gareth had fought the French from Oporto to Bayonne, been decorated nine different times, and was promised a colonelcy. His career seemed ready to outshine even the first duke's. Then disaster had struck, and in the most unexpected of forms.

Gareth didn't know what he had expected after the British forces were disbanded. A marching band would have been nice, a bit of bunting for the lads who had survived, a warm welcome from a grateful king. Instead, his men had been gathered upon a dusty plain outside Bordeaux. There the regimental colors had been furled and the company dismissed. No word of how they were to return home. No reward for having saved the British empire. Not even a receipt of back pay. His men made it home only because Gareth hired a vessel with his own purse. He had lost three wounded during the journey, due not so much to illness as to a loss of spirit, defeated by their own king.

They had returned home to find the nation in delirious joy, yet beneath the elation was misery of a shocking scale. Many disbanded soldiers had to beg their way back to homes and families. Gareth used his family carriage to transport the wounded. Upon the journey he saw just how his beloved homeland suffered. The land enclosures, the destitute, the mill hands, the miners, the suffering of children. He returned to London shaken to his core, only to learn that here as well the news was bleak. The king was ill, and in his place the land was ruled by the prince regent and his cronies. The regent was a wastrel who cared only for gambling and carousing. It was he who had caused the Treasury to treat Gareth's men so badly.

Finally Gareth Powers had a focus for his ire.

He resigned his commission in disgust and traded his sword for a pen. The established press, or broadsheets as they were known, were all controlled by allies of the Crown. So Gareth had written his regiment's tale and gone to a private printer. He paid for the pamphlets himself, then used the printer's runners to sell them at a halfpenny apiece.

In two weeks he had sold more than a hundred thousand

copies—nearly the number of copies sold of the nation's second most popular newspaper.

He wrote a second pamphlet. And a third. By the time he penned the fourth, his pamphlets required the printer's entire output to run right around the clock. He bought out the old man and the shops to either side, then sent word to his old military mates that work was available if they were willing. The sight of his old friends, and the state into which most had fallen, caused Gareth to weep.

The Powers Press became a voice recognized even by the Crown and the ruling Tories. Yet Gareth's rage would carry him only so far. He had seen ahead and envisioned where he was going, gradually falling into bitterness and a cynicism that no triumph or achievement could overcome. He was terrified by his own helplessness, which seemed only to grow with his rising popularity.

At about that time a friend took him to church. Gareth had gone mostly because the church's name appealed to him; they were called Dissenters, and no label had ever suited him so much. What he had found inside those simple unpainted doors of the church changed his life forever.

Now Gareth stared down at the swirling mass of humanity surrounding their carriage. "Remind me to ask my aunt not to make her next return from the Continent upon such an inauspicious day."

Daniel studied the pair of speakers haranguing the crowd from a makeshift stand. "I smell trouble on the wind, I do."

"Then we must not take a moment longer than necessary before starting our return. Soon as we arrive at dockside, you see to the offloading of these pamphlets. I will track down my aunt and cousin." Gareth could scarcely make himself heard over the roaring crowd. "Can't you draw a bit more speed from these nags?"

"It's not the horses that are slowing our pace, sir." Even so, Daniel cracked the whip high over the steeds' heads. "Make way, there!"

The London docks formed the largest city Erica had ever seen. But it was not a city at all, simply a sprawling mass of people and ships and rowboats and wharves and warehouses. On and on the city sprawled, spreading across both sides of the river and completely overwhelming an island in the middle of the Thames. The Isle of Dogs, she heard it called, a wretched name for a miserable looking place. Two rowboats were now lashed to her ship's bowsprit, and the rowers sang a horrid ditty as they hauled upon the oars. The ship berthed alongside a broad cobblestone lane. Along the shoreline people massed and struggled and shoved like human bees flooding about a great dirty hive. The other vessels were too many to count, far more than at Portsmouth, but of every conceivable size and shape. The noise and the stench were overpowering. Many of the other ladies held perfumed handkerchiefs to their faces. Erica's eyes watered from an acrid smoke that drifted about in the still air. But she would not meet this new world with her face half hidden.

When the ship was lashed to the quayside, all the other passengers began pushing and shoving their way down the twin ramps. Erica felt a similar hunger to have solid earth beneath her feet once again. Yet at the same time, she could not stop the occasional quake from wracking her. There was so much unknown ahead of her, so much new, so much to be afraid of.

"Orright, missy?" One of the sailors gave her a gap-toothed grin and pressed a knuckle to his forelock. "Where's your carriage, then?"

"What, no, that's quite . . ." Erica stopped her protest because the sailor had already lashed her three valises and one trunk together and hefted them upon his broad back. He shouted a warning and began bulling his way forward. The wooden ramp bowed under his weight. Erica had but two choices: to follow him or to watch her luggage disappear in the maelstrom.

Even with her eyes held steadfastly upon the sailor, she had difficulty keeping track of him. Twice the hordes seemed to make the most casual of shifts, and suddenly she was being swept off in one way while her luggage headed in another. She struggled to keep to her feet. One hand remained fastened to her hat and the other gripped the hem of her dress. She cried for people to let her pass, but her voice was lost in the bedlam.

Erica Langston was not used to such brutal indifference. She shoved back at the crowd and forced her way through. By the time she caught up with her luggage, the sailor had almost arrived at the long rank of carriages flanking the warehouses.

"Which is your'n, missy?"

Erica almost had to shriek to be heard. "I seek a carriage that will take me to West London."

"None to be found, miss."

"I beg your pardon?"

"It's the trouble, see."

"The what?"

The sailor's explanation was shattered by a heightened pitch to the din. Two male voices shouted like guns being fired. Her entire body tensed in response. Erica could scarcely hear herself think. For an instant she could not say exactly what had caused such a surge of panic. Then she saw the glint of sunlight upon burnished metal and understood.

Soldiers. British redcoats.

Two ranks of mounted cavalry came first, ramming their way through the masses. People shouted and shrieked and struggled to find safety. Erica found herself so compressed by this wave that her feet actually left the ground. Even the sailor was shoved about. The cavalry horses were trained to stand fast in the face of artillery and shells and gunfire. They whinnied as high as a woman's scream and pressed forward. Behind them stomped rank after rank of redcoats, their long-bore rifles tipped with bayonets. The forest of steel marched stolidly past, the muscled threat so vast it choked off the air from Erica's lungs. She knew the noise about her went on unabated, but for the time it took for the soldiers to pass she heard nothing at all. She could not take her eyes off the brutal force on display. All the terror and agony she had known back on that horrible day in Washington returned.

Then they were past, and the crowd relinquished its crushing grip. Still Erica could not draw the world back into focus. What, oh what, was she doing here? The sailor was shouting at her, but she could not derive any sense from his words. Then a face came into view.

He wore the dark suit of a working gentleman. His topcoat was of fine material. He wore a frilled shirt, sparkling waistcoat, pressed dark trousers, and polished boots. He was merely one of many such men milling about the docks. Perhaps he was more handsome than most. He possessed the sharply defined features of one accustomed to harsher realms than mere parlor life. But that was not what caught her attention.

She had seen him before. Erica recognized him instantly. Perhaps if his appearance had not been preceded by the military's passage, she would have required more time.

He glanced her way. His clear green eyes clouded over. Clearly he felt he should know her.

Erica felt such revulsion the word was clawed from her throat. "You!"

Recognition dawned in his eyes. "The lady in Washington. Can it be?"

Erica wanted to turn and fling herself away. Where did not matter. What worse collection of portents could she have imagined for her arrival in England?

But the sailor interrupted her anguish. "I'm glad to see you, sir," he shouted above the din. "Didn't have a hope of finding a carriage for the lady."

"A carriage? Here?" The man was still having difficulty adjusting to Erica's appearance. "Today?"

"What I said exactly, sir." The sailor was puffing from still holding the luggage aloft. "But I dursn't leave the lady's things just sitting here."

"No, of course not." The unspoken request was what the man seemed to have required. He turned and pointed behind them. "Third coach in line. There's a good man."

"Right you are, sir."

Erica's mouth was so filled with bile she could scarcely shape the words. "I would rather die."

"If you stay here today, that is precisely what will happen," her would-be rescuer shouted back. He took a step toward her but halted when she drew back. "The riots threaten to cut us off from the city proper."

"What?"

"Riots!" the man repeated. "Bread and blood, they're called, for that's the crowd's rallying cry." When Erica continued to shy away from him, he cried impatiently, "Look about you! The place is a half step away from full alarm!"

It was true. She saw a man wave a sheaf of bank notes in the face of a carriage driver. Three women clutched one another and wailed pathetically. Drivers cracked long leather whips and shouted at horses and people alike. Panic was a palpable force in the air.

This time, when the man stepped forward, she did not retreat farther. He stood very close and spoke loudly to be heard. "You can spend the rest of your life hating me, miss, but only if you first survive this day!" He gripped her upper arm. "We must fly!"

Erica flinched. "Unhand me, sir!"

He did no such thing but instead pulled her roughly through the crowd to a carriage, where a driver took her valises and lashed them to the upper transom. "Pay your man!"

When she clearly did not understand, he shouted, "Your sailor. Give him a coin!"

Erica fumbled for her drawstring purse, handed the sailor a coin she did not see, and allowed herself to be bodily lifted and inserted through the open carriage door.

The man leaped up behind her, slapped the carriage's side, and shouted, "Make haste, Daniel!"

"Right you are, Major!" The driver settled into his seat, raised the whip from its stand, and released the carriage brakes. "Heyah!"

The streets of London closed in about them. After weeks of frothy waves as the only interruption to endless sea and sky, the tightly compressed walls with their coverings of soot were grimly claustrophobic.

Erica and the officer sat facing forward. She looked at the other passengers. Across from them was a young woman, perhaps a year or so older than herself, and an older woman. Both looked gray from fear.

The officer was never still. He scouted the streets fore and aft, slipping over to glance out the windows on her side. Twice he trod on Erica's toes, but she stifled her protests. The carriage rocked and jounced upon rough-hewn cobblestones, and the horses' metal-shod feet clattered and echoed back from the walls to either side, as loud as military drums.

The older woman winced when the man's boot came down upon her instep. "I do wish you would seat yourself, Gareth."

"Forgive me, Aunt. But I must remain vigilant a while longer." Even so, he lowered himself to perch upon the seat's edge.

"The least you can do is introduce our traveling companion."

"I beg your pardon. My aunt, Mrs. Clarissa Bellows, and my cousin Karity. This is a young woman from America, Miss Langston—"

Erica's face registered her surprise. She had not expected that the man would know her name. But he was still speaking.

"—although I fear we have never been properly introduced."

Now it was his aunt's turn to look startled. "Then what—"

A faint rush of noise rose ahead of them. Gareth cried, "Down on the floor, all of you!"

The two women opposite Erica flung themselves down in a swirl of petticoats. Erica was not so speedy, however. As a result, she found herself staring out the window at pandemonium.

A crowd larger than the one portside filled a gigantic square. Two of the buildings at the square's opposite end had been set ablaze. The throng was so noisy it was impossible to make out more than a single word, one shouted over and over: *Blood*.

As soon as the carriage raced into view, the crowd bayed. Fists and staves and farming implements and a few rusty swords were lifted into the air. The multitude swarmed toward them. The driver whipped the horses and shouted so loudly he could be heard over the baying throng. The horses, as frightened by the raging surge as Erica, sprang forward. They managed to outrun all but the fastest. One man scrambled onto the carriage's nearside door. He wrapped his arm about the stanchion, then poked his head and thrust his other hand through the open window. The hand held a knife as long as Erica's forearm. It was stained with something dark and glinted like a taste of death itself. The assailant opened his mouth to reveal a great maw of rotting teeth and roared at them. Erica might have screamed back. Someone in the carriage certainly did. She could not be certain it was she who had made the sound.

Gareth responded with cool precision. He ducked beneath the slicing blade and hammered one solid fist directly between the attacker's eyes. The assailant blinked very slowly, and his knife clattered to the carriage floor. Then Gareth did something that amazed Erica as much as anything that had happened that strange and terrifying day. Just as the assailant's arm began to unravel from the stanchion, Gareth reached out and gripped the man's collar. "Steady on, chap."

He pushed the man's head and arm back through the window, then leaned so far out the window he seemed almost to topple from the racing carriage. He lowered himself, supporting his own and the unconscious attacker's weight by propping his knees against both carriage seats. Then he dropped the man into the street.

He glanced fore and aft, then called, "All right topside?"

"Aye, sir," the driver sang out. "One tried to climb aloft, but we saw him off right smart."

"Excellent. All right, Auntie. You can rise up now."

"Are you quite sure?"

He helped the two women rise from the floorboards. "We are almost to Parliament. The crowds don't dare come this far."

Erica looked at Gareth. Why had he gone to such lengths to keep their assailant from slipping beneath the carriage wheels? She couldn't keep her astonishment to herself. "That man wanted to kill us!"

"Yes. He was also starving." Gareth leaned forward for another scouting ahead and behind. " 'Blood and bread' is their rallying cry for good reason, I'm afraid. The enclosure laws have forced thousands of stout British farmers off their land. The fortunate ones are doomed to working sunup to sundown in the new mills, spinning flax and cotton and wool. The others . . ." He waved out the window. "You see how desperate the others have become."

Erica took a moment to slow her breathing and observed how the two women watched Gareth. More than family ties bound these people, of that she was certain. The aftertaste of terror and danger left her able to see the carriage's interior with a crystal clarity. "Desperate," she repeated.

It was the older woman who answered. "Were you to see your children starve before your very eyes, a rage such as what we have just witnessed might be forgiven."

"Forgiven but never condoned," Gareth said, rising for another check out the window. "Not violence. Never violence."

Erica turned in amazement to the young man. "That is quite a remarkable comment to hear coming from a soldier," she snapped.

Gareth said nothing but wore a look of very deep sorrow.

The older woman was clearly affronted. "That seems a rather strange tone to take with a man who has just saved your life."

"Is it indeed?"

Gareth continued to stare into her face, his look so poignant she felt it in her very marrow. It would be so easy to like this man. The sudden thought left her dizzy with a conflicting surge of repulsion and appeal.

He said very softly, "It's all right, Aunt Clarissa."

"Really, Gareth. You just saved the young lady's life."

"Twice," her daughter added.

"Quite so. There at the harbor, had you not come to her aid, she might still be stranded."

The lane they followed had opened into one of the grandest panoramas Erica had ever seen. The tall spires of Parliament rose into the cloud-flecked sky. She observed the fine parade of carriages and well-dressed people, the carefully tended green at the square's center, the utter calm. The scene was a world away from the chaos they had just left behind but which remained so close that her heart still stuttered and her breath caught in her throat. She felt herself ensnared by the carriage and these watching eyes. "Let me out here, please."

"I am quite happy to take you wherever—"

"I demand that you let me out!"

"Very well." Gareth leaned out the window. "Pull up to the line of coaches, Daniel!"

"Right you are, sir."

The two women watched as Erica opened the door and alighted before the carriage had come to a full halt. "I must say your behavior astonishes me, young lady," said Mrs. Bellows.

"Aunt, please." Gareth got down and said to the driver, "Give me a hand carrying the lady's valises."

But Mrs. Bellows would not be dissuaded. "I think the young lady owes you some expression of gratitude."

"Do you?" asked Erica. "Tell me, madam. If a gentleman stood by and watched as one of his soldiers felled *your* father with a blow from his rifle, what do you feel would be the proper response?"

The woman's mouth worked but no sound came out. It was the daughter, Karity, who responded, "No doubt he had good reason."

"Oh, most certainly. My father was rushing across the street to fetch a pail of water. You see, these same soldiers had just set our family's business on fire. So my father rushed for the water trough carrying buckets for weapons. One of this gentleman's soldiers struck my father so hard he fell and never rose again." Her eyes burned from the telling, such that she might as well have been fighting the flames anew. "I am unfamiliar with the British concept of proper etiquette. No doubt the gentleman's response was most fitting under those circumstances."

When neither of the women chose to respond, Erica nodded. "I thought as much. Good day."

Gareth and the driver handed her valises up to the carriage's driver. Gareth's man turned his back on Erica's offered coin and returned to his carriage. Gareth, however, stood upon the emerald square and waited as she boarded.

Erica said to the driver, "I wish to go to the United States Embassy."

"Very good, miss."

The driver clicked once and flicked his reins, and the horse drew away. Erica glanced back, then immediately wished she had not. For Gareth remained as he was, standing foursquare upon the green, watching her. There was a defenselessness about him, a proud man brought low through his own willingness. A man who would neither defend himself nor deflect her verbal attack. A man who seemed to apologize just by his stance.

Erica set her jaw. Why should she feel such regret over having spoken nothing but the truth?

Chapter 12

Erica's carriage took a series of broad lanes leading north from Parliament Square, past grand plazas and impressive buildings. They entered Piccadilly Circus, which was not home to any festival as she had once imagined but was simply a name derived from the frilly collar called a pickadil and the Latin word for circle. A spider web of lanes spread out in all directions. Innumerable carriages made their way around the central fountain, while the sidewalks were packed with well-heeled pedestrians.

The circus opened onto a boulevard named Piccadilly as well. The street was lined on the south by a well-tended park and on the north by shiny new mansions. The United States Embassy occupied a manor about midway up the grand boulevard.

Erica gave her name to the porter stationed by the gate lodge. The man tipped his hat in recognition and scurried to help the driver unload her cases. She paid the driver and followed the porter, extremely grateful for the escort. The manor's drive was filled with gentlemen, nearly a hundred of them she guessed, standing in tight clusters and smoking their long clay pipes.

Still more gentlemen lined the broad staircase leading to the tall entrance doors, as well as the building's front foyer. Four doors led off this vestibule, three of which were shut. A secretary's desk was stationed before each door. Men hovered about the three desks, talking in urgent whispers. The foyer's rear double doors were open, revealing a large open room very similar to the one in which the Langston clerks once worked. Embassy officials rushed back and forth, important and urgent in their manner and speech.

Erica found herself strangely reassured by the air of tension that surrounded the entire ground floor. Clearly these were men of power and wealth. They would only give their time to stand and wait here if they felt that there was something to be gained. The idea gave her hope that her mission too might result in her obtaining justice for her family's cause.

The porter led her up a sweeping circular staircase to yet another set of double doors. These were quite new, Erica realized, because she could still smell the fresh-cut timber and paint. The doors were very heavy, and the wall both solid and thick. The porter shut the door behind her, and the atmosphere abruptly changed. Gone were the noise and the tobacco smoke and the huddled conversations. In their place were the smell of fresh-baked bread and the sound of a child's laughter.

"I'll just go see to your other cases, miss."

Erica took that as a signal and reached for her purse. "Wait just a moment, let me see . . ."

"That won't be necessary, miss."

"But I insist."

"Mr. Aldridge doesn't permit such, miss." He touched the rim of his bowler. "Won't be a moment."

A new voice piped up from behind her. "Hello. Are you my new governess?"

Erica turned to face a young redheaded girl of perhaps eight. She had a lively expression and the poise of one born to rule . . . and she looked so much like Abigail Cutter that Erica found all hint of reserve vanishing. In the midst of so much turmoil and strangeness and fear it was so good to see a familiar face—even if it did belong to a total stranger.

It seemed the most natural thing in the world to drop to

her knees so that she was at the same level as the child. "No, I am afraid I am not. But I must say it would be my great pleasure to teach a young lady as poised and intelligent as you."

The child did indeed have Abigail's pointed chin, as well as the same abrupt cut of her nose and the keen blue eyes. "My mother says I am far more trouble than any two girls should ever be."

"I'm certain she would not say any such thing."

"But she does. She says I'm the reason why our first governess ran away to get married. She says if I were not such a handful, our life here would go much smoother."

A woman's voice interrupted. "You have said enough, Abbie."

"But I was just explaining to the new governess—"

"I said that was enough," she said gently.

Erica stood up to greet the woman she presumed to be Abbie's mother. "Mrs. Aldridge?"

She was a tall woman, comfortably padded by recent childbirth. Her day dress was high-collared and elegant but liberally dusted with flour. She offered her hand. "Yes. Miss Langston? We have been looking forward to your arrival for well over a month now."

"The journey was endless and horrid."

Abbie piped up, "Ours was as well. Sixty-one days. I kept a record in my little book. Mama was sick the entire way. She was carrying my baby brother, Horace. Mama would eat because Daddy insisted, but it never stayed down very long. Then—"

"I think our guest understands exactly what transpired, Abbie." But there was no scolding to the words. "I see you have met my daughter."

"I have indeed. She is a wonderful child," Erica said and meant it sincerely.

Abbie looked pleased. "I could show you to your room."

Her mother asked, "Do you know which one it is?"

"I heard you and Daddy talking about it. She is to have the

one beneath the stairs at the back of the house, where the but-ler would live if we had one. Which we don't." She caught her mother's eyebrows rising and added hastily, "Mama says we need to remember how we have been raised, as proper Amer-icans who don't need a houseful of servants at our beck and call."

"I think that is a splendid principle."

"Oh, good." The little girl made an effort to heft the largest of Erica's cases but was relieved to allow Erica to take it from her. She then selected the smaller square traveling case. "Mama is ever so busy, and that worries Papa. She has the new baby and all. I'm not quite certain the baby is worth keeping. He wakes us up at all hours and frets ever so much. But Mama says once a baby arrives we can't give him back to God. No matter how much bother he is in the middle of the night."

"I would tell her to be still," Mrs. Aldridge offered from Erica's other side, "but it would only be a temporary reprieve. Sooner or later you will hear every detail, whether you wish to or not."

"I must tell you," Erica replied, "your daughter's company is the brightest and most beautiful gift I have received in weeks."

Both mother and daughter showed great pleasure at her words. "I can see why my mother thinks so highly of you. You must call me Lavinia."

"And I am Erica."

"Does this mean that we are to be friends?" Abbie queried.

"That is for time and God to decide," Lavinia replied. "But were I pressed, I would think perhaps yes."

"Oh, good. I haven't many friends. I did once, but they're all sixty-one days away, across the Atlantic." Abbie clutched the square valise with one hand as she pointed up a narrower set of stairs. "Upstairs where we live is ever so far from the garden. And Mama is always busy now with the baby. Do you have children?"

"No, I am not married."

"If you were to have a baby like Horace, I think you might wish never to marry and have children. When he cries, his face looks like a stewed prune. And he cries a great deal."

"Abbie, please."

"It's fine. Really." To Abbie, Erica said, "But what if I could be certain that I might be blessed with a daughter as fine as you?"

The little girl flushed bright pink. "I suppose that might make things all right."

"Then I guess I shall have to consider finding myself a husband, at some point in time," Erica said. To her astonishment she found herself blushing. Not at the confession. But because to her surprise she found herself recalling the officer who had stood with such sorrow on his face and watched her carriage disappear.

Gareth Powers, former major in the fusiliers, stood on the balcony overlooking his own shop and tried to remember what he was supposed to be doing.

He had a very full evening ahead of him, what with the news waiting to be written and the bills of lading to be paid and the contacts at Parliament to be seen on the sly. . . . No matter how he tried, he could not manage to accomplish everything each day required.

And it did not help matters a whit, his standing over the clattering din with his head in such a muddle. But he could not help himself. He stared down at the parchment with its half-finished sentence and couldn't recall what he had intended to say. The quill in his ink-stained hands dripped India black onto the floor by his feet. His ears were filled with the clattering presses and the cry of his busy mates. All the world waited what next would come from the Powers Press. But all Gareth

Powers could think about was an American maiden with flashing brown eyes.

Gareth had torn down the interior walls of the old print shop and opened the printing area into one giant corridor with an open balcony that ran the length of the printing room. There was a small shop in the front that sold pamphlets and books. A cobbler's house out back had been acquired and turned into a small warehouse. Another hovel, formerly housing a tinker and his family, now served as a sort of barracks. The stables across the rear courtyard had also been purchased and turned into a smallish apartment where he resided. He could afford something much nicer. Gareth's business now sped pamphlets as far north as Inverness, as well as out to Brussels and Madrid and Berlin. He tried hard not to think of such things, or how his poor spelling and paltry grammar were being read throughout Europe. It only made his task more difficult.

Gareth had two desks. One was housed inside the office he rarely used. It was covered with ledgers and bills of lading and journals and broadsheets and pamphlets written by others, both here and abroad. The other, an old-fashioned scribe's table perched on tall legs, was situated on the balcony. The table rose at a slant, with an inkpot and stack of parchment resting at the back. The men called this balcony the major's station and did not mount the stairs unless called. Gareth disliked retreating to his office. He had always led from the center of his battalion, always entered battle first, always stood with his men in the thick of things. At the moment his feet were surrounded with strewn scraps of paper and balled-up pages, as usual. His staff knew better than to touch anything. Often he would be down on his hands and knees, going through what he had written and discarded earlier, searching out a forgotten phrase that might be just right after all.

Outside the rear window, the sky was streaked with a glorious sunset of gold and rosy hues. Smoky pillars rose from London's narrow chimney pots to join the copper cloud overhead. Gareth turned back to the blank page and wished he knew what to do.

He leaned over the railing and called, "Where's Daniel?"

"Here, sir!"

"A word, if you please."

The barrel-chested former gunnery sergeant took the stairs two at a time. "You wanted me, Major?"

"I have asked you a hundred times and more not to call me that."

"Sorry, sir," the huge man replied easily. "Won't happen again."

"Right. Cast your mind back a ways. The Washington foray."

"Nasty bit of business that was."

"We certainly agree on that point. You recall our entry into the city?"

"Like it was yesterday. You marched at the front of the men, same as always. I was shepherding the wagons."

"So you did not see when we felled the old man."

"The one you asked me about before, on the troop ship to Oporto?"

"I am astonished you should recall."

"You asked me to check with the men, see who felled him."

"And you came up with nothing."

"At the time." Daniel hesitated a moment, then added, "Heard later it was McCusker."

"Did you now."

"His mates let it slip after he was beyond punishing."

"That's it, then." They had buried McCusker in the rocky soil of northern Spain.

"Hope I didn't make a mistake in not passing that on." Daniel gave his beard an idle scratch. "We had more pressing business at the time. Nip and tuck it was, those battles raging on all sides and the Americas so far behind us."

"No, no, think nothing of it." Gareth fiddled with his quill.

"If you remember, there on the outskirts of Washington some-one fired a warehouse."

" 'Course I do. That fellow came running out of his build-ing carrying buckets. Had words with one of the other ser-geants and then proceeded to run through the marching lines. Or tried to." Daniel shook his head over the tragedies of war. "One thing, Major. It wasn't our men what set the place ablaze."

"Are you certain?"

"Soon as I smelled the smoke, I checked the squad what were carrying the firebrands. Your orders were clear as day. None save the government buildings were to get the torch."

"You're telling me none of the men had lit their brands?"

"None that I saw, and I checked every one I found."

"Did you see anyone else around the building?"

"Hard to say, Major. I was trying to watch in all directions at once. People were shouting and ladies screaming, folks rush-ing about hither and yon. Right mess that was."

Gareth pondered that hard and long. If Daniel said he had checked the soldiers' torches, he had done a thorough job of it. Which meant . . . what? He cast his mind back to that day, but his recollections were as scattered as Daniel's. They had marched through havoc. Which of course was why McCusker had struck the old man though he had been armed with only two buckets. They had been marching into enemy territory, with orders to fire upon no one save enemy troops, and were surrounded by the chaos of a city in panic.

To have fired the building just as his troops were passing would have required very careful forethought. And a very solid reason. One so important that the attackers would risk being assaulted by the invading soldiers.

He realized Daniel was watching him avidly. "I saw the man's daughter today."

"You don't mean the lovely lass we saved from the harbor riots?"

"The very same."

"Thought I'd seen her somewhere before." The man's eyes gleamed. "That explains why she showed you the sharp edge of her tongue, I suppose."

"It does indeed."

"What brings her to old London town?"

"I have no idea. But I wonder . . ." Gareth rubbed his chin thoughtfully. "Pass word around. Ask if anyone recalls seeing who it was that set the fire."

"Aye, Major, that I will." The former sergeant grinned. "A fetching lass, if I do say so myself."

"She is most certainly that." Not that it would do him any good. Gareth studied the still-empty page, sighed, and set his quill into the inkwell. "If anyone asks for me, I shall be attending the evening service at Audley Chapel."

Chapter 13

Erica was daily surprised by the household where she now resided. The deputy minister plenipotentiary, Samuel Aldridge, held power more casually than Erica had ever thought possible. Samuel Aldridge was both intelligent and keenly aware, yet patient so long as people did not cross him. He did not suffer fools or manipulative pleaders, not for an instant. But he never revealed such acidic tones before his family. To them he was a man who always had time, always spoke kindly, whose very gaze softened at the sight of his children. Yet so far as Erica could tell, Mr. Aldridge utterly lacked a sense of humor. He never smiled unless it was at the antics of his baby son. In the nine days she had resided with the family, she had never heard him laugh.

It had taken Erica a few days to become accustomed to the unusual layout of the embassy. The middle floor originally had three formal chambers, matching the ones downstairs, with high ceilings and crown moldings about the chandeliers. One of these now saw duty as the family kitchen, another as Mr. Aldridge's private office, and the third as the family parlor. The sweeping staircase and the landing that had been closed off to give the family privacy resulted in the remaining area being somewhat disjointed.

Erica was often downstairs, running errands for the household and acting as an intermediary between the private world above and this one that was so terribly public. Abigail Cutter's daughter was many things, but she was most definitely not a public person. Lavinia deplored the way people used her presence as a means of gaining contact with her husband. She disliked the smoke and the noise and the subterfuge of politics. She would far rather remain intent upon the affairs of her home and her children. She was a perfect hostess when necessary. She could command respect from a dozen servants brought in for a large function such as the one they had hosted the night before. But her own home remained free of servants, though it meant a great deal more work for her. And yet, in spite of her having a personality and interests utterly unlike those of Erica, Lavinia showed no sense of resentment toward her young guest and her aims. Instead, Lavinia Aldridge seemed to like the fact that they were so different.

Erica had formed the habit of rising before the rest of the household. She took her breakfast at the large kitchen table where they ate all meals when Mr. Aldridge was not present. Then she did the rounds of the Shepherds Market shops. In the early morning light, the ancient lanes held a comforting air. In bygone centuries, according to Lavinia, this village had stood surrounded by vast pastures. Drovers had brought their animals to feed the ever-hungry city and stayed at the multitude of Shepherds Market inns. But the village had been swallowed by the expanding city, and these inns were now used for more notorious ends. Quite often Erica was awakened late at night by the sounds of boisterous revelry.

In the early mornings, however, the fancy men and their ladies were all abed. The sunlit air was filled with the fragrances of fresh-baked bread and new vegetables, and Erica could imagine herself walking through a medieval English village, far removed from the fears and woes that had brought her halfway round the world.

Erica knew she was in hiding. She involved herself increasingly in the affairs of this household because she did not want to venture out. The farthest she had been from the embassy so far was to this very market. She spent her days cleaning and playing with the children, as no governess had yet been found who satisfied both parents. Erica also knew that the minister and his wife were watching her and waiting for a fuller explanation for her visit. But what could she say? That she was terrified of confronting the banker and being defeated? That the very thought of entering the giant city with its riots and violence and chaos upset her so greatly that she spent most nights staring at the ceiling and wishing she had never come?

Every morning a trio of old drovers brought their cows into Shepherds Market, where they would settle their stools upon a corner and milk their cows into battered metal pails. Erica bought fresh milk from them, along with bread and whatever fruit looked best at the one stall that opened before dawn. She returned home and set the table for breakfast, then sliced the bread and cut a bowl of good English strawberries that she would take down later for Mr. Aldridge. He rarely stopped for breakfast and would often forget to have lunch unless there was some event he was required to attend.

But this morning, as she let herself back into the upstairs apartment, Erica heard the sound of weeping. She found Abbie crouched beneath the stairwell leading to the third floor, sobbing as though her heart was broken. "Abbie, dear, what is the matter?"

The little girl only wept harder.

Erica got down on all fours and crawled into the tiny space. She could not quite make it the entire way in. The stairs were supported by a broad beam that split the gloomy space in two, and Abbie was small enough to move in behind the beam. She was curled up like a calico mouse, her face entirely hidden.

"Have you hurt yourself?"

Abbie gave a tiny shiver that coursed through her entire body. "No."

Erica breathed a bit easier. She reached out and caressed the silken hair. "Won't you tell me what's happened?"

Abbie whimpered words that were so mangled by her sobs

that Erica could not understand them. She tugged gently on the one shoulder she could reach. "Come here, Abbie. Please. I can't make it back in there to you. Wouldn't you like to be held just now?"

For a moment Erica thought Abbie would refuse, then the little girl swung around, crawled beneath the plank, and flung her arms around Erica's neck. It was a most uncomfortable position, but Erica dared not move. She held the little girl and eased out one leg so that she was not quite so cramped. If only she knew what to say.

Only one thing came to mind. "There have been many worries and concerns I have brought with me to London. And some new ones I have discovered since my arrival. One of these has been to know how to speak with you. I have never had much contact with young ladies, you see. So I decided on that first day that I would speak to you as I would to someone of my own age."

Abbie whimpered, "I'm just a baby."

"Why would you say such a thing?"

Abbie started to reply, but just at that moment there came a sound of footsteps from overhead, and the child's eyes opened wide with alarm. Clearly she did not want her mother to see her thus.

Erica understood perfectly. She released Abbie and slid from beneath the stairs, then pulled the little girl out after her. Swiftly she led her into the kitchen, where she wet a towel and scrubbed the little face. She untied Abbie's ribbon, swept back the child's tangled locks, and tied them into as neat a bundle as she could manage in such haste. She then began to brush briskly at the girl's skirt.

"Good morning, all. Abbie, whatever do you have on your frock?"

"She was helping me with something." Erica smiled at the mother and baby. "How did you two rest?"

Erica chattered through breakfast, allowing no space for Lavinia to speak more than a few words to her daughter. After the dishes had been washed, Lavinia went upstairs to change Horace. Abbie put a finger to her lips, took Erica by the hand, and led her down to the end of the hall.

"I'm not supposed to go in here. But I wanted to surprise Papa."

She pushed open the door to her father's upstairs office. Erica could not quite stifle a gasp at what she saw.

The sound was enough to cause Abbie's lip to tremble. "I made a terrible mess, didn't I?"

The entire room was awash in papers. "Tell me what happened." Documents spilled from four massive piles that blanketed the large desk. Another pile grew from the settee by the tall side window. Papers covered the seats of the chairs placed before the desk and spilled across the carpet around the chairs.

"Mama refuses to come in here even to dust. She says the disorder is just too alarming. Papa says bills have not been paid because he can't find them. So I thought I would surprise him by tidying up—only the papers wouldn't stay in piles, and now it's worse than before."

"So you came in because you wanted to help."

"Yes. Papa has been so worried. Before you came they had to dismiss the embassy clerk because he did such a bad job. Papa and Mama think I don't understand, but I do. Sometimes if I'm quiet, they forget I'm here and talk about all manner of interesting things."

"Is that so."

"Mama said I must wait until I grow up before I can help Papa as I want to. But he needs help now." The words became somewhat fractured with Abbie's attempt to hold back more tears.

A voice behind them both said, "My dear sweet wonderful daughter. Come here."

"Oh, Mama." Abbie flung herself at her mother. "I'm so sorry."

"I know you are. And I love you very much."

Erica waited until mother and daughter had regained their

composure to say, "If you like, I think I might be able to help."

Samuel Aldridge came upstairs late that afternoon wearing the tight expression of a particularly difficult day and found Erica at work in his study and Lavinia seated at a chair next to the desk. "What's this?"

"Erica has offered to help you, dear." Even his wife seemed tentative, affected by the cold sternness that trailed after him like a vapor. "You know how worried you have been about the unpaid accounts. And I am no help whatsoever."

"You do too much already." He walked over to Erica. "You are comfortable with ledger work, Miss Langston?"

"I handled all the accounts for my father's firm, sir."

"Since the tragedy?"

"Actually, sir, my father began training me in this regard some time before."

"There are confidential papers here that no one is permitted to see."

Despite the fragrance of the meal being prepared, Erica could still smell the odor of old smoke upon his clothes. "Everything that is not specifically related to a charge against the embassy or your family, I have set aside without reading."

"Where are these papers?"

"Here, sir." She handed him a heavy felt folder and could not quite keep her fingers from trembling.

"I see." He unbound the blue silk ribbon and studied how the pages were set face down. "Well, do you have anything you wish to discuss with me?"

Despite having spent all her life in Washington, despite all the politicians and hangers-on who had whiled away the hours in their coffeehouse, despite all the soirees she had attended, Erica felt intimidated by Samuel's severe demeanor. "If you will permit me, sir, I would prefer to work through the remainder of these papers. Then I can offer you a full accounting and not waste any of your time."

"How much longer will you require?"

"This evening and tomorrow morning should suffice, sir."

He carefully rebound the ribbon, then hesitated a moment before setting the folder back upon the desk. He patted it twice, then gave a nod to some internal decision. "Shall we say tomorrow afternoon at half past two?"

"Whenever you wish, Mr. Aldridge."

If he found anything strange in her formal manner of address, he gave no sign. "Very well." He straightened and worked at setting aside whatever it was he had encountered downstairs. "My dear, something smells marvelous."

"The butcher saved me a lovely cut of veal."

"Then we should waste no further time."

Only when Samuel stepped from the library did Erica notice Abbie. The little girl was hiding behind her mother's skirt, so that only the upper half of her face showed. Her eyes were as round as two blue saucers.

Ledgers were books of great interest to Erica Langston. She read them the way some of her mother's friends read novels. Normally she could look at numbers and see the hidden story, the mystery that knit together a person, a family, a company. But the embassy's finances were an utter muddle. She spent hours after the family had gone to bed, trying to work out why nothing she saw was making any sense. The papers were all there before her, or so it seemed. It did not look as though a single thing in the office had ever been filed away. She had even found the original documents for their acquisition of this manor, the costs of registering it with the Crown as an embassy, the legal fees, the bank's documents, the builders' papers, everything. Yet none of it made any sense. What she found upon the papers did not correspond with what she saw in the ledgers.

Finally sometime after midnight Erica gave up and went to bed. Two sleepless hours after she had lain down, she finally came up with the answer. It was, she realized, the only solution that made any sense. She rose from her bed and dressed, made a fire and heated the kettle for tea. She knew now what she had to do. She was going to set aside all the account records made up to that point and start afresh.

She began by lighting every candle she could find. Then she began to make piles according to dates, going all the way back to the minister's arrival. Stacks began to march down the hall. She used the kitchen table for all the initial documentation, then lined the hall with the six kitchen chairs and dated them by months. The two horsehair settees in the front parlor were stations for the latest documents.

Finally, as the rising sun began painting the eastern horizon with lovely strokes of rose and violet, she understood. The answer was so shocking she could not even apologize when Mr. Aldridge appeared. He stopped in the process of buttoning his vest and stared open-mouthed at Erica's work. "What on earth?"

"I need a new ledger."

He forced his gaze away from the chairs and their burdens that stood in military precision down either wall. He glanced at the four piles rising like pillars from each corner of the kitchen table. He glanced into the parlor. Then he looked at Erica. "I beg your pardon?"

"Might I have a ledger?" Sand had imbedded itself behind her eyelids, and her throat was raw from dust and lack of sleep. The numbers were marching into a precise order inside her head, so many she thought her poor brain might burst from their weight. And the realization that she had been correct was almost too much to bear. "An accounts book. A fresh one."

"My dear Miss Langston." Samuel Aldridge was clearly at a

loss for words. "No one expected you to build Rome overnight."

"This is important, sir."

"I am quite aware . . . Have you been to sleep at all?"

"No, but . . . I cannot stop now."

"Right. A ledger, did you say? Very well, come with me." He slipped into his long black coat and opened the door leading to the principal rooms. As they descended the long circular stairs, he confided, "This present arrangement is not particularly suitable for anyone. I had never expected to live above my work. My wife decided on this because there are such enormous difficulties in finding decent housing. We are having a house built not far from here, one of the new structures rising alongside Grosvenor Square. But it will not be completed for another eight months, possibly longer."

Erica realized he was trying to put her at ease, but she found it difficult to concentrate on anything other than the numbers in her head.

Samuel pulled down a broad volume bound in gray hide, checked to see that it was empty of writing, and handed it over. "Will this do?"

"Perfectly. Thank you. Now if you will please excuse me . . ." Erica hurried away. She *had* to get those numbers down.

"Half past the hour of two o'clock, Miss Langston," Samuel called after her. "I shall await with great anticipation the telling of your tale."

And tale it was. As soon as the numbers were set down in proper order, the story was there for her to read and understand. Just as she had expected. Just as she had feared.

Erica worked through the morning and straight on past the noon hour. She was aware of the family moving quietly about her, but she could manage no more than a simple word of acknowledgment. She knew she would be unable to clarify the entire picture, but that was not necessary. What she needed was proof.

Finally she set down her quill. In the distance she heard the clock chime the hour. Her brain was so weary it was difficult to even count the bells. Two o'clock. The hour meant something. But what was upon the page left little room for thought of anything else.

A hand tugged upon her sleeve. Again. Erica glanced over to see Abbie watching her. "Yes?"

"Mama sent me."

"She did?"

The shining curls bounced as the child nodded confirmation. "She says you have to come now."

"Come? Come where?"

"She's fixing you a bath."

"Bath?" The word seemed to have no meaning. Then the world shot back into focus. The clock had just struck two. Erica bounded from her chair. "The meeting!"

"Mama says you mustn't worry. There's still plenty of time."

"But I have to get ready! These books aren't complete. . . ."

"Papa won't know," the little girl said confidently. "Papa says he'd rather dance a jig with King George himself than add a row of figures."

Erica looked down at the little girl. "Your father said that?"

"Yes, he did. Do you like jam with your bread and butter?"

Erica realized she was positively famished. "Oh, yes."

"I thought you would. Mama says a lovely young lady like you must guard her figure. But *I* knew you'd want something special after all this work."

Twenty-seven minutes later Erica was bathed, dressed in her best frock, armed with her books, and filled with three slices of home-baked bread liberally slathered with fresh-churned butter and strawberry jam. Lavinia Aldridge held the baby, and Abbie stood beside her as Erica came down the stairs. "How do I look?"

"I sincerely doubt that my husband will even notice," Lavinia replied.

"You look beautiful," Abbie declared. "Papa is going to be so proud."

"Proud? Of me? Whyever so?"

"Because—"

"Shah, child, that's enough."

Abbie looked up at her mother. "But why shouldn't she hear that Papa has called her an answer to prayer?"

Lavinia smiled down at her daughter. "I should think the young lady already has enough on her plate, wouldn't you?"

Chapter 14

It must have been Erica's imagination that everyone in the embassy's foyer was watching her descend the staircase. After all, Mr. Aldridge would not have spoken to anyone else about her activity. Was it that unusual for a woman to enter these environs? How she wished she had something better to wear, something newer and without the carefully stitched tear on the skirt or the salt stain on the sleeve that she could not completely remove no matter how hard she scrubbed. How she wished for sleep and more time to prepare. But there was none of that, just the moment at hand and the staring eyes. She avoided looking directly at anyone as she crossed the foyer and approached the clerk standing before the doorway.

"Good afternoon, Miss Langston. Mr. Aldridge is ready to see you now."

The minister had an antechamber to his office, where a second clerk worked and where several men in formal daywear stood and muttered. At least, they usually did. Never before had she felt so many eyes upon her.

The clerk knocked once and did not wait for a response. He slid open one of the heavy double doors leading to the inner sanctum and announced, "Miss Langston has arrived, Mr. Aldridge."

"Right on time as well. Let her in."

As she passed, the clerk asked Erica, "Will you take tea, Miss Langston?"

She did not trust her voice and so made do with a tiny shake of her head.

"Nonsense. The good woman has been up all night working on these matters. Of course she shall have tea. With a dollop of milk and two sugars, if I recall." Samuel Aldridge was already up and moving around his desk. "Here, take this chair. You will be far more comfortable."

"Thank you, sir." Her voice was scarcely above a whisper. She carried the two ledgers tight against her front, a shield against the tirade she knew her revelations would release.

"You know Mr. Carnathan, do you not?"

"Indeed, Mr. Minister." Carnathan was one of four Englishmen who worked in the embassy. He was a sharp-nosed gentleman who walked with a slight stoop. He was also the only man there who regularly wore a powdered wig. It was the height of fashion among those attached to the royal court, but Erica thought it looked rather foppish. "Good afternoon, sir."

"Really, sir, I scarcely see how this could possibly be so vital as to draw me away from the matters of such pressing—"

"Attend us a moment, if you will." The words were mild, the voice calm. But the steel was most evident.

"Oh, very well. Although I hope this will not delay us long."

"I am quite certain Miss Langston will not keep us a moment longer than necessary." Samuel talked of inconsequential things while his aide poured Erica a cup of tea. "Perhaps you would care to begin?"

Erica found herself very glad after all for the tea, which helped to unseal her throat. "I fear I must impart some bad news, sir."

"Do you, now."

"Very bad news indeed."

"How extraordinary." He laced his fingers across his vest front. "Please go on."

The realization hit Erica with a jolt. He already knew. The shock was enough to draw the entire room into focus. She sensed that the aide must know as well. She saw how he crossed and uncrossed his legs, the silver buckle on his shoes catching the light as he bounced his foot up and down. His hands were never still. His two rings danced in the light as he adjusted his cravat, the frills of his shirtfront, the buttons on his embroidered vest, the lay of his powdered wig.

She returned her gaze to Mr. Aldridge. He was waiting in utter stillness, apparently willing to give her all the time she required. Oh yes. He most certainly knew.

So she used a far blunter tone than she had planned. "Mr. Aldridge, you have been robbed."

"Have I, now."

"I fear this is something that has been going on for some time. Perhaps all the way back to your arrival."

"Are you certain?"

"Yes, sir."

"Most remarkable. You may continue."

She opened the two ledgers on the desk before her. "If I may draw your attention to these pages, you will see—"

"I fear the exposition of figures will serve no end save to baffle me entirely. Please let us go straight to the heart of the matter."

She settled back into her chair. "The clerk you employed was stealing from you."

Carnathan exploded, "Preposterous!"

"I fear not, sir."

"Minister Aldridge, this woman is quite mad."

"Humor me a moment longer, Carnathan. Do go on, Miss Langston."

"The ledger entries were absolute nonsense, sir." Erica drew strength and confidence from Mr. Aldridge's manner. Enough to speak aloud the mystery she had discovered hidden in the piles. "They served no purpose save to mask the fact that moneys supposedly being paid to your creditors were in fact landing straight in someone's pocket."

Carnathan bolted from his chair. "I shall stand for no more of—"

"Sit down, Carnathan."

"Really, sir, I must protest in the strongest terms."

The steel in Samuel Aldridge's voice and gaze emerged a fraction farther from their scabbard. "Sit."

Erica continued. "There is a regular pattern, sir. A bill comes in. An entry is made into the ledger that it has been paid. A period follows—sometimes weeks, in some cases several months. Then another bill. Then oftentimes a letter follows. Sometimes this is from a solicitor, other times from a bank. Some are very strongly worded."

"Yes," Samuel Aldridge murmured. "I remember seeing one such letter not long ago."

"These bills and letters have been hidden in the most remarkable of places. I found them inside books on your shelves. One folder was tucked beneath the carpet. Another folder rested under the settee cushion. They were slipped among your personal documents and in your desk drawers beneath all manner of other items. What I do not understand . . ."

"Yes? What is unclear?"

"Well, sir, I could not understand why these bills were not simply destroyed by the person stealing from you."

"A most astute question. Would you not agree, Carnathan? Why on earth would such damaging evidence be left lying about my private study?"

Erica realized that the aide was sweating. His eyes seemed unable to rest upon anything for more than a fraction of a second. "I-I can only suppose it is because the matter is not at all as this woman proposes."

"Do you? Do you indeed? Could it not be something else entirely? Could this entire procedure be part of a careful scheme? One intended to discredit me and my station?"

"That is utter—"

"Could this have been designed not to enrich the clerk in question but rather to have me publicly branded a scoundrel? One who lives by means of defrauding his creditors?"

Carnathan had grown as pale as his wig. "What you are proposing, sir, is nothing short of scandalous."

"Scandalous. Yes. I agree. A scandal would most certainly have erupted. Is it not true that there are parties among the royal court who would dearly love to see the minister put to shame?"

"I can think of no one who would dream of such a thing." Carnathan withdrew an embroidered handkerchief from his sleeve and mopped his brow. "Forgive me. I find this chamber quite stifling."

"You are well acquainted with everyone at court, are you not?" Mr. Aldridge did not give his aide a chance to respond. "You were also the one who advised me to hire this clerk in the first place."

"The man came with the most glowing recommendations." He attempted to draw himself up sternly. "I hope you are not implying that I had anything to do with such a dastardly scheme."

"Naturally not. Instead, to demonstrate my trust for you, I shall place these critical matters into your care. First, I wish for you to take this matter before the court and have a warrant issued for the clerk's arrest. Second, I shall hold you personally responsible for tracking down whoever it was behind this scheme. For conspiracy it was, of that I have no doubt. And then you shall make the entire affair public and seek to bring these scoundrels to swift justice."

"Of course, sir," Carnathan replied weakly. "If you are certain this is the direction you wish to take."

"Quite certain."

"Then I shall do as you command."

"Very good. I shall keep you no longer."

As Carnathan rose to depart, he shot Erica a look of purest malevolence.

"Oh, and be so good as to transfer your duties to Harwell on your way out."

Carnathan froze to the spot. "I beg your pardon, sir?"

"Did I not make myself clear? This matter is of utmost importance. Vital to America's good name. Of course you will make this your sole activity until all the matters are satisfactorily resolved."

"But—"

"There's not a moment to lose, Carnathan. Off you go."

Samuel Aldridge waited until the door had closed behind the dismissed aide, then looked at Erica. "He was a gift from the prince regent."

Erica felt the band of tension squeezing her chest gradually ease. "You mean a spy?"

"Something of the sort, would be my guess. Naturally, I could not dismiss someone so closely linked to the royal court. So perhaps some good has come out of this rather expensive debacle." He glanced at the open ledgers. "Dare I ask how costly this will prove?"

"I have not completed my tally, sir. But I suspect in excess of three thousand pounds."

He winced. A gainfully employed bank clerk could expect to earn no more than a hundred pounds a year.

"If you will excuse me, Mr. Aldridge."

He refocused upon her. "Yes? There is more?"

"I fear so. You see, some of these more recent letters are quite, well, demanding."

"Threatening, you mean."

"Yes, sir."

"Which means we must hasten to make amends."

"That would be my advice."

"Would you be willing to help further with this matter, Miss Langston?"

"Of course, if that is your wish, I—"

"Excellent." He raised his voice and called, "Harwell!"

The door opened instantly. "Sir."

"The document I requested has been prepared?"

"It has indeed, sir."

"Bring it here, that's a good man. My dear, permit me to introduce my chief aide, Jacob Harwell."

"A pleasure, Miss Langston."

Aldridge read the document over carefully, took up his quill, signed it, and dusted his signature. "Is the carriage ready?"

"By the front portico, sir."

He handed the document not to Harwell but rather to Erica. "You will accompany Miss Langston to our bank to ensure there is no question about this matter."

"Immediately, sir."

Erica had difficulty comprehending what she was reading. "You are giving me full authority as signatory for the embassy's finances?"

"Who else am I to trust? You see what happened when I left such matters to the Crown's own man. Upon whom should I depend? Harwell cannot work with figures, can you, Harwell?"

"Rather face a regiment of cavalry than a line of numbers, sir."

Erica stared across the table. "Then you already knew, sir?"

"I suspected. But it took you to confirm it." To Harwell he continued, "You will proceed with Miss Langston to whatever destinations she requires. Escort her the remainder of the day."

Samuel Aldridge rose to his feet, drawing Erica up with him. "I fear your well-deserved slumber must wait a bit longer. But it is already Thursday, and there is no way of knowing what mischief our so-called allies might wreak by Monday."

Sleep was the furthest thing from Erica's mind. The thrill of such responsibility left her giddy. "I shall not let you down, sir."

"Of that," he replied, beaming at her, "I have no doubt whatsoever."

Chapter 15

When Erica arrived outside, she found Lavinia Aldridge standing beside the carriage's open door, holding a closed parasol in one hand and a hat with a long silk ribbon in the other.

"I thought you might care for a bit of company today."

"Of-of course," she stammered. "But what of the children?"

Lavinia allowed Jacob Harwell to help her into the carriage. "The children are fine. A friend is watching them for me."

But when the aide started to climb in after them, Lavinia said, "Would you mind terribly granting us a bit of privacy?"

"Not at all, madam." Whatever surprise Jacob Harwell might have felt over the request was well hidden. He backed from the carriage saying, "Nice a day as this, I'd relish a bit of fresh air."

"Jacob is a fine young man," Lavinia said, settling herself comfortably into the velvet cushion. "I don't know how my husband would manage without him. Or you, for that matter."

"Me? B–but I have just arrived."

"Precisely. And I don't mind telling you, your delay troubled us mightily."

The driver cracked his whip, and the carriage started forward with a jolt. Erica was pushed back into the seat as they rolled through the stone gates. To her right lay the expanse of Hyde Park. Because the day had turned so nice, a steady stream of carriages, coaches, open landaus, and riders on horseback took the air along what was known as Rotten Row. Piccadilly was a broad thoroughfare that connected the park and the boroughs on its opposite side—Knightsbridge and Kensington and Belgravia—to the city. The carriage turned left out of the gates, away from the park and toward London's heart.

Erica realized that Lavinia had spoken to her. "I'm sorry, I was drifting."

"I said that as soon as we received the letter from my mother describing you and your desire to come, my husband was convinced you were the answer to prayer."

Erica didn't know how to respond. She watched out the window as they entered the bustling Piccadilly Circus and turned toward the river. The last time she had come this way had been in the carriage after fleeing the riots. "Where are we headed?"

"Our bank is located at the city's eastern edge, just downriver from Parliament."

"Do we need to concern ourselves with the Troubles?"

"The unrest has been stifled, at least for the moment." Lavinia's tone caught a slight edge, though her features did not crease. "Would you prefer not to speak of the disturbances right now? You look far too weary to enter into such a complex issue."

"I am rather tired."

"Then let us remain with the matter at hand." Brilliant sunlight glanced between the buildings and illuminated the carriage's interior. At that moment Erica could see how much Lavinia was like her mother; the same upright stance, the same easy intelligence, the same direct manner. "Ever since your arrival, we have waited prayerfully in hopes that you would be the help my husband so desperately needed."

"I'm sorry," Erica said. "I have difficulty accepting that anyone would consider me an answer to prayer."

"Shall I tell you what my mother said of you in her letter?"

"I expect she said I had managed to run off every young

man who ever turned in my direction, including your brother."

"Oh, dear Horace spoke of little besides you for months on end. Until the tragedy. But let's not dwell upon that today." Lavinia's tone was light, her features cheerful. "My mother wrote that she found you an utterly astonishing young woman."

"She did?"

"She said that one of your most endearing qualities was how completely unaware you were of your own beauty. And that you counted your intelligence as a liability, along with your forthrightness. Despite the fact that you and your mother were of very diverse natures, you still held your parents in the utmost respect and love. In effect, my mother said, you were every inch a lady."

"But I am so poor at what is required of a lady. My mother once told me I was the only girl she had ever met who was mystified by the process of making a proper cup of tea."

Lavinia coughed discreetly. "And this is what you feel defines a proper lady?"

The fatigue rose and fell like the waves Erica had lived with for weeks on end. One moment the world was clear and her thoughts lucid. The next it was hard even to hear what came from her own mouth. "I could not follow a needlepoint pattern if my life depended upon it. I do not dislike the company of other women, but sometimes . . ."

"Yes? Sometimes what?"

"I have said too much already." Erica turned her face to the sun. The light was strong enough to cause pinpricks of real pain at the back of her eyes. Or perhaps it was simply because she was so tired.

Lavinia slipped across the central space to sit beside Erica. She took the younger woman's hand in her own and said, "You detest the empty chatter of most social gatherings. You despair of other women's ability to talk for hours on end about nothing at all. You look into your own future and see little beyond being chained to a life that does not suit you one iota."

Erica could only stare into Lavinia's smiling face.

"My mother said the only risk she saw for you in life," continued Lavinia gently, "was your tendency to make your own way to such an extent that it is difficult for you to call another person friend."

"All too true, I fear."

Lavinia's voice took on a thoughtful tenor. "My husband and I find it difficult to identify our friends in this land. You have seen how testing this assignment has proven."

"You knew of the theft also?"

"There are few secrets between Samuel and me, I am happy to say. We knew there was trouble with the accounts. How serious the matter was, we discovered only by chance, when a merchant approached me at a banquet. A member of the opposition party and a Dissenter."

"Excuse me, a what?"

Lavinia hesitated. "I fear there is so much bundled together that if I begin I shall never end. The Dissenters are a church group. For years they were treated as outlaws because they vehemently opposed the war against the United States. Most of their members belong to the opposition party. As I said, a merchant approached me at a banquet. He told me of the unpaid bills and of rumors that were circulating. How those who resented our nation sought to use this matter to undo our good name."

Erica found herself unable to hold the weight of such matters in her weary brain. "I am glad I did not know all this when I began."

"As you can see, when Mother said you were an absolute genius with figures, the prospect seemed almost too good to be true." She glanced over as the driver called to the horses and their carriage pulled to a halt. "We have arrived."

The lane was far too narrow for the height of the surrounding buildings. The stern edifices turned the road into a shadow-filled valley. Erica was out of the carriage and starting up the front steps when the name above the door fully registered. She came to a sudden halt. "I can't go in there."

"Whyever not?"

The oiled door looked fine enough to belong upon a palace. The lead-paned windows to either side were bordered by stained glass. A beam of dark wood ran the length of the building just above the doorway. And upon it was embossed in gold lettering, "Bartholomew and Sons, Merchant Bankers."

Erica felt the world shifting beneath her feet. "I-I am not ready."

"For what?"

"To meet them. To confront . . ." She shuddered.

Lavinia returned down the step to where Erica stood. "Is there something I should know?"

"These people, this bank . . ."

"Yes?"

What was she to say? A uniformed footman was holding open the door for them. Lavinia stood before her. Jacob Harwell was at her side. Erica rubbed a weary hand across her forehead. How could she tell the world that this was the bank that had sought her family's ruin? Had cheated them of their wealth? Had left them at the mercy of creditors? Had led to her father's final rage?

Lavinia stood watching her somberly. "We are friends, yes?"

"Y-yes, that is . . ."

"Friends," Lavinia said quietly. "We will do this together. Not merely this one act. But all that is to come. You, me, my husband, our staff. We are allies. Do you understand what I am saying?"

In truth, Erica's addled mind had difficulty accepting the words. But her companion's strength, resolve, and calm fortitude were enough to help her regain her balance. "All right," she said softly.

"Shall we enter?"

"Yes."

"You need say nothing. Jacob and I shall handle everything.

Come along, my dear." She took Erica by the arm and, after a word with a clerk, proceeded to a banker's station at the rear of the high-ceilinged chamber, behind a waist-high partition of stout oak inlaid with a Grecian pattern of rosewood and birch. There was nothing sinister about the bank. It smelled of beeswax and coal smoke and India ink and papers. The main chamber was lined in ancient wood and brass. Pictures of sailing vessels and stern-faced gentlemen hung on the walls. The talk was quiet, respectful, and full of latent power. In any other place, in any other time, Erica might have said the room possessed an enchanting flavor.

After taking their seats at the chairs in front of the banker's desk, Jacob began by requesting a book of sight drafts. Clearly he planned to act as messenger, going about with the papers she signed and delivering proper payment.

"It's too late for all that," Erica interrupted. "You have not read the letters."

"Which letters are these?" Lavinia inquired.

"It doesn't matter. Believe me when I say there is only one thing that will end these problems. And that is gold."

The gentleman behind the desk was balding and senior enough to pooh-pooh Erica. "My dear young lady, you can be quite sure that trade in gold coin is not—"

"One moment, if you please, sir." Lavinia said, holding up a gloved hand with the authority of one well used to being obeyed. "Do go on, Erica."

"We are facing not one crisis but two. There is the issue of overdue payments. Then there is the problem of the minister's good name. Rumors are swirling. We need to go personally to those creditors with whom the embassy is most seriously in arrears. Payment must be made in gold. I remember my father saying . . ."

"Yes? What did your father tell you?"

Speaking of her father in this hall left her feeling both the weight of loss and the burden of future strife. Erica forced herself to respond. "My father said nothing turned aside the retribution of one wronged like a sincere heart and a payment in coin."

"I can well understand," Lavinia said slowly, "just how much your father must have valued you." She turned to the banker and announced, "Gold we shall have, sir."

"But, madam—"

"If you will not accommodate us, no doubt we can find someone else with whom we might conduct our business," Lavinia replied. "Here or elsewhere."

The banker rose stiffly to his feet. "As my lady wishes. How much will you be requiring?"

"Erica?"

She had the number ready. "Six hundred pounds."

"Six hundred . . ." He pushed through the swinging gate. "One moment. I must put this matter before Mr. Bartholomew."

"Bankers do so dislike parting with their coin," Lavinia observed. "Almost as much as I despise paying for things twice over."

"There will be further requirements," Erica said quietly, "but some of these less pressing debts can be paid by promissory note . . ."

She felt the breath freeze in her throat as the first banker led a slender gentleman across the gallery. This was the very same man she had last seen on her seventeenth birthday.

Mr. Bartholomew showed no reaction to Erica. Why should he? After all, he had scarcely seen her at all. She would have been a shadowy figure inside Forrest Langston's front hall. A young girl, scarcely more than a child, certainly not anyone worth noticing.

Yet the man could not help but notice Erica's reaction to him. She knew her horror and revulsion were clear on her features. The banker bowed a greeting to Lavinia, yet his gaze kept returning to Erica. "Forgive me. Have we met?"

Erica felt an aversion so great it forced aside the blanket of fatigue. "Not formally."

Lavinia introduced them. "Miss Erica Langston is assisting my husband in matters related to the embassy's finances."

The name registered deep in the banker's gaze. "You are . . ."

"Erica Langston." For Erica, the moment was etched with the crystal clarity of ancient rage. "The daughter of Forrest Langston. Surely you remember my father."

"Your . . . father."

"While it was not for that purpose that I came here on this particular day, I have come to England with the sole purpose of collecting the moneys you owe my family."

"Moneys . . ." The man was already stepping away. "I'm sorry, I recollect no such payment due."

"No. Of course you would prefer to forget such a debt. But debt it most certainly is. I have the documents, you see." She stalked him now, matching him step for step as he backed away. "The documents signed by your very own hand. Stating that you would hold my father's gold in trust until—"

"No!" The man pushed through the gate and hurried off. "I wish all of you well away!"

The entire chamber remained caught in a breathless hush. Then Lavinia announced to the befuddled junior banker, "I believe there was the matter of a withdrawal, my good sir. One we intend to take in gold."

Two of the embassy's creditors simply could not wait, not even a day, the letters they had sent were that alarming. Thankfully, both were in the direction of home and bed, for Erica's frayed nerves were finally giving way to fatigue. Twice her eyelids began to fall before the carriage jounced her awake.

When they pulled up in front of the solicitors' offices, Lavinia offered, "Perhaps I should do this myself."

"No. Really."

"My dear, you remind me of a washed and starched bed sheet. I insist—"

"Lavinia, please." It was the first time she had called Mrs. Aldridge by her given name. "Please trust me concerning this."

Something in Erica's tone caused Lavinia to pause. "You suspect there may be trouble?"

"I hope not. But if there is, the minister's wife cannot be seen to be directly involved." Erica allowed Jacob Harwell to assist her from the carriage. "Do you have the gold?"

"Indeed, miss."

"Then let us do this thing." She nodded a greeting to the footman standing by the ancient double doors. "I seek the offices of Richmond and Richmond."

"Straight across the quadrangle, first door on your left." As she passed, he added, "They are called chambers, miss."

"Thank you." Everything about this system was so confusing. She was entering a place called Lincoln's Inn, but it was not an inn at all. Instead it was one of a collection of ancient structures called the Inns of Court, where the London attorneys had their offices. Which, as she had just learned, were not called offices at all. The inn's center was a narrow square with an emerald green lawn and a stone fountain in the middle. To her left stood a small chapel from a time beyond time. The other three sides were lined with peaked medieval doors, the wood blackened by age.

She entered the proper door. A clerk so young he could not shave yet stood in striped pants and long black coat. "May I assist you, my lady?"

"I wish to have a word with Mr. Richmond, Senior."

The lad had been carefully trained, for he responded formally, "Might I ask the good lady's name?"

"Please tell Mr. Richmond that I come on behalf of the United States Embassy."

"One minute, my lady."

She stood in the tiny front alcove for quite some time before a portly gentleman in half-moon Franklin spectacles and a stained morning coat appeared at the head of the stairs. "I do so hope this is not leading to more empty promises."

"I assure you not, sir."

"Because my patience is at an end, I tell you. I won't stand for another letter, another false payment, nor another worthless chit. I am taking this matter up with the proper officials, and it is my intention to publicly denounce—"

"I bring gold."

The solicitor's mouth shut with a snap. He lowered his head so as to inspect her over the top of his spectacles. "Your name?"

"Erica Langston, at your service."

"That is not the name I recall from earlier correspondence."

"That particular gentleman is no longer in the embassy's employ."

"Ah. A thief, was he?"

"That is not for me to say, sir."

"No, I suppose not." The man seemed reluctant to believe his troubles were at an end. "I don't mind telling you, another two of your creditors have come to me this very morning, seeking a writ against the embassy."

"Then I shall offer payment in full to them as well if you would be so good as to tell me the total amount owed."

He studied her a moment longer, then seemed to collect himself. "Perhaps you would care to sit down?"

"Thank you, sir. But we are involved in matters of some urgency here, as you can no doubt understand."

"Very well." He turned to a clerk standing in the open doorway. "You have the accounts?"

"Yes, Mr. Richmond."

"Well, let's be having them, man. Don't keep the lady waiting."

"Two hundred and seventeen guineas, fifteen shillings and four pence."

Erica said to Jacob, "Pay the gentleman, please."

As Harwell counted the money into the clerk's hands, Erica said, "I must extend Minister Aldridge's most sincere apologies, both to you and to the creditors you represent. This entire matter has been a most serious affront, and we can only hope that no lasting damage has been caused to his good name."

Mr. Richmond continued to examine her over the top of his spectacles. "You will excuse an old gentleman for observing that you look exhausted, miss."

"We did not discover the fault until just before dawn." Erica steadied herself with a gloved hand upon the side wall. The coins made a musical clink as they were counted. "Perhaps you would be so good as to sign a receipt."

"One moment." When he returned with the chit, he offered, "The Inns are terrible places for rumors. It's hard to tell what is real until it is written in the books. But some rumors show a certain strength, if only through how long they hang about. One such is in regard to your employer. Apparently there are some within the royal circle who would rather see him fail."

Erica knew she should be paying stricter attention and asking intelligent questions. But all she could think of just then was how much she yearned for her pillow. "I shall pass on your helpful observations, sir. And now I must wish you a good day."

She did not recall the second appointment, nor the journey home, nor even how she climbed the back stairs and entered her little room. She worked at her dress stays and buttons, then decided it was all just too much bother and fell into bed still clothed. She awoke in the middle of the night, feeling famished. She found a plate of food waiting for her on the kitchen table. She ate hungrily, then undressed and slept until dawn.

Erica and Jacob Harwell spent all Friday and Saturday making the rounds. By the close of business on Saturday, all but three of the creditors had been paid. Word had circulated of the young lady bearing gold and the embassy's apologies. Her carriage was met by butchers and stationers and silversmiths and carpenters, all wreathed in smiles. To each one Erica offered full payment and sincere apologies. Both nights she slept like the dead.

Sunday morning dawned clear and bright. Erica had slept ten hours. Yet she awoke still feeling as though her head were encased in a fog of weariness. Her dreams had been a constant chase from one creditor to the next, a never-ending array of eager creditors with outstretched hands.

Sunday was the one breakfast all the family took together. She washed and dressed in her one remaining clean frock, then joined the others at the big breakfast table in the kitchen. Only when she saw the piles of papers stacked beneath the window did Erica realize that she had never tidied up after her discovery. "Oh, sir, I am so sorry."

Samuel looked up from his tea and bread. "Sorry? Sorry for what?"

"Sit down, my dear." Lavinia patted her shoulder as she passed. "Let me serve you this morning."

"But this mess I've left lying around," Erica protested. She could scarcely believe she had let it sit about their beautiful kitchen for three days. "I feel so ashamed."

Samuel dabbed his lips with his napkin and rose from his chair. He scraped back the one alongside his own and said, "Allow me, Erica. May I call you that?"

"Sir, of course, but . . ."

"Please. Sit yourself down, my dear." He returned to his seat. "Did you sleep well?"

"All right, I suppose. Sir, about the papers, I shall clean them all up immediately after breakfast."

"You shall do no such thing."

"But—"

"Rest yourself, Erica. Have a bite to eat and be calm." He spoke to her with the same tone he used with his children, serene and strong and deep. "Won't you have some of these strawberry preserves? How about a slice of Wesleyan cheese?"

"Y-yes. Thank you." Being served by the minister's own hand, while his wife poured her a steaming cup of tea, was most disconcerting. "Really, I can manage quite well on my own."

For some reason the two other adults found that most amusing. Lavinia said, "Of that I have no doubt whatsoever."

Samuel slid his chair back a fraction. "Now, then. I hope that in the days to come I shall find a way to express my gratitude. Just at the moment I find anything that comes to mind most inadequate."

"Sir . . ." Erica hesitated, feeling Lavinia's hand upon her shoulder. A gentle squeeze, then gone. But enough of a message for Erica to still her tongue.

"You may well have saved our family's good name. What is more, our fledgling embassy is also protected. We have had a stream of visitors come by the office already. People who have avoided my requests for business, traders with whom we would like to establish relations, merchants from different nations. The business of America is business, as you well know. The royal court may frown upon merchants, but we know their worth and thus are granted a level of access and welcome seldom if ever given even to the prince regent. Or we would be, so long as our good name remains unsullied."

Erica found herself following his direction. "To damage our credit means cutting off our access and thus our ability to serve our country."

Samuel's look was as strong a compliment as Erica had ever received. "Precisely. And thus you can see why your work over the past few days has been so vital." He reached over and patted Erica's hand. "I, my family, and the country we serve owe you a great debt. You are indeed a friend."

Abbie could contain herself no longer. The little girl had sat wide-eyed and beaming throughout the exchange. Now from across the table her little voice piped up, "I said it first, Papa! The day Erica arrived, that's what I said. That she was going to be our very good friend."

Chapter 16

A lovely June Sunday greeted them when they entered the manor's forecourt. Samuel Aldridge plucked the timepiece from his waistcoat and flicked open the gold face. "I believe we have time to walk. My dear, would you care to take a turn?"

"Nothing would suit me more," Lavinia replied.

Samuel pushed the perambulator while his wife held his arm. The pram was built with the precision of an elegant carriage. The wheels joined a complex spring system that gentled the baby over rough spots. The apparatus was framed in gilded mahogany and covered with a starched linen skirt that matched the blanket laid over the sleeping infant. Erica walked behind the couple with Abbie attached to her hand like a bouncing balloon.

Abbie's chatter had a musical gaiety to match the birdsong rising from Green Park. "Winter was ever so long here. Wasn't it, Mama? We arrived in a storm that lasted for months and months."

"I wish my daughter were exaggerating," Lavinia said over her shoulder. "But I must say the weather was quite vile. The worst winter in years, or so we were told."

"It's all the little smokestacks," Abbie confided to Erica. "All the little chimneys, they go all the time. Just puff and puff, night and day, and they feed the clouds. You can see it if you look closely. The clouds eat up all the new smoke, and it comes back down as rain."

The child looked from one adult to another. "Why is everybody laughing?"

They all grew quiet as they neared a manor, one far larger than the embassy. Sounds of revelry emerged from a number of open windows. Lavinia said uncertainly, "Perhaps we should cross to the other side."

"Certainly not," said her husband.

"But Samuel, the child."

"It's all right, Mama. I know not to look." And she didn't. Abbie kept her face pointed straight ahead as they passed before the high metal fence fronting the road.

But Erica was not so resolute. A peal of female laughter was followed by a shriek and a higher sound—perhaps words, she could not be certain. She looked over to see two women seated upon an upstairs windowsill, glasses and thin cigars in their hands. Erica had never seen women smoke before. Through a downstairs window she could see a large crowd of people encircling a table. A man slapped something down hard upon the table, and there came another great shout of laughter. Gambling, Erica realized. They were gambling on the Sabbath. She was so shocked she would have halted in her tracks had Abbie not tugged her forward.

"It's not nice to stare," the little girl reminded her.

"No, we must allow Erica to see this." Samuel's tone was as grim and cold as Erica had ever heard it. "Let her observe the state of this realm. It is only right and just that she understand. Is Erica not a valued member of our little band? Of course she must see. Are we not passing the residence of a prince of the realm?"

"Samuel, please."

"King George the Third was most certainly America's enemy," Samuel continued to Erica. "He forced us to pay taxes without representation, which led to our colonies revolting and becoming a nation under God. He then tried to choke off trade with us and finally attacked us a second time. All this is most certainly true. But George the Third was also a moral man. No friend to America, certainly, yet a man who valued family and church. His son, the prince regent, is another matter entirely. Since his father became ill, the prince regent and his little clan of wastrels have made a mockery of decent men. And of God."

"Enough," Lavinia said firmly. "It is the Lord's Day, and we are enjoying a stroll in this glorious sunshine."

Erica's last glimpse of the manor was of a woman leaning out an upstairs window to speak with someone in the front garden. Erica was not certain, but she thought the woman wore nothing save a petticoat. No. It must be her imagination.

They rounded a corner and passed from Piccadilly onto Audley Street, walking past an odd assortment of ancient farms and beautiful manors. Everywhere there were signs of new construction. Off to her right she could see the northern border of Shepherds Market, where she went each morning for fresh milk. The older buildings were Tudor inns and merchants' houses with lime-washed walls and beamed upper floors. These were dwarfed by newer structures in the style known as Georgian, named after the king who was now gravely ill and his father and grandfather. They looked just as Samuel Aldridge had described the monarch—stolid and square and ponderous.

The church up ahead was drawn from an earlier era. On the previous two Sundays since Erica's arrival, the family had been once to St. Paul's Cathedral and once to Westminster Abbey, which was very close to the Houses of Parliament. This church was something else entirely. The people milling about outside were dressed in a severe manner that reminded Erica of the Mennonites she had seen about Washington. The difference was that the men here were clean shaven, and the clothing was not homespun but simply unembellished. The men wore black overcoats and breeches and polished black shoes. The women were in either black or dove-gray dresses with starched crinoline sleeves and matching white caps. The children were miniatures of their parents. They played little games on the stairs leading up to the church but kept close to their parents, and for good reason. Farther along Audley Street was another establishment, this one lined with elegant carriages and benches full of rowdy folk.

A man with gray muttonchop sideburns moved down to greet them. "Your lordship, you do us a great honor by joining us for the Sabbath."

"I am not a lord, and it is you who do us the honor," Mr. Aldridge replied. "Might I introduce you to my wife? My dear, this is the elder of whom I spoke, Mr. Clarkson."

The gentleman bowed over Lavinia's hand. "Your humble servant, my lady."

"Please, sir. We are all servants of the one true God; I ask that you not set any titles before my name."

Mr. Clarkson bowed a second time, then turned to Erica and Abbie. Before Samuel could make the introductions, Abbie piped up.

"I'm Abbie. I'm eight years old. And this is Erica. She's come all the way from America, just as we did, to be our friend."

Mr. Clarkson smiled tolerantly. "I am pleased to meet you both. Our Lord was good to send you such a special friend, was He not?"

"Oh yes," Abbie continued. "Papa says she was an answer to prayer." Before the elder could think of a suitable reply, Abbie spoke again. "Have you lost all the hair on your chin because you're so old?"

The man's eyes widened. "I beg your pardon, miss?"

"I was just wondering, because you have the space there between your sideburns." She rubbed her own little pointed chin. "My papa has lost some of the hair on the top of his head. I thought perhaps that was why you couldn't grow your beard all the way around."

Samuel Aldridge coughed as Lavinia placed a gentle

restraining hand on her daughter's shoulder. "My apologies, sir. My daughter has a most remarkable manner of viewing the world."

"On the contrary, I find her most charming." Stiffly Mr. Clarkson bent in closer to Abbie. "What did you say your name is, young lady?"

"Abigail, sir." She gave a little curtsy, glancing at her mother for assurance. "I'm named after my grandmother. But everyone calls me Abbie."

"Well, Abbie, my manner of sideburns was that of a very famous theologian. A man I admire so much I choose to emulate both his dress and his style."

"My daughter meant no disrespect, sir," Lavinia offered.

"Of that I have no doubt." He offered the child a hand coarsened by age and hard work. "Might I have the honor of escorting you inside, Miss Abbie?"

A lady from the children's nursery relieved Samuel Aldridge of the pram. The other families on the church's forecourt made a passage through which they might enter. As they started up the stairs, however, a raucous cheer erupted from the inn next door.

Samuel Aldridge glanced over. "I confess to thinking little of your neighbors, sir."

"I do my best not to think of them at all," the elder replied, keeping his gaze fastened upon the doors ahead.

So it was that Erica walked up the church's outer stairs by herself. Mr. Aldridge and his family had already entered the central doors before she realized who it was standing just inside the entrance, acting as greeter.

She recoiled from the man's hand.

The man was equally shocked by her appearance but managed to recover more swiftly. He dropped his hand to his side and bowed stiffly. "Miss Langston. Do I recall the name correctly?"

"You do indeed, sir."

Gareth Powers wore his black suit as he would an officer's

uniform. The severe cut and shading suited him well. He was tall and striking, with the stern jaw of a man used to leading men in the harshest of circumstances. Yet his gaze held the same calm wounded state that Erica recalled from their last encounter, as she had stormed away from his carriage on the day of her arrival.

He bowed a second time. Only then did she notice the scar that traced its way along his hairline to his right ear. "It is an honor to welcome you into the Lord's house."

She knew she should thank him, but her tongue felt wooden. She made do with a stiff nod and turned away. Only then did she notice how Samuel Aldridge was watching her. For an instant she feared he was upset that she had been no warmer in her greeting. Evidently this church held some importance beyond a Sabbath visit. Yet there seemed to be no censure in the man's expression. He did not look angry with her at all. No, on the contrary. He seemed quite pleased.

Erica found herself repeatedly struck by the thought that her mother would love this church and these people. Erica's early Sundays had been spent in the closest thing Washington had to a cathedral. It was a place of high fashion and concentrated power. Seldom did a Sunday pass without the presence of several cabinet ministers and numerous lackeys. Yet her mother's new church was known for its quiet severity and austere surroundings. It was, in fact, very similar in atmosphere to this Audley Chapel. Strange that Erica could sit here, an ocean away from home, and feel as though her mother were seated right next to her.

She felt her eyes sting with longing for her family. Her brother and his funny ways and lopsided smile, her mother and the quiet manner she had adopted over the last harsh years. They seemed so close to her now. And her father, of course. Erica closed her eyes and felt as though she could see Forrest Langston standing there in the aisle, smiling proudly at her.

A hand slipped into her own. Erica opened her eyes to find

Abbie staring up at her. The child's eyes were solemn and ready to weep in sympathy. Erica forced herself to smile. She whispered, "I find myself missing my mother."

"If I were here across the ocean all by myself," Abbie whispered back, "I would miss my mama very much."

Erica wore summer gloves of linen knit with little buttons fastened at the wrist. She traced one gloved finger down the side of Abbie's face. "You are the most special child I have ever known."

The little girl turned scarlet with pleasure. She started to say more but was hushed by a single glance from her father. She faced forward again. But she never let go of Erica's hand.

Erica returned to her reflections. The sermon was delivered by a young man whose whiskers resembled those of the elder who had met them outside. He spoke of something called home churches, which apparently meant small groups of believers who met during the week. Erica was not particularly held by the message itself. Instead, it was the atmosphere that entranced her.

Three men sat in high-backed chairs behind the pulpit. They observed the vicar intently. There was a calm intensity to the simple place and these dark-suited people. A few others besides the Aldridge family were dressed in colors of higher fashion, but most kept to black and gray and starched white. The interior of the church was plain and unadorned, with a large U-shaped balcony supported by slender white pillars. The pews were of pale oiled wood, as were the floors. The windows were smoked glass framed with simple stained-glass imprints of Scripture passages. Compared to the ornate houses of worship where the family had gone the previous two Sundays, the Audley Chapel was austere.

"We long to be granted a clear vision of eternity," the pastor was saying, "yet we do not take the necessary steps. The path of healing is laid out before us. But we refrain from lifting the veil that shrouds our eyes."

Erica glanced at Samuel and Lavinia. They appeared totally

caught up in the man's presentation, completely at ease with the place and the people. She turned her casual inspection to the congregants seated across the central aisle. Her gaze fell upon the former major. Gareth Powers' chin was tilted upward, accenting the strength of his jawline as he listened intently to the vicar. Dark hair fell in abundant curls over the back of his collar.

Erica felt a slight catch to her breathing and forced herself to turn away. She sighed quietly. Of all the men in the world to find attractive, she had to be drawn to this one.

"The kingdom of God is here among us, yet we are blind to its presence. How are we to seek the illumination required to see what is beyond earthly vision? By releasing all that locks us into the mire of this world. Lust, anger, a desire for vengeance . . ."

For the first time, Erica found herself paying attention to the message. She halted her casual inspection of the surroundings.

"We have all the proper reasons for feeling as we do. But whoever said that life as Christians was to be ruled by logic? Was it logical for God's own Son to give His life to erase sins He did not commit? Was it logical for the heavenly Father to offer us a salvation we do not deserve? Was it logical for Him to love us in our lowly and utterly unlovable state?"

Erica found the atmosphere growing somewhat thick. It was more than the tight gathering of people in this airless chamber at the height of summer. She glanced across the aisle again, and this time she met the gaze of the dark-haired former military officer. Gareth Powers quickly averted his eyes, and Erica forced her own gaze back to the front of the chapel.

"We know what we are called to do. We must confess our sins; we must release ourselves from the bonds of our old self. We must seek forgiveness of God and our fellow men. We must stand before others who seek the same divine illumination in their lives, with whom we share our secrets and our needs. We must reveal that which we might otherwise keep hidden, that which holds us apart from God."

The vicar did not raise his voice, as Erica's pastor in Washington sometimes did. His tone was conversational. Once more she felt herself deeply connected to her mother, only this time it was not in a comforting manner. The congregation rose to sing the final hymn and receive the closing benediction, and Erica fumbled her way to her feet. But she neither read the verses nor sang the music. Instead she recalled her mother's parting message: *Do not become mired in the same desire for vengeance that wreaked such havoc in your father's life.* Erica watched the vicar pass down the central aisle. How could this utter stranger speak words that threatened to shatter her heart?

The parishioners began to walk out, and Erica found herself face to face with Gareth Powers. Only this time she could not bring herself to withdraw at his approach. Gareth seemed to recognize the change, for he bowed and said, "I would be most grateful for a word, Miss Langston."

Samuel murmured as he slipped by, "Take whatever time you require, my dear. We shall wait for you outside."

Erica permitted the tall gentleman to draw her into an empty pew. He made a slight gesture, inviting her to be seated, but he registered no surprise when she remained standing.

"I shall not keep you long. But I wanted to take this opportunity to speak of two matters. First, I wished to ask your forgiveness for the most regrettable actions of my men. We were driving them hard. They had marched all night and knew we were entering dangerous territory. The risk of such terrible errors was as great as the threat of attack from any quarter."

Erica found her voice. "That is no excuse."

"Nor is it intended as such." Though he spoke with stiff formality, there was no mistaking the exposed and wounded nature of his gaze. "Nor is there any way I might undo the tragedy. Nonetheless, I wished to offer my deepest regrets for the loss of your father and the hardship this must have caused your family."

The same silent intensity that had surrounded her while

listening to the preacher's final words remained with her now. Erica shut her eyes, not to close out the church and this handsome gentleman, but rather to heighten the closeness of her father. How she missed him. A space in her life remained empty and exposed, so keen an absence it might have happened yesterday, rather than two years earlier.

She opened her eyes. "Why are you not in uniform?"

Gareth seemed taken aback by her query. He fumbled with his watch chain as he responded, "I resigned my commission in protest."

"Over the attack on my city?"

"No, Miss Langston."

She could tell that he wanted to lie, to say what she wanted to hear. Yet for a reason she could not explain, Erica felt great comfort in the honesty of his response. "What, then?"

"It is a long story. One I would rather not recount here in this hallowed hall."

She heard the resignation in his voice and knew he had accepted that there would be no forgiveness from her—not now, not ever. "You said there were two things you wished to speak with me about?"

"Indeed. I wanted you to know that my men did not start the fire that destroyed your family's establishment."

"I . . . do not understand."

"I have investigated this very carefully. A number of my men work with me now. I am a pamphleteer. I write—" He checked himself. "That is not pertinent to this discussion. I have sought out as many of my men as I could find, and word has come back from a variety of sources. Not a single man in my regiment carried a lit firebrand. We were instructed to fire the government buildings only. It would have made little sense to race through the streets with burning brands. The men cannot carry a lit torch and handle a rifle, you see."

Erica's mind struggled to make sense of what she was hearing. "And you believe them?"

"What reason do they have to lie? We were miles from our

destination and had no reason to burn anything that far from the Capitol—much less set fire to one structure in the midst of so many others."

"But then, who . . . ?" In her confusion, Erica couldn't even frame the question.

"I cannot answer that. One of my men claims to have spotted two figures racing off from the blaze, but what with the fact that we were surrounded by the enemy . . ." Gareth realized what he was saying and stopped short. "Forgive me, miss. I forget my place utterly."

But she was too caught up in the implications. "This could only mean that someone knew of your plans far in advance."

"And took advantage of both our presence and our intentions," he agreed. "My thoughts exactly."

She started to turn away. But in spite of her thoughts whirling with the implications of what she had just learned, the austere chamber's silent intensity held her still.

Gareth Powers had already dropped his head in resignation. Which meant he did not immediately see her hand when she extended it. When he did, he slowly lifted his head until she found herself staring back into eyes now filled with hope.

She found her voice had grown somewhat strained, but still she managed to say, "I am indeed most grateful that you would go to all this trouble on my family's account, sir."

"Miss Langston . . ." He grasped at her hand, then bowed so low she thought for a moment he was going to kiss it. Instead, he merely held the pose for a long moment. When he straightened, she saw that his features were struggling to contain a most powerful emotion.

Erica walked down the aisle and reentered the brilliant summer sunshine. She smiled as Samuel and his wife greeted her arrival. She must have spoken some words of parting to the gray-bearded elder. She allowed Abbie to take her hand once more, and they descended the stairs. Yet all she could think of in that moment was how strange it was to feel both light-hearted and burdened by all that had happened inside. Erica lifted her face to the sun and for reasons she could not begin to fathom struggled with a sudden desire to weep. Out of joy or sorrow, she could not say. Only that she fought against tears pressed from an overflowing heart.

Chapter 17

Sundays held to a very stable routine in the Aldridge household. After church the family returned home and ate a light meal of cheese and fruit and bread. Samuel then took what he called his weekly indulgence, which was a nap in the middle of the day. They did no entertaining on the Sabbath nor accepted any visitors. The guard by the embassy gates had been specifically instructed in this regard.

Today as usual Erica spent this quiet hour penning a letter to her mother and her brother. She spoke of the week's multitude of activities, including her meeting with the banker. She dwelt for several paragraphs on Audley Chapel and how close she had felt to both her mother and her brother. The memories brought a renewed sense of homesickness and longing. Only concerning her meeting with Gareth Powers did she remain silent. Erica sat for a time with her quill poised over the parchment. But her emotions were so tumultuous she finally penned her love, sealed the envelope, and rose from the table.

Afterward she joined Abbie and Lavinia in the kitchen, where she helped wash and scrape vegetables. Erica did not want to assume anything incorrectly, but she sensed a new flavor in their company. She was indeed being treated as one of the family now.

Abbie was seated at the kitchen table cutting out biscuits from dough. Flour streaked her arms and face. "Do you know why we don't have any servants up here, Erica?" She didn't wait for a reply. "It's 'cause Mama doesn't want me being raised with any airs. She told Daddy this before she agreed to come. She wants us to be a proper family. She wants us to know our place in this world and remember we are to be servants to our Lord and our nation."

"Very good, child," Lavinia affirmed with a smile.

"Daddy didn't want to agree. He worries about Mama working too hard, especially with my brother. Did you hear Horace cry last night? He woke me up seventeen times."

"Don't exaggerate, Abbie."

"It was seventeen, Mama, really. I counted. Are you sure we can't ask God for a replacement who is a bit quieter?"

"Quite sure. Are you done with those biscuits yet?" Lavinia turned from the basin and her vegetables and picked up the rolling pin. She did not say a word about how Abbie had managed to flour herself almost as much as the biscuits. "Here, let me take these scraps and roll the dough up for you."

"Daddy has been in houses with lots of servants, hasn't he?"

"As have I. Armies of servants."

"They have gold on the walls and gold in the uniforms. They have slaves too, don't they, Mama? Slaves dressed up in fancy uniforms and turbans with peacock feathers and jewels." Abbie was too intent upon her biscuits to notice the change in the room's atmosphere. "Just like little dark dolls."

They had not noticed Samuel's arrival. He now stood in the doorway buttoning his waistcoat. "Servants standing at attention in every doorway," he agreed. "Slaves serving dinner wearing gold waistcoats and curl-toed shoes, as if I were seated in a harem rather than dining with a prince of the realm."

Lavinia smiled a greeting. "Did you sleep well?"

"Very nicely, thank you. Abbie, you are wearing so much flour I cannot tell if we are baking biscuits or a little girl."

Lavinia used a clean finger to brush the hair back from her daughter's forehead. "She has been such a big help. I don't know what we would do without her."

"Splendid." In the same conversational tone he asked Erica, "Speaking of such, I do not believe we have ever asked how your family feels about the slavery issue."

"We have been part of the abolitionist movement for several generations, sir."

"Have you indeed." He nodded slowly, as though checking something off an internal list. "My dear, might I have a word with Miss Erica alone?"

"Of course. We are quite done here."

"Miss Erica, perhaps you would be so kind as to join me in the parlor?"

As she passed the hall mirror, Erica noticed that her hair was tumbling down once again. She hesitated, suddenly very nervous. She wanted to race into her room and unpin her tresses, brush them out, and re-pin them neatly. No, she decided. It would be best not to make Samuel wait. She hastily tucked the worst of the strands back into a semblance of order, then erased the streak of flour across one cheek.

She had made the proper decision, she saw, for Samuel Aldridge was standing by one of the tall horsehair chairs by the front window. It was here he sat with his wife in those spare moments he was able to wrest from the unending pressures. Now he held the back of the chair for her. Erica seated herself and tucked her ankles in together at the chair's base, just as her mother had taught her.

"I shall launch straight in, for that is my habit," Samuel said even before he had seated himself. "Your answer about the slavery issue was a splendid one. But it failed to address the matter of how you yourself feel. And because of what I wish to say to you, I must be very clear on this point."

"I-I have inherited my father's despair over the entire issue." Erica swallowed, trying to erase her nervous tremor. "The United States is a nation founded upon the principle of freedom. My father believed this freedom was intended for all men, of all races and creeds. I share this belief."

"Excellent." He leaned back, apparently so pleased by her

response he was able to relax. "I regret anew that I never had the opportunity to make your father's acquaintance. He sounds like a remarkable gentleman."

"He was indeed, sir. Might I ask why this is so important?"

"I will come to that in a moment. First of all, I wish to address another issue. Miss Erica, might I ask how long you intend to remain with us?"

"I wish I could say myself, sir. I do not wish to overstay my welcome."

"You misunderstand me. My wife and I have discussed this at length. We would be happy to see you remain with us indefinitely."

"Remain—"

"Lavinia's mother was correct. You are a most remarkable young lady. I need a clerk, an official who can help with all the underpinnings of running such an establishment. You are aware that we are building a new residency?"

Erica's head was spinning from what she heard. "Y-yes, sir. On Grosvenor Square."

"Work is proceeding at far too slow a pace. No one is supervising either the work or the expenses, which continue to mount at a most alarming rate. You have seen the bills?"

"I paid the carpenter and the bricklayer just yesterday, sir."

"Indeed so. I can scarcely occupy myself with such matters. I need someone I can trust with the embassy's finances. I have requested an aide from Washington, but it will take a full six months, possibly more, before someone can be chosen and sent over. I would like you to accept this position."

"Sir, you do me great honor."

"Nothing you do not deserve. Think upon it; that is all I can ask."

"Very well, sir." Erica started to rise, assuming their discussion was over.

"No, please remain where you are. I have another matter to discuss with you, one of far greater import." When she had settled back into the chair, he asked, "Might I ask what your relationship is with Mr. Gareth Powers?"

Hearing the name spoken in these surroundings was yet another jolt. "That is not an easy story, sir."

"I thought as much. Miss Langston, I will be perfectly frank. The Good Book tells us that when we arrive at heaven's reward, those who have done well with the small things will be given far greater gifts and responsibilities. I find this a solid way to lead my work in the here and now. So I will entrust you with secrets of national import."

He took out his vest watch, opened the face, shut it, wound the stem, and opened the face a second time. But it was unlikely he even noticed the time. Erica waited patiently. It was remarkable how comfortable she felt at this moment, despite her utter lack of understanding of what was to come. One thing she knew she could say with certainty: she could trust this man. It was a defining moment for her. She could trust Samuel Aldridge enough that it was possible to let him fumble with his watch and collect his thoughts and know that whatever was said, the words he spoke were a gift of trust she would treasure all her days.

"Since George the Third became ill and the prince regent took up the reins of court, this nation's government has been in turmoil. The ruling elite are a cluster of ne'er-do-wells. They behave in the most licentious manner imaginable. They ignore the desperate plight of many of their own citizens. They are blind to all but their own pleasures and entertainments. I despise them and all they stand for. But I must deal with them. What is more, I am being watched constantly."

He rose and turned to stare out the front window. "The only reason our embassy has been permitted to open is because the merchants demanded it. They are represented in Parliament by the Whigs, the opposition. The Tories hold power and are steadfast allies of the Crown. But the Whigs are gaining power. They wanted an end to this disastrous war and renewed relations with our country. Reluctantly the Crown agreed. But the Tories would love to see us fail. They watch us constantly.

What is more, they have intimated that any connection we are seen to have with the Dissenters will be seen as an act of treachery."

"Dissenters," Erica repeated. "The name of the people at church this day."

"Precisely. They have been declared enemies of the realm. In times gone by, some of their numbers were hanged for treason, others deported to the Americas and Australia upon the worst of prison vessels. Nowadays the realm is more subtle in its condemnation. For a representative of a foreign nation to have contact with them, however, would still be considered an affront. I took the risk of visiting one of their churches, as this could happen for any number of reasons and because there was a matter of gravest urgency. I had hoped to meet a most remarkable gentleman by the name of William Wilberforce. Unfortunately he did not appear. Have you ever come across his name?"

"No, sir."

"No matter. William Wilberforce is a thorn in the side of these rulers. He is a staunch Christian and a man who fights the good fight within the very Houses of Parliament. He leads the battle to eradicate the British slave trade. And he seeks a change in the morals of this land." He turned so as to look down at her. "Gareth Powers is a principal spokesman of this movement. He has started a printing business that has made him one of the most powerful pamphleteers of this nation. His words are read in all the capitals of Europe and beyond. I have recently heard that the czar of Russia himself relies on Mr. Powers as a means of maintaining a connection with the pulse of Great Britain."

Erica licked at dry lips. "You wish for me to make contact with Mr. Powers?"

Samuel returned to his seat. "First I would like you to tell me what precisely has transpired between you and this gentleman."

She hesitated. "You have heard of my family's difficulties?"

"Only the barest of facts. Something to do with a fire and the war."

"Our problems actually began earlier, during the trade embargo."

"Well can I understand. My own family suffered mightily."

"My family was approached by a British merchant banker. He had recently acquired two ships and a substantial cargo, or so he claimed. He offered to sell all these goods to my father at prices we could scarcely afford to ignore. He had all the required permits. He promised swift delivery. In return, he demanded payment in advance, and in gold. We already had the money here in England, gathered from earlier transactions. Because of the embargo, it was difficult to transfer it back to America. We assumed this was why we were approached."

"This merchant bank, it was the same one our embassy uses?"

"Indeed so. I first saw Mr. Bartholomew himself the night of my seventeenth birthday. The ships were long overdue at that point. He and my father argued. Something about Mr. Bartholomew's attitude left us both certain that he was aware of the coming war."

"And intended to use it to his advantage," Samuel intoned. "Did the supplies ever arrive?"

"No, sir. Neither ship ever docked."

"Did the bank repay the gold owed to you?"

"Not a penny."

"Then perhaps they never meant to supply you at all."

"Just so," Erica solemnly agreed. "That and more."

Samuel bolted upright. "You don't mean to say they had a hand in your father's demise?"

"Not directly, no." The resurrection of all the old wounds only added to her weariness. "But new evidence that Mr. Powers gave me this morning suggests things I am only beginning to fathom."

She recounted what Gareth had told her about the battalion's unlit firebrands.

Samuel pondered this at length before saying, "All I have heard about this Gareth Powers suggests he is a man of his word."

"I believe him," Erica quietly agreed.

"Which means someone else started this fire. And instigated this multiple tragedy that has besieged your family." He turned to the window and mused, "The Bartholomew Merchant Bank is closely allied to the prince regent and his court. As unscrupulous a band as ever I have known."

They sat for a long moment in silence. Finally Samuel shifted in his seat and said, "You know we will do all in our power to assist you in your efforts to reclaim your family's gold."

"Sir, I cannot thank—"

His upraised hand silenced her. "I would ask a favor of you, Miss Langston. Between friends. We shall do away with the attempt to express what words will always fail to articulate. And that is the gratitude between friends."

"Between friends," she solemnly agreed, though she had to fight the words through a suddenly constricted throat.

"Know that I shall endeavor to aid you whatever you decide in regard to this second request of mine. Had I known what reasons you held for despising this gentleman, I would not . . ." It was Samuel's turn to hesitate. "No. I cannot say that. My need is so great, I would have asked in any case. But I understand if you cannot do this thing."

"I will do it," Erica said promptly.

"You do not understand. I am not asking for a single connection to be made. I do not merely wish for you to meet with this Dissenter movement or even just to speak with Wilberforce himself and sound the man out. I need an ongoing relationship. Just as I strive to be between this nation and our own."

Lavinia Aldridge knocked upon the parlor's open door. "Samuel, the dinner will soon be so overcooked as to be inedible."

"How can that be?" He opened his watch again and cried, "Great heavens above, we have talked the day away!

"My sincere apologies, Lavinia. We will be only a moment more."

"Very well."

When Lavinia disappeared, Samuel continued, "All I can ask is that you think upon this request of mine."

"I don't need to," Erica replied. "I will do it. Or at least try. If you truly think I am worthy of the charge."

"My dear Miss Erica." Samuel Aldridge smiled, such a rare occurrence that Erica found herself blushing. "I can think of no one on earth who would make a finer envoy."

Chapter 18

Samuel Aldridge carried himself with stern reserve. But Erica had been raised in the new nation's capital. She knew all about men of detachment. Erica had long since decided that Samuel held himself back because people were constantly requesting favors and help he could not honestly grant. So he built walls. The deputy minister plenipotentiary also knew the temptation of power, where the entire world seemed eager to tell him just how grand he was, when in truth they merely saw the power he wielded. He accepted everything the public showed him through the lens of his very strong character and faith.

Lavinia, Erica could see, endured the public meetings and receptions and teas because she was required to do so, but she did not enjoy them. In truth, Lavinia was most herself at home. She loved nothing more than to sew and cook and tend her house and children. When the servants assigned cleaning duty in the embassy came up to assist in their private quarters, Lavinia did not protest, but Erica knew even this was an unwelcome presence. Over time Erica was realizing just how fortunate she was to have been accepted into the Aldridge family household.

On Monday morning Lavinia found Erica working in her husband's upstairs office. She stood in the doorway for a time, bouncing Horace on her hip and observing the younger woman. "Am I disturbing you?"

"Never," Erica replied and meant it sincerely.

"Our new governess is due to arrive tomorrow. I asked Abbie what she might like to do with her final day before beginning her lessons. She replied that she would like to take a tour of London and then have tea and cakes at the confectionery on Berkeley Street."

"That sounds lovely."

"Would you care to join us?"

"Me? But . . ."

"Abbie specifically said she would like to include you."

"Then I would be delighted."

Erica returned to her room and hastened to prepare for the outing.

There was a light tap on her door, and Abbie entered. "Mama said you are coming with us."

"If you would like me to."

"Of course." Abbie walked over and seated herself in the room's only chair. "Why do you keep it so plain in here?"

"What do you mean?"

"There are no pictures on the walls. You could put up some prettier curtains. You could have the extra bedspread Mama kept for my room when it got so cold last winter. It's much prettier than this old thing."

"But this is not my room."

"Of course it is."

"I am just a guest here, Abbie."

The little girl became completely still. "Are you going to leave me?"

Erica turned from pinning up her hair. "Why, sometime. You know that I must go home eventually."

"But why can't you stay and make this your home?"

"Because I have my own family waiting for me in America."

"Do you miss them?"

"Very much."

"What are they like?"

"My mother is, well, in many ways she is like your grand-mother Abigail."

"Then I would like your mother, Miss Erica. I think my grandmother is the finest person in the whole wide world, after Mama and Papa."

"And my brother is the nicest young man God ever made, with a smile that makes me laugh just looking at him."

Abbie watched Erica take the powder puff and dab at her nose. "Why do you do that?"

"To hide my freckles."

"I don't see any."

"They are on my nose. I think they make me look ugly."

"I have freckles. Lots more than you do."

"That's because you have a redhead's fair skin."

"Are my freckles ugly?"

"Of course not. They look beautiful."

"But how can they look beautiful on me and ugly on you?"

Erica set down the powder puff and looked more intently at her reflection. "I suppose," she said slowly, "I have never much cared for my face. Particularly my nose."

"I think you are beautiful." Abbie tucked her feet up on the chair's edge and pulled her long dress over her shoes. "Why don't you like your nose?"

"It is very straight, you see. I think it makes me look severe. And men like small, dainty noses." Erica took one finger and mashed her nose down flat. "I used to do this when I was your age. I thought if I pushed my nose down hard enough and long enough it would stop growing. But it didn't work."

"Mama says you have a very intelligent-looking face. And Papa calls you a striking young woman."

Erica found herself blushing. She turned away from the mirror. "They said no such thing."

"Oh yes they did. I heard Papa say it again last night." Abbie watched as Erica stepped into her dress and began doing up the long row of cloth buttons.

"I can do your last buttons if you like."

"Thank you." She stepped across the room to where Abbie now stood upon the chair.

"Mama says she envies you your hair."

Erica touched the dark tresses. "It is always falling down. I can never seem to make all the pins stay in their proper place."

"Mama says you should leave it down over one shoulder. Or double it up behind your back."

"What else does Mama say?"

"She says a lovely bright silk ribbon woven into your hair would do wonders. Your hair is so thick, you see. Mama wishes she had such thick hair. And she worries because she has seen some gray. She says it's from joy over being so blessed with me and my brother. I think it's because she's kept up all hours of the night with Horace's crying. Mama says I fret almost as much as he does. But I know that's not true."

Erica waited until the last button was done up, then returned to her mirror. She had always worn her hair up because that was how her mother wanted it. But in truth she had never much cared either for how it looked or how it concentrated all the weight of her hair at the top and back of her head. Slowly she raised her hands. She hesitated a long moment.

"What are you doing?"

"Thinking." She removed one long hairpin. Then another. The curls seemed to spring out as though liberated. "Would you please ask your mother if I might borrow a ribbon?"

When the three emerged from the rear of the embassy they found the carriage had been brought around back, and Jacob Harwell was there waiting for them.

"A very good morning to you, ma'am. Miss Langston."

Abbie demanded, "Aren't you going to greet me too?"

"Of course, my lovely young miss." He smiled at the young girl. "You look as bright as a new penny this morning."

"My mother is taking me for a drive. We are going to see

all of London and then have a grand tea with cakes."

"So your father has informed me. I was wondering if I might be permitted to ride along and enjoy the day."

Lavinia stepped forward and allowed the sweep of her skirt to come between them and Abbie. She asked quietly, "More troubles?"

"None that we are aware of, ma'am," Jacob said, all too brightly. "But Mr. Aldridge felt it might be wise all the same."

"Of course. We are grateful for your company and sorry to draw you from more important duties."

"Think nothing of it, ma'am. It's a slow day, and that's the honest truth."

He bowed Lavinia on board, swept up Abbie and lifted her into the carriage, then turned and offered Erica his hand. "The minister is most pleased with your work, Miss Langston."

She blushed, not from his words so much as from the look in his eyes. "Mr. Aldridge is too gracious." As she was entering the carriage, Erica inquired, "Would you mind terribly if we went by Grosvenor Square on our way? I wish to see something. And, well—" Erica hesitated, then blurted out—"I feel that Mr. Aldridge has laid a great trust upon me, and I do not wish to start by ignoring it this very first day."

Lavinia seemed to find nothing amiss with that. Instead she said to Jacob, "Be so kind as to ask the driver to take us by the new house."

"Of course, ma'am. With your permission, I'll ride up top where I can keep an eye out."

They rumbled through the manor's front gates, turned right on Piccadilly, and carried on to the same turning they had made on their way to church. They passed Audley Chapel, then farther on entered into a broad square of green and sheltering elms. A grand manor anchored the end closest to Hyde Park, with two others standing directly opposite. Several townhouses were under construction along the two remaining sides.

When the carriage pulled up in front of the ambassador's new residence, Erica needed but a single glance to see that things were not right. "I knew it!"

"Knew what, my dear?"

"They are cheating you."

To her surprise, Lavinia halted her with a firm grip upon her arm. "Are you positive?"

"It's right there before our eyes!"

"Yours perhaps, but not mine. Never mind. I want you to sit back and take a deep breath."

"But—"

"Do as I say." Lavinia waited until she was certain she had Erica's full attention. "One thing I have learned from my husband is how to deal with such issues. Do not confront this directly."

"What do you mean?"

"How do you think it would be for you to accuse this builder of fraud and trickery?"

"But he is doing just that!"

"I have no doubt. My husband has suspected as much for weeks. But my dear, we must still deal with him."

"Deal with him?" Erica felt like one of those tropical birds that could mimic only a few words.

"We need him to finish the house, do you see? If you, a young woman, publicly shame him with accusations that cannot be denied, we will have no end of trouble." Lavinia waited for that to sink in. "Diplomacy is an art. It is a means by which the impossible issues of life, the things that are so serious and severe they can lead nations to war, are instead dealt with in polite conversation. And that is what you must do here."

"You want me to be diplomatic."

"Just so." Lavinia leaned out the carriage's open window. "Jacob?"

"Ma'am."

"Be so good as to ask the master builder to join us for a moment."

Erica watched Lavinia settle back into her seat. Anyone

who mistook Lavinia Aldridge for a simple housewife was making a most serious error.

She observed Jacob approach the master builder and wondered frantically what she was to say. As the two men picked their way out of the building site and approached the carriage, it seemed as though her mind was being compressed by a demand that was beyond her abilities. Then she recalled her meeting downstairs in Mr. Aldridge's office. She saw anew how Samuel Aldridge had handled that strange man in the powdered wig, how Mr. Carnathan had been confronted with all his misdeeds without Samuel saying a single word of accusation.

Erica repeated, "Diplomatic."

"Smile if you are able. It sweetens the most bitter of words."

So it was that when the master builder approached the carriage, he found himself greeted by Erica's most brilliant of smiles. "Miss Langston." He swept off his cap and revealed a few blunt and yellowing teeth. "Good day to you!"

"A good morning to you, Master Dobbins. I hope you are well."

"Aye, miss. Couldn't be better. Now that the arrears have been settled I'm doing just fine. Had my first decent night's sleep in a month, I did."

"I'm very glad to hear that." Erica felt her smile was cemented into place. "I do so hope your men are going to recover swiftly from their ailments."

"My . . . Excuse me, miss, I don't understand."

"I can only assume that an epidemic has swept through this building site, Mr. Dobbins. My bills from you show you have had twenty-four workers on this site every day, week in and week out, for almost three months. And today there are only, how many? Forgive me, sir, the sun is so bright I have difficulty counting."

His eyes widened, as though he too was having difficulty focusing clearly. "How many men?"

"Are there four workers there? No, forgive me. Five counting yourself, of course. And just two of them bricklayers, and they are both mere children. How old are these apprentices? Nine? Ten?"

"I'm not quite—"

"Which is astounding, of course, since every bill has shown four master bricklayers with seven apprentices. And they have worked, rain and shine, every day without pause. So I can only assume it was a sudden epidemic that has swept across the site this day." She leaned through the window and let him see a trace of the steam behind her sweet tone. "And no doubt your bill for this day's work will show as much."

He fidgeted with the hat he held within his two dusty hands. "My bill."

"Naturally I shall hope and pray for your entire team's speedy recovery. And I shall return every day to ensure that they are well."

The builder squeaked, "What?"

"As the ambassador has left me responsible for paying you and your men, my concern for their health could not be higher." She let that hang in the air between them, then said, "Good day, Master Dobbins."

Erica leaned back in the carriage, utterly spent.

Lavinia called out, "Off we go, Jacob."

When the carriage was once again under way, Lavinia reached forward and patted Erica's knee. "Shall I tell you something, my dear? My husband, in his finest hour, could have done no better."

The day was with them from the start. Abbie hung from the windows, bouncing back and forth across the carriage, trying to see everything at once. She sang out the street names and a constant barrage of questions. Erica felt like singing along with her.

They crossed the royal parks, with Buckingham Palace rising through the trees. They traversed Westminster Bridge in both directions because Abbie liked the view so. They rode along street after street of new terraced houses, testimony to a nation eager to put the war behind it. Of course, Lavinia reminded her, it was not the American war she referred to. The British hardly gave that one a thought. She meant the war against Napoleon. The war that had consumed over a thousand ships and almost half a million men, a war that had stretched over seventeen countries and almost as many years. Erica sat and watched and listened gratefully as Lavinia placed the sights in a modern context.

They passed through one of the many harbor areas, for London was above all a city that lived from its connection to the Thames. This one was called Scotland Yard, a name from beyond time. Long lines of ancient willows gave way to reeking inns where barge captains and harbor workers hung their hammocks. They continued on past the vast sculptured gardens of Northumberland House, where it was said that more than two hundred men worked year round to keep the grounds as perfect as a queen's drawing room. They passed Somerset House, an imposing structure designed like a Venetian palace. Beyond that rose the crown of St. Paul's Cathedral. They wound their way back by the Houses of Parliament and Westminster Abbey, the gothic structures of rose and ochre and cream glowing like jewels in the sun.

They crossed the river any number of times, so often Erica lost count and forgot all the bridges' names. Abbie loved these crossings most of all. She loved the gray waters sweeping through the heart of the city, the multitude of brick factories springing up along the docks, the swarming workers, and most of all the boats. The river was packed with commercial crafts and pleasure seekers. There were barges and lateen-sailed square-hulls and great trading vessels being rowed upstream by longboats packed with oarsmen.

The one troubling moment came on the river's Surrey side, just beyond the stretch of new warehouses that crowded in close to the bank. According to Lavinia, this was a region known as St. George's Field, but Erica saw neither meadow nor any green whatsoever. Instead their carriage passed through a boggy lowland that stank of mud and humanity. The open plain was now covered with an endless sprawl of hovels.

Erica watched as Abbie moved back from the window. Lavinia did not say anything but gathered up her child and let Abbie nestle her face into her dress. Erica understood then. This portion of the journey was for her benefit alone. She forced herself to study the tragedy stretching out on either side of the road.

"The squatters' town extends out all the way to Southwark," Lavinia said quietly. "No one knows how many live here. They have never been counted."

Here and there rose brick edifices, so covered by soot it was hard to tell their original color. Streams of men and women came and went through doors that loomed like the maw of some great beast. "Why have these people come to live here?"

"The Land Enclosures Acts. You have heard of these?"

"The name only."

"Entire villages have been emptied and shuttered because of them. This is the result."

"I don't like this, Mama," Abbie complained.

"No, child. Nor I."

As though in response to the child's complaint, the carriage took a turn around the obelisk at the junction of Borough and Greenwich roads, and they headed back toward the river.

Erica asked quietly, "Why did you want me to see this?"

"The Dissenters have two great causes, both of which make them the enemy of the prince regent. First, they wish to outlaw slavery." Lavinia shifted so as to allow Abbie to burrow her head into her shoulder. "Many of the regent's staunchest supporters are drawn from the East India Party. This group represents the plantation owners throughout the Caribbean and southern colonies, as well as those who grow fat from the miserable traffic in humanity."

"And their second cause?"

"Mr. Wilberforce calls it the reformation of manners. By this he means to change the morality of British society, one person at a time. The Dissenters work tirelessly among the poorest of the poor. They have established the first hospitals in history where no one is turned away, no matter if they are able to pay for their care. They have begun a new system that has spread throughout England called Sunday school. They teach any who care to learn how to read and write, using the Bible as their guide. Wilberforce is also seeking to change the nation's laws. He is the voice of the voiceless you see living here."

Only when they passed back through the line of riverfront warehouses and began across the Thames did Abbie slide down from her mother's lap and return to the window. But the atmosphere within the carriage remained subdued. From her perch overlooking the river traffic, Abbie said, "I want to help the voiceless, Mama."

"As do I," Erica added solemnly. "Very much."

So it was that when they pulled up in front of the confectioner's shop, Erica found herself unable to leave the carriage. "I think I should perhaps see to one more thing today."

"You're not coming?" Abbie was astounded. "But you must."

"There is a matter your father has asked me to help him with, you see."

"But this is the most beautiful place in the whole world! And there are four people who sit in a corner and play the most beautiful music. And the waitresses come around in starched aprons and pinafores and they bring you so many things the little tables look like they hold mountains of teas and chocolates. And there are little sandwiches and bits of the most delicious salmon and fruit tarts and tea cakes and strawberries and jams and fresh clotted cream." Abbie had to stop because she had run out of both breath and words. She waved her hands about for a moment, then added, "You said you would come!"

"Abbie," said Lavinia. "You know how Papa works ever so hard, and sometimes he needs others to help him."

Abbie looked from one adult to the other. "Is it about the poor people?"

"We hope so."

"I suppose you must go, then." Abbie brightened. "Shall I bring you out a tea cake and fresh jam to give to them?"

"There's a splendid idea," Lavinia said. "Why don't we go inside and have a lovely time, then we can bring home a packet full of goodies for Papa and Erica. Would you like that?"

"I suppose so," Abbie said. "But I will miss you just the same."

Jacob Harwell moved from the perch beside the driver down to share the carriage with Erica as they traveled. He did not ask where they were going or why. Erica sat across from him and pretended to watch the people and buildings with fascination. In truth her mind was all a muddle. She should have been thinking about the coming encounter. And she did feel a flutter of nerves over seeing Gareth Powers again. But whether it was from fear or anger or excitement, she could not say. What she knew for certain was at this moment a young man was seated across from her, watching her avidly and waiting for the chance to speak.

Should she be diplomatic, she wondered. And if so, how to do this without opening herself to further approaches? Erica sighed. Life was such a bewilderment. When the carriage stopped before the printer's, she made no move to alight.

Jacob took her stillness as his chance and called out to the driver, "We'll wait here a moment, if you please."

Erica studied the young man. Strange that she should

consider him that, for Jacob Harwell was certainly four or five years older than she. To be placed in such a position of responsibility, acting on behalf of the embassy, he must also be intelligent. And no doubt from a good family, otherwise he would never have received such an appointment. But young was how she thought of him. He was evenly featured and stylishly dressed, far more than she for that matter. In any normal lady's eyes he would be considered an excellent catch.

"Miss Erica, I hope you might permit me to pay suit to you."

She held back a sigh. "Jacob . . . May I call you that?"

"Of course." He brightened at the prospect. "I am honored."

"This morning I have been given my first lesson in diplomacy. And perhaps I should use it here. But I feel I would fail, and then I should look foolish, especially in the eyes of one who is clearly so experienced in the ways of this world."

"I am hardly that."

"With your permission, I would prefer to speak honestly."

"Nothing would please me more, Erica."

She saw the thrill it gave him to address her thus. And it saddened her that she felt nothing in return. Why should she be destined to walk through life alone? This time the sigh did emerge.

"Jacob, I am here because when the British invaded Washington, my father was murdered and our family business burned to the ground. Perhaps you have heard of these misdeeds from Mr. Aldridge."

His face paled in surprise and consternation. "I have heard nothing save that you are a family friend and from a highly thought-of merchant clan."

"Once we were well thought of, certainly. But no more. Bartholomew's Bank has stolen almost every cent our family had to its good name. That is why I am here. To try and wrest back what is owed us." She gestured toward the printer's front door. "Inside that office works the former officer whose men murdered my father. Mr. Aldridge has asked that I use this connection, however dark and tragic, to aid him in making contact with the group known as Dissenters. I do hope I can trust you to hold these matters in strict confidence."

"Of course, Erica."

"Mr. Aldridge trusts you, and so shall I." She discovered she was twisting her fingers tightly together and forced her hands apart. "I came to England with one matter that I feared was already more than I could manage. Now Mr. Aldridge has asked my help with another, one that is clearly greater in scope and magnitude than my own family's needs. I feel beset by responsibilities and challenges that threaten to overwhelm me."

The young man straightened in his seat, as though rising to attention. "I would be most honored to assist you in any way possible."

"But in what capacity, Jacob? You see, I am trying my utter best to be completely honest with you. My life is set upon a course that seems fraught with peril. If I succeed, I must return and aid my family in rebuilding what was lost. If I fail, I must do the same. I am here but for a brief instant. Then I must depart for Washington. Whether I succeed or fail, I must turn from this challenge to another."

The ardor in his gaze gradually faded. "You are refusing my entreaty?"

"I am saying that to do anything else would be an utter dishonesty. My family depends upon me. My father is gone. My brother is the finest man in the world, but he needs my help. My mother . . ." She swallowed down a sudden longing for all she had left behind, both in distance and in time. "I love them very much, you see."

"I understand," he said stiffly.

"I fear you do not."

"No, Erica." He stopped, then corrected himself. "Miss Langston. I understand completely."

She shook her head. All she could see from his expression and his tone was that he had been hurt by her rejection. A diplomat she would most certainly never be. She moved for the door. "This should not take long."

Jacob recovered enough to ask, "Shall I accompany you?"

"Thank you, Jacob, but I think I will be fine on my own."

She stepped from the carriage and passed across the walk. A bell chimed as she pushed open the lead-paned door.

"Help you, miss?"

She recalled the servant as the driver of Gareth's carriage who had helped with her valises the day of her arrival. The man was a giant, standing head and shoulders above Erica, with smudges of ink from the toes of his boots to his nose.

A light of recognition dawned in his eyes as well. "The lady from Washington, isn't it?"

"Yes indeed, sir."

"Then you must be after the major."

"Is he here?"

A voice from the balcony overhead called down, "That's all right, Daniel."

Hobnailed boots beat a rapid tattoo down the wooden staircase. Gareth Powers wore well-cut breeches and a starched white shirt opened at the collar. His sleeves were rolled back to reveal muscled forearms and ink-stained hands. He did not realize he still held his quill until he offered his hand to her.

"Forgive me, Miss Langston. I was not expecting visitors."

"I apologize for not sending word in advance of my coming," she replied formally.

"Not at all. I am delighted to see you."

"Might I please have a word in private?"

"Of course." He motioned to the stairs. "Would you care to join me on the balcony? Daniel, pop around to the shop and see if they can brew us a fresh pot. Do you like tea, Miss Langston?"

"I don't want to be any bother."

"No bother at all. Tea for two, Daniel. Oh, and some cakes if she's got any fresh. Do you like fruitcake, Miss Langston?"

The big man offered, "The shopkeeper's wife is a devilish fine baker, miss."

"No, really, I don't wish—"

"Cakes for all, Daniel. See if the men wouldn't like to down arms and have tea as well." He made a sweeping motion with his quill. "Let us all take a moment's respite."

"Right you are, sir. I'll have this lot cleared out in a flash."

Erica allowed herself to be seated by the balcony's only table. Gareth Powers gathered up the clutter of quills and paring knife and papers and blotter and dusting powder and newssheets. The downstairs racket gradually grew silent. "I did not wish to bring your entire establishment to a standstill."

"To be perfectly frank, Miss Langston, my men are glad for the breather. We push them rather hard around here."

"So I am led to understand." Something in the way he spoke caused her to say, "Your men."

"Yes?"

"You said that as a military man would."

"Ah. Yes. Well. I suppose I did. And for good reason. Many of them came from my old regiment. Like old Daniel. He was one of my best sergeants."

The big man chose that moment to clump up the stairs. "Aye, miss. The major saved me from Squatters Fields. Though I don't suppose you know what I'm talking about."

"I was there just this morning."

Both men took great interest in that fact. "Were you indeed," Gareth murmured.

But Daniel was not finished. "When old Georgie finished using us to crop the Frenchies, he let us go without a by-your-leave. Only way we managed to make it home was because the major here hired a ship with coin from his own pocket."

Gareth waved away his friend's speech. "No more, Daniel."

Daniel settled the teapot and saucers and cups upon the table. "The baker's got a fresh apple cobbler just ready to come out of the oven." As he started back for the stairs, he added over his shoulder, "They don't make 'em any better than the major, miss. You can bank on that."

Gareth puttered about with the cups and pot, clearly embarrassed by his friend's praise. "How do you take your tea, Miss Erica?"

"This is fine, thank you."

"It's not the Berkeley Street Confectionery, but . . ." He stopped because of the smile that bloomed upon Erica's face. "Yes?"

"It's just that I was invited there this afternoon."

Gareth paused in the midst of pouring his own cup. "You gave up tea and cakes to visit me? Here?"

"Here is fine, sir. I assure you."

"It is anything but. It is a squalid little shop that reeks of ink and newsprint and hard work."

"Sir, I am the daughter of a merchant and raised on the fragrances of trade and honest labor."

"Ah yes. Of course." His features darkened. "How could I forget."

"I did not come to cause further discomfort, sir." She glanced around, uncertain of how to proceed. "I shall never be a diplomat. Never in all my days."

"Why do you say that?"

"Oh, today I have been given a lesson in diplomacy. And no doubt I should use it now. But I know not how."

"Why should not honesty and directness serve you just as well?"

"No, no, I just tried that also, and it failed me miserably."

"When was that?"

"Just outside of your establishment. In the carriage."

"I don't understand."

"No, and there is no reason you should. Or any reason why I should be discussing it."

"But I would very much like to hear."

"Would you?" She was insane to speak thus. After all, this man was essentially a stranger, and she still thought of him as her family's enemy. But somehow she could not keep herself from recounting the conversation with Jacob. She finished with, "I know there is a better way to say what I did."

"No, there is not."

"But he was so disappointed with me."

"Of course he was." Gareth Powers toyed with the handle on his cup. "But if he is half the man you describe him as, he shall come around. In time, his disappointment will be replaced with respect. And because you have treated him so honestly, he may well become both a staunch supporter and a friend. You can never have too many friends, Miss Erica."

"Yes. I have heard that before." She sipped from her cup. "Forgive me. I should never have spoken thusly. I don't know what came over me."

"Your words were a gift. Shall I confess something to you as well? I loathe the empty chatter that passes for polite conversation in most circles. As a result I am considered oafish and uncouth. My brother's wife despairs of my ever marrying, for I insist upon discussing at every turn such matters as this business and my writing and even the world of politics. Which of course is frowned upon by proper society."

Erica could scarcely believe this was happening. Here she was, seated across from a man who logically should remain her lifelong enemy. Yet she spoke with him as comfortably as she would a dear friend. She studied him. Some might not consider him handsome, with his strong, almost taut features. Even when seated he held himself with the precision of a bird of prey. His eyes, even downcast, were ever watchful.

"I should imagine," she said carefully, "that you are a writer of cutting intelligence."

"Have you ever read one of my pamphlets?"

"I fear not."

"Would you care to?"

"Nothing would give me greater pleasure." And, to her astonishment, she meant it sincerely.

He sprang from his chair. "A moment!"

He bounded down the stairs, and Erica could hear his

hobnailed boots cross the plank flooring. He stopped and began muttering, "No, this is old news. And certainly not this one; the writing was crass and ill-informed. No, no, this won't do at all."

She looked down from the balcony. "Sir, Mr. Powers, I assure you—"

"Miss Langston, I really must find one that . . . No, the first paragraph is horribly penned. Perhaps . . ."

"Mr. Powers," she said, louder this time.

"Yes?"

"Any of them will do, I assure you. They will be fine."

His footsteps were far slower upon their return. "Here you are, then."

"You must release them if I am to read even the first words." When his fingers unclutched the papers, she said, "Thank you kindly. I look forward to reading them."

He sat down across from her. "Might I ask what brought you here today?"

"I fear that to say anything would require a diplomacy I do not have."

"Then let us discard diplomacy entirely."

"Very well. The embassy wishes for me to act as its envoy and make contact with the Dissenters. Can you help me?"

"Of course."

She stared at him. "Truly?"

"It would be my distinct pleasure. There is a meeting the day after tomorrow at seven in the evening. Can you come?"

"I suppose . . . yes, of course I can."

"I shall come round and fetch you."

"No, Mr. Aldridge, well . . ."

"Of course. Forgive me. It would do none of us any good were I to be seen at the embassy." He rose and scrabbled about for pen and ink and paper. He wrote busily, then handed the paper to her. "Give that to your driver."

"Very well." She rose. "Thank you so much for the tea, Mr. Powers."

"Please, call me Gareth."

She hesitated, then tasted the word. "Gareth, then. And you may call me Erica. Thank you very much."

"Daniel will be disappointed that you did not remain for the apple cobbler."

"Perhaps another time." Erica descended the stairs and crossed to the front door. There she stopped.

"Was there something more?" Gareth asked as he followed her.

"Yes." She swallowed hard. "Yes, there was. The other day you asked for my forgiveness."

The wound opened anew at the center of his gaze. He said dully, "Indeed so."

She offered him her hand. "Gareth, it is I who must ask your forgiveness for my wrongful accusation."

She did not wait for him to reply or to open the door, which was just as well, as Gareth Powers appeared frozen to the spot. Erica hastened across the walk and into the carriage, then turned her face to the opposite window. She did not want him to see her sudden tears.

Chapter 19

The next day flashed by in a stream of hurried consultations, reviews of documents, and two further visits to the building site. In the afternoon Jacob Harwell was assigned to accompany Erica to pay the final three overdue accounts. She pretended not to see his glum countenance and chattered as cheerfully as she would with a good friend. She returned to the embassy weary from the strain but satisfied she had given it her very best effort.

The next morning she was busy with her ledgers when there came a knock on the door. Lavinia had taken the baby out for a walk. Abbie was upstairs in the family's private sitting room, where she was allowed to leave her dolls out and form her imaginary mansions and make the cheerful messes of a happy eight-year-old.

Jacob Harwell stood at the doorway. "Mr. Aldridge's compliments, Miss Langston," he said stiffly. "He wishes to have a word."

"What about?"

"I'm sure it wasn't my place to ask."

Suddenly the man's punishing reserve was too much to bear. "Jacob, are we to be friends?"

He was clearly taken aback by her bluntness. "Miss?"

"I am not the lady of the house, and you know full well

you need not address me as such. I asked you a simple question. Are we to be friends?"

"You were the one—"

"Who said I was too crushed by pressures from all sides to permit you to court me. As it would be dishonest to us both, and I cared too much for you to do otherwise."

"As a friend," Jacob added unhappily.

"Precisely. But I find that you are treating me as though I have wronged you, and it hurts me very much. So I must know. Do you intend to act thus forever? If so, I must learn to be less open with you and adopt a stern and cold resolve myself. So please tell me. Are you refusing my offer of friendship?"

"I had wished that it would be something more."

"But it can't be, as I tried my very best to explain. Yes or no, Jacob. You owe me an honest response."

"Very well." His chilly façade gone now, all his face pulled down with gloom. "If that is all I am to have, I suppose I must accept this small boon."

He looked so endearing at that moment, Erica was hard-pressed not to relent. Instead she gave a great sigh, as in relief. "I am so glad. For you see, I am quite certain you would make a very fine friend. And I am in such dire need of friends just now."

"Were that it would be more."

"But it can't be and never will," she replied firmly. "And so as friends I must ask that you do not consider this a possibility or ever speak of it again."

"But—"

"Of course I am able to make such a request of you. One friend to another. Now please excuse me while I go and prepare myself."

"You look lovely as you are."

She chose to ignore that comment. "I'll be just one moment."

Erica was not yet ready to appear in such formal

surroundings with her hair down. So she brushed out her tresses and pinned them up, and because she did so with too much haste she had to unpin one side and do it all over again. She powdered the freckles across her nose and straightened her dress, then rushed back down the hall for the two ledgers she had been working on. "All right, I am ready."

"Might a friend be permitted to carry these tomes for you?"

"Thank you, Jacob," she said and meant it sincerely.

When she arrived downstairs, Erica found to her surprise that Samuel was joined in his private office by the stout solicitor from Lincoln's Inn.

"Mr. Richmond, I hope I made no error in my payments."

It was Mr. Aldridge who responded. "On the contrary, my dear. Mr. Richmond is here at my request. Sit down here, why don't you. Jacob, we will not be requiring those ledgers."

"Very good, sir."

"Will you take tea, Miss Langston?"

"No sir, thank you."

"Very well. To business, then." The two gentlemen resumed their chairs when Erica had seated herself. "I made a number of inquiries yesterday. The word I have received was unequivocal. In the matter of overdue accounts and reluctant payers, there is no better man to have in your corner than Mr. Richmond."

"The minister is too kind." The portly gentleman wore the same stained waistcoat as when Erica had visited his chambers. "Although I must tell you, it is a far finer position I find myself in today than at this time last week."

"Yes, well, thanks to the efforts of Miss Langston here, I trust the threat has been averted."

"More than that, sir. Far more. Throughout London they are now speaking of the lovely young lady who travels about in the American Embassy's carriage dispensing gold and fair words." He cast an approving eye upon Erica. "Anyone would be hard-pressed to find fault with your actions, Miss Langston. Or your accounts."

"Thank you, sir."

Samuel told her, "I have taken the liberty of asking Mr. Richmond here to aid in your family's cause. I wanted him to understand that I consider this a matter of utmost importance, and all the powers of my office, such as they are, remain at his disposal."

Gratitude swamped her such that she felt unshed tears sting at her eyes. "You are too kind, sir."

He waved that aside. "Pray take a moment and explain to Mr. Richmond the situation."

Erica had seen the press of dark-suited men waiting for Mr. Aldridge or one of his aides. The air of the outer chambers and the front portico was thick with talk and smoke from their cigars. "You have far more urgent matters—"

"How am I to know what is required of me if I do not hear Mr. Richmond's response? Do go on."

So she told her tale once more. Long before she had concluded with the confrontation with the banker the previous week, Mr. Richmond's plump features had folded themselves down into a somber mask.

"I fear the situation is rather more serious than I expected," he said.

"On the contrary," Mr. Aldridge replied. "The evidence seems to stand all on the side of Miss Langston. Did you not hear her remark that she has documents substantiating all her claims?"

"I did indeed, sir. But I must also tell you I have numerous other claimants, all with such excellent documentation, who have endured losses because of the wars."

"But her claim is not war-based!"

"That is the case that they will develop, sir. The court is swamped with supplicants who have suffered during the war years. It will be very easy for these bankers to find a sympathetic judge, one who resents the American colonies calling themselves a nation at all. And Miss Langston would find no joy in an appeal, sir. None at all."

Samuel studied the smaller man. "The Crown?"

"Bartholomew is merchant banker to the regent and his clan, as you well know," Mr. Richmond confirmed. "They will protect their own."

Erica looked from one man to the other. "What are you saying?"

The solicitor glanced at the minister. When Samuel remained silent, the solicitor replied, "I would be honored to take your case, Miss Langston. But I must tell you that in order to win, we must have more than evidence on our side. More than right."

"What about the famous British justice?"

Mr. Richmond blew out hard, causing his pasty cheeks to ruffle like sails. "Yes, well. I fear the war—"

"The war, the war! Every flaw I find in the system, every failing of right versus wrong, all of it is blamed upon the war." Mr. Aldridge thumped the arm of his chair. "Do you know, I was well into a meeting last week when I realized he was referring not to the war with my good nation at all but rather with the French! It was as though our own conflict never existed!"

"And to many it did not," Mr. Richmond confirmed. "They heard of it in passing but paid it little or no mind. Most found it hard to worry about the sting of an American bee while the French knife remained at their throats."

"I don't understand," Erica interjected, trying to return the conversation to her own family's cause. "You say I need more than right and evidence on my side. What more could there possibly be?"

The solicitor's gaze was wearied by all that he saw, all that he was forced to work against. "I am saying, Miss Langston, that you need an ally."

"The deputy minister plenipotentiary is not enough?"

"Not insofar as the courts are concerned. Not when your

opponents will be able to call upon the Crown to pressure the judge and quash this case."

"Impossible," Samuel muttered, no longer able to meet Erica's gaze. "The situation is utterly impossible."

It felt as though her will, her energy, the very air of her lungs had been sucked away. She asked weakly, "But what am I to do?"

The men's silence was the worst response imaginable.

Erica carried the gloom with her through the rest of the day and into the evening. Her dinner was a subdued and solitary affair. Samuel was held downstairs by business, and Erica had to prepare for the evening event with Gareth Powers. She did not want to go. She wished for nothing more than to remain in her room and weep. But Mr. Aldridge was counting on her. She repeated that to herself a number of times. Lavinia and Abbie both asked what the matter was, but she said nothing. She could not lie but had no wish to burden them with more of her own personal dilemma. When the carriage driver knocked on the rear door and said he awaited Erica, she was almost glad to go, for it meant not being there when Samuel recounted the matter to his wife.

The night was balmy and Erica was quite comfortable with just a light shawl about her head and shoulders. It was very rare for a single woman to ride alone, particularly in the evening, and she should have been relishing this escapade. The thrill of setting off on such an adventure, particularly one to which Mr. Aldridge attached such vital importance, should have heightened all her senses. But she saw nothing. They passed through Berkeley Square, where the air was suddenly filled with birdsong. Yet the music was unable to pierce the cloud that Erica carried with her.

The carriage turned away from the fashionable West End

and meandered into a region she did not know. The streets turned rough in places, and the buildings were clustered together in no real order. This area obviously marked the city's edge of growth—here a farmhouse, there a stone structure in the grandiose new style called regency, after the current monarch. The carriage halted before an older house of wattle and split timbers, with a roof of thatch. Before the driver could come down to hold open the door, Gareth Powers had sprung from the house entrance.

"Right on time, Miss Erica. A genuine pleasure to see you." He offered his hand. "Is this not a lovely evening?"

"I suppose it is."

The driver asked, "When will the lady be requiring me to return?"

"If you like," Gareth offered, "I could take you back in my carriage."

"I don't wish to inconvenience you."

"No bother at all. I am returning with a family that lives quite close to the church; the embassy is right on our way."

"Very well." To the driver she said, "Mr. Powers will see to my return."

"Right you are, my lady." He clicked to the horses, and the carriage rolled away.

"A moment," Gareth said, blocking her entry into the house. "I sense that you are sorely troubled."

"Do you know me so well?"

He hesitated, then spoke very deliberately. "I know you hardly at all. But I treasure the gift of honesty you offered me almost as much as I do your words. So I shall respond in kind. Though I do not know you, Erica, I somehow feel a very deep bond."

Erica found herself unable to reply. For to do so would have meant agreeing with him, something she was not prepared to do even to herself.

But her silence was enough of a response for him to take a

step closer and speak in a soft and intimate matter. "What is the matter?"

"I feel wretched!"

"You are unwell?"

"In spirit and mind, not in body." She motioned toward the door. "Should we not go inside?"

"They can wait a moment longer. Mr. Wilberforce has not yet arrived. Tell me what is troubling you, Erica. Please."

She had no reason to do so. If Mr. Aldridge could not help her, what could a mere pamphleteer do? But the words came of their own accord, all the hurt and the wounded frustration. She concluded miserably, "I have failed."

"You have done nothing of the sort."

"But how am I to find an ally within the royal court?"

"You cannot. They are opposed to anything and anyone attached to the American cause. But there is one other possible avenue."

This was a different Gareth Powers, one she had not seen before. Decisive and quick. "Not according to Mr. Richmond," she replied.

"No, he would assume the Crown's power is unstoppable in such matters. On the surface, that is how it appears."

"What are you saying?"

"The tide is shifting. The Crown is not as powerful as it once was. As it was even last month, for that matter, or last week."

"How do you know this?"

"Because this is my business, Erica. The Crown has overstepped its own boundaries. The prince regent has acted as though he can do whatever he wants, live however he pleases, and thumb his nose at the nation and its morals. But those days are gone. We are gaining in power. We have learned in such times as these we must express our principles and our convictions. We must stand up for what is right and live as beacons both in the public arena and in our private lives."

"I-I don't understand."

"No. Of course you do not." He offered her his arm. "Come. Let me introduce you to my friends."

Despite Gareth's fine words, inside the home she found no hope. The gathering itself was fine. Yet after living and working about the embassy, even for this short space of time, Erica had come to know the feeling of power. And this place held none of it.

The parlor, which ran the entire length of the front of the house, was quite full. There were perhaps two dozen people perched upon a variety of chairs and stools and settees, with teacups and plates of home-baked dessert close at hand, chatting with the calm deliberation of longtime acquaintances. They welcomed Erica because she was introduced by Gareth, whom they counted as a dear and trusted friend.

Their host was a surgeon at some hospital in the West End, and two of the other guests worked there as well. There was a councilman of some ilk, a pair of widows in matching dark gray, and a young man fresh from seminary with a wife who looked at him adoringly. There were a solicitor and a clerk. There was a new parliamentarian just recently arrived from a rural constituency and eager to take his place at Westminster.

All this would normally have been enough to make for a most enjoyable event. But she sat in her corner by the unlit fire and surveyed the room with the eye of one seeking what could not be found—possibly not anywhere, and certainly not here. She felt herself shrinking farther and farther back into the pall of gloom that had entered with her.

The others accepted her silence and granted her space. Only Gareth glanced at her repeatedly, concern written deep on his face. Even in her despair Erica could see he was a good man, strong in his own way and very genuine. But her heart continued to lurch along, counting the minutes to a hopeless evening.

The tea was finished, the plates and cups gathered. Bibles were brought forth. Several people read passages. A discussion swirled about her. For Erica, the talk and the strong sense of prayerful bonding among these people only served to push her farther inside herself.

She had failed her family. The words became a litany that plunged into her heart with the strength of a poisoned dagger. Her trip to England was a sham. Her pretensions of being able to return home in triumph lay revealed for the fraud they were.

The group bowed their heads in prayer. Erica followed their lead but was unable to hear a word that was spoken. Instead, behind her closed eyes she found herself staring at the banker. The man who had brought her family to the brink of ruin. The man whose web of power was so strong not even the embassy could help her regain what was rightfully hers. Erica felt her heart become enflamed with a fury so fierce it burned away all else, including her feelings of failure.

The prayer ended, but Erica was reluctant to lift her head. She opened her eyes and kept them focused on her hands in her lap. There was a knock on the door, but she did not lift her head to see who entered. In truth, it mattered little. Her rage at Mr. Bartholomew remained at the center of her thoughts. She could feel her heart clenched by a fist of burning coals, branded by the anger she felt pouring forth like steam. This man had defeated her. He and his connections had rendered all her plans and her journeying and her hopes futile.

Erica was so intent upon her internal tempest that she did not realize that the entire roomful of guests had risen to their feet. She looked up to find all the people turned toward the entrance. They had crowded around so Erica could not see who was at the center of all this attention. She stood up, but whoever it was must have been so small, or so young, or perhaps just seated, that she still could not see.

But what did it matter? Another person had come to join

this group of nice and useless people. It was not their fault that they were useless. Erica turned her face slightly away so as to hide from this kind group of strangers the thoughts that swirled through her head.

"Erica . . . Miss Langston."

She lifted her eyes. "Yes?"

Gareth towered over the man standing by his side. "Might I have the pleasure of introducing William Wilberforce?"

"How do you do." She gave a full curtsy, not so much out of respect as to hide her dismay. She could feel how drawn her features were, how tight the muscles across her forehead and cheeks and even down her neck. Her frustration and anger had left her unable to show any other emotion.

Why Samuel Aldridge wished her to know this man was a mystery. William Wilberforce was a tiny wisp of a fellow, with an odd way of cocking his head to one side. He looked like a gray-headed sparrow. His skin had an unhealthy pallor, and his features looked ravaged by an old ailment. Only his eyes seemed untouched, for they burned with a piercing fire.

Then he spoke, startling her with the force and depth that emerged from that frail little body. "My dear friend Gareth tells me that you are sorely troubled, Miss Langston."

She cast him a startled glance. "I am not certain it was proper for him to share such confidences."

Neither man seemed touched by her ire. "Perhaps our host would be good enough to grant the three of us a moment alone?"

"But—" Erica's protest was stifled as the surgeon and his wife instantly began hurrying about. The three of them were swiftly ushered into a small antechamber at the rear of the house. Erica had time for just one glance at the faces she passed. The entire gathering looked at William Wilberforce with a reverence that bordered upon awe.

The room was filled with books and charts and papers, scarcely leaving room for three chairs. Erica's knees almost touched those of Gareth and this little stranger, whose own legs were so short his feet scarcely touched the carpet.

"Really, this is not necessary," she protested.

"You have trusted me enough to grant me the gift of honesty," Gareth responded with the force of absolute confidence. "Please trust me with this."

"I would be honored to hear of the matter that troubles you so, Miss Langston," Wilberforce said.

She sighed and did not reply. When Gareth realized she was not going to respond, he repeated what she had told him, both that evening in front of the house and the previous day in his printing establishment.

Erica kept her eyes downcast and tried not to fidget. She counted herself as a very private person. Gareth had broken a confidence by speaking in this way. She wished for nothing but for the night to end and to be away, but her benefactor Mr. Aldridge considered a connection with this strange little man to be very important. She could not simply rise up and walk away.

Gareth stopped speaking. Wilberforce said nothing, and eventually Erica was forced to look up. The little man held his head at a slight angle and gazed at her unblinkingly, a most intense luminosity in his eyes. She felt her shame increase.

"It is certainly not wrong for you to seek what is rightfully yours. Most particularly something that has been taken from you and your family in such a false and wrongful manner."

The man's voice held a quality Erica could not recall ever having heard before. It was rich in timbre and clearly could rise to fill the grandest hall. Yet there was none of the pomposity that she had come to associate with politicians used to shouting their message as a tinker would announce his wares. Instead, the man was as gentle in his words as he was in his gaze. Erica found herself able to examine him openly, and she forgot for a brief instant all the tumult she had felt throughout the endless evening.

"What is wrong, and forgive me for being so blunt, Miss

Langston—what most certainly is wrong would be for you to seek what is *not* yours."

She finally spoke. "I have no desire for anything that is not due to my family, sir."

"Do you not? Are you certain on that point? For we must never forget that some things are claimed by our God as His and His alone. To seek what He has claimed is more than wrong. It is dangerous. Our God does not refuse us out of covetousness. No, that is Adam's flaw, Adam and all his sons. No. God denies us what can devour us. And He does so out of love."

For some reason the words spoken with such gentle strength stripped her bare. Erica felt the flood of angry tears pushing at her throat and eyes so that her words came out strangled. "Was it love that kept our enemies safe while I and my family suffered?"

"No, alas, that was man. Man and his endless desire for more." He took no offense either at her words or her tone. Instead he smiled, and his entire face was gentled by a caring concern. "But let us remain upon my warning for just a moment longer. Can you think of anything you might wish to claim as yours that God has already said must remain only His?"

"Sir, I seek only my family's good name and my father's hard-earned gold."

"Do you? If so, I am most glad. But I fear—dare I say it? Yes, I feel I must speak. Forgive an old man for addressing you in such a fashion, particularly if I am proven wrong in my concerns. But I seek only to offer counsel to another of our blessed clan. Do you perhaps also seek something that is not yours and never can be? Something he has forbidden us?

" 'Vengeance is mine; I will repay, saith the Lord.' He has claimed this. It is His right to do so. He does this to protect us. Why? Because the lust for vengeance and punishment can destroy us." He examined her a long moment. "Do not remove yourself from His protection by seeking what is not yours and never can be."

A strange quaking came upon Erica, rocking not her physical form but her innermost being. It felt as though her spirit were a chime or a bell of early dawn, set to ringing by this man's words. She raised one hand to wipe away her hot tears. "My mother told me the same thing just as I was preparing to leave my homeland."

"No doubt she is a wise lady who seeks only the best for her daughter." Wilberforce reached over and patted her hand. "As do I, Miss Langston. As do I."

Chapter 20

The next morning the embassy's cleaning ladies gave the Aldridge home its weekly scrubbing down. Lavinia worked twice as hard as anyone, and Erica and Abbie pitched in as well. They knew that the harder they worked, the faster the jobs would be done, and then everything could go back to the private atmosphere Lavinia preferred. All the windows were open to let out the smell of lye being used upon the floors and kitchen surfaces. The house seemed completely surrounded by birdsong and sunshine. A fresh breeze blew in from the park across Piccadilly as Erica and Abbie sat on the parlor carpet, surrounded by newspapers and scrubbing hard at a pile of silverware.

"I don't mind this, really," Abbie confessed when her mother had gone upstairs to check on the baby. "Governess was told not to come today."

"But you like your studies. I've heard you tell your father that."

"I do, I suppose. Sometimes, anyway. But I'd much rather be off playing with you."

"I have little time for playing these days."

"What are you doing?"

"Well, let's see." Erica set down the soup ladle and selected the pie wedge. "I am trying to complete work on a problem that vexed my father very much."

"And you're also helping Papa with something. I heard him say so."

"You're not supposed to eavesdrop on your parents, Abbie."

"I didn't mean to hear them. But Papa was standing in Horace's doorway while Mama was changing him. And they were talking about you."

Erica was most eager to hear what Mr. Aldridge had said about her, but she debated whether or not to ask. After all, she had just told the child not to listen in. But curiosity got the better of her. "What did they say?"

"Papa wishes his staff would move with the same ala . . . I forgot the word."

"Alacrity?"

Abbie gave her a look of pure pleasure. "That's it. Alackity."

"Alacrity. It means swiftness."

"He says he would not have expected you to meet some person in less than a month. Instead, it is done in two days. Was the man terribly important?"

"He didn't appear so, at least to me. His name is William Wilberforce. And he looks like a little bird. Very small and delicate. He doesn't stand quite straight. You'd expect him to drop his arms and go hopping around the room."

Abbie looked delighted. "Did he?"

"No." Erica sobered at the memory. She looked up to see Lavinia entering the room but continued, "No, but Mr. Wilberforce did something else quite extraordinary."

"What, then?"

Erica reached for the last of the serving platters. "He looked right into my most secret heart."

"How on earth did he do that?" asked Lavinia.

"I'm not sure." It was a measure of the comfort Erica felt around these people that she could be seated upon the parlor carpet with her skirts tucked in tightly about her ankles, polishing silver with river sand and soap, and speaking about such private matters. "But he did."

"What did he say?" Abbie asked eagerly.

"That . . . that I was to do what my mother said before I came to stay with you."

"I do what Mama tells me," Abbie announced.

"Most of the time," her mother amended. "A very great deal of the time. Now up you come and go freshen yourselves for lunch." She walked over and handed Erica a sealed note. "This was just delivered for you."

Erica broke the seal and withdrew the note, wondering aloud about the sender. She quickly scanned the writing and announced, "Why, Gareth Powers asks that I go for a ride with him in the park this afternoon."

"An admirer. How splendid."

Abbie clapped her hands. "If you fall in love you won't ever have to go away!"

"This is nothing of the sort," Erica replied, folding the note and stowing it in the pocket of her skirt. "Mr. Powers is the gentleman who arranged for my meeting with Mr. Wilberforce."

Abbie demanded, "Is he handsome?"

"You saw him, daughter. He shook your hand when we entered the church last Sunday."

The child's eyes grew round. "The man with no hair on his chin?"

Erica smiled. "No, that was Mr. Clarkson. The younger man, in the black suit, whom I spoke with after the service."

"Oooh, he is a dashing man. Like a prince from a fairy tale! Does he live in a castle and have a big white horse?"

"He works in a printing shop and wears ink up to his elbows. And he never walks anywhere; he always runs."

"But he had the most wonderful smile," Lavinia offered. "Like the sun was coming out inside the church."

"I have a hundred reasons to dislike this gentleman," Erica reminded herself aloud. "And a thousand reasons more not to go courting with any man."

Lavinia laughed at that. "Whenever has a woman's heart listened to her head?"

As promised, Gareth Powers awaited her a short distance down Piccadilly, standing beside a carriage known as a landau. Its roof looked permanent but could be lowered and stowed behind, as it was now. He doffed his hat and said, "A very good afternoon to you, Miss Langston."

"Are we to stand upon formality again?"

"Ah, no. Of course not." Gareth was dressed in a dove-gray suit with a matching top hat, frilled shirt, and sparkling black boots. He clearly had given a great deal of thought to his dress. "Forgive me, Erica."

"There is nothing to forgive, I assure you. I simply wished to know what decorum to follow."

He studied her anew. "Are you always this self-possessed?"

"Hardly ever. It must be the beautiful weather affecting me so."

Gareth smiled, opened the door of the landau, and offered her a gloved hand. "Allow me."

She settled into the rear seat. The carriage was most elegantly upholstered in shiny brown leather. It had brass fittings and polished wood framing the seats and doors. The top was open to the splendid afternoon sky. The driver perched upon a very high seat well in front, granting them an intimate space from which to watch the world and speak uninterrupted.

Gareth settled into the seat opposite and said, "Once around the park, Jimmy."

"Right you are, sir." He clicked the reins once, and the pair of matched bays ambled off.

When the carriage began its gentle rocking, Erica was put in mind of a boat on wheels. One lined in luxury and wealth. "Is this carriage yours?"

"No. Well, yes. I suppose it is, in a way. My brother gave it to me on permanent loan. My older brother, the duke." Gareth fiddled with the top of his cane. "It's quite complicated."

"So many things involving family are."

"Well put. My brother was furious when I resigned my commission. He threatened to disown me. He felt I had let down the family name, and in a way I suppose I had. Ours is the third generation to hold royal title, you see. The next brother in line has always gone into the military, and the one after into the church. Only in our generation there are just the two of us."

"Were you happy in the army?"

"For the most part. I suppose I never gave it much thought. It was not a matter of happiness; it was simply what one did. But after the war, when I saw how the Crown treated my men, those fine soldiers who had risked life and limb to preserve our nation, I wept. I truly wept. I could no longer remain true to my oaths. So I resigned."

They trotted along in companionable silence until they arrived at the great circle where several large roads came together. A crew was erecting some large statue in the middle of the way. The crowd of carriages and pedestrians and riders on horseback was so dense that their landau was forced to slow to a crawl.

"I'm sorry," Gareth said. "I have no idea how I came to discuss that topic."

"You were explaining how your brother gave you this magnificent coach."

"And the horses. They are all his. My brother the duke is a collector of horseflesh and carriages. He has so many it is unlikely he even notices this one has gone missing." He looked at the milling throng. "My brother and I did not speak for over a year. It was Mr. Wilberforce who urged me to renew contact. I did not want to, of course. After all, my brother was the one who had claimed I dishonored the family name. But Wilberforce can be most persuasive."

"I know," Erica said, speaking so softly it was unlikely Gareth even heard her.

"Apparently my brother elected not to make his threat of

disownment official. He is childless, you see. He has been married twice and both women have died, one of the flux and another in childbirth. He is a lonely man, wrapped up in a web of possessions and titles and court. He is infuriated by what I say in my pamphlets, so he continues to rail against me and threaten further action. But I try to hear the lonely man crying out for family and companionship, and forgive him all else."

"What an unusual man you are."

The words surprised them both. Erica wished she could take them back. But they were out there now, as was the look Gareth gave her in return.

"Might I ask how you are feeling about last night's conversation with Mr. Wilberforce?" he asked.

"I was mortified when you began disclosing my secrets."

"I feared as much."

"And quite angry."

Gareth nodded slowly but said nothing. The carriage turned off the circle and passed between ceremonial gates. They took another turn, this one beneath broad sheltering elms, and entered upon a wide lane fashioned from sand and sawdust. The result was a total muffling of sound, both from the horses' hooves and the carriage wheels. They had joined an endless line of riders, many of whom called greetings back and forth from one carriage to the next.

"This is known as Rotten Row," Gareth explained. "The king and his family often came here for their afternoon jaunts. But of course you must have been here before."

"I have had little occasion to do anything of a social nature since my arrival."

It was a remarkably public sort of gathering, with hundreds of riders and carriages all streaming beneath the oaks and chestnuts and elms. Sunlight flickered through the branches, and the air remained so quiet Erica could hear the multitude of birds overhead. The air tasted of horses and perfumes and wild flowers.

Many people glanced her way, and Erica was glad she had

taken time with her appearance. Her hair was done only partly up, with two tresses linked in a ribbon of midnight blue that matched her dress. It was the nicest of her dresses now, the one that had best survived the journey and constant use. Yet it seemed shabby compared to the parade of fashion she saw about her.

"Everyone here seems so elegant."

"Do they?" Gareth scarcely glanced at the next carriage, where four young women in frills of pastel silk flirted openly from the safety of their coach. He turned back to Erica. "Because the king does this, the height of society feels it is a necessary part of their regimen."

"You do not care for this society?"

"I feel very little about such matters one way or the other." He hesitated. "Do you mind my being honest?"

"It is one of the most refreshing qualities I have found since arriving here," she replied. "This sense that you and I are able to speak on so many topics and in such an open manner."

For some reason, Gareth blushed at her words. "Then might I return to my earlier question and ask what you thought of Wilberforce and his comments?"

"You said earlier that I seemed self-possessed. I suppose it is because ever since hearing him last night, I have thought of little else. And the result has been a paring away of much that I have carried inside myself."

For the first time since their journey began, Gareth stilled his fidgeting. "Indeed."

"I was asked by my little eight-year-old friend what I thought of your Mr. Wilberforce."

"I'm sorry, by whom?"

"The child you greeted at church. Her name is Abbie, and she is the most wonderful little lady I have ever met. I told her that the gentleman looked into the very depths of my soul and told me things I desperately needed to hear. But there was more to the night than that."

"Yes?"

She took a breath. Her logic said she had no reason to entrust such deep secrets to this man. But logic did not hold her just now. Gareth had been right to divulge her confidences to William Wilberforce—just as she was right to speak now. "When the group began to pray last night, I found myself swamped with a rage stronger than anything I have ever felt in my entire life."

Someone hailed Gareth from a passing carriage. Neither of them even glanced over.

"Do go on," he said.

"My hatred was as vast as a great molten sea. I stood upon the brink. I wanted to cast myself in, to give myself over to the rage and the hurt. I knew it would consume me, just as it consumed my father toward the end. I knew it, and yet I did not care."

She looked into Gareth's face and saw a man capable of hearing the very worst she had to offer. A man who neither judged nor hurried her along. A man who did not wish to speak down to her but would take her seriously. A man who listened.

"Why would this anger rise up in me just as others were praying? Was it because I have been such a poor believer? Am I so horrid a person that I can bow my head and see only the darkness, hear only the tempter's call?"

"Please don't think that," Gareth protested. "Not even for an instant."

"But I did, Gareth, and with reason. But no, I do not believe that is the case. I think God's hand was upon this."

"I do as well."

"God showed me what was my greatest temptation, and He did it to prepare me for the meeting that came after. I could not deny my desire for vengeance, because I had just witnessed how easy it would be to let it devour me. It left me not merely defenseless to Mr. Wilberforce's words. It left me hollowed."

"Ready to be filled by a greater wisdom," Gareth agreed. "Ready to listen with a heart and mind truly open to receive."

They passed around a narrow lake and turned at the far end, beginning the return journey. After a long silence, Erica said, "Tell me about this friend of yours."

"Wilberforce was introduced to me at a terrible point in my life, one where I was tempted by much the same vindictiveness as what you have just described. He helped me greatly, not merely in terms of faith, but also in seeing my life and my future as instruments that could be applied to a higher and greater purpose. Since then he has become a friend. I suppose I see him as much as anyone, for many of my pamphlets are based upon our discussions or matters that he asks me to delve into."

"But who *is* he?"

"He is a Member of Parliament, of course, you know this. And a leader of the struggle to outlaw slavery. He believes that his need to follow God's guidance on every issue holds him from swearing allegiance to anyone save the Master above." Gareth took a moment to gather his thoughts.

"The Dissenters consider him their foremost spokesman on matters ranging from poorhouses to the immorality of our leaders. But he remains a very private man, too humble about his own failings to speak often about his faith. I for one consider him to be a man who possesses an undivided heart and mind."

"I don't understand."

"Jesus criticized the Pharisees for being like beautiful jeweled cups on the outside, yet filthy within. An undivided heart and mind means there is no duplicity. To my mind, William Wilberforce acts the way he thinks. He lives a very public life with his most private thoughts and heart focused upon God and God alone. It is from this single-minded quality that he draws his strength. That is what I think. He sees you clearly because his vision is focused not on you but rather on the Father." Gareth stopped. "Forgive me. I have not expressed this at all well."

"On the contrary." The carriage jolted to a halt. To Erica's surprise, she found they were two houses away from the embassy. "Are we back already?"

"We have been gone almost two hours."

"It seems like a few minutes only."

Gareth smiled then, transforming his entire face. The taut features lost years, and the solemn weariness vanished from his gaze. "Shall I take that as a compliment?"

"You should indeed." Erica did not want to leave the carriage. She did not want to leave the company of this man. "Thank you for inviting me."

He climbed down from the carriage and held out his hand. "Might I have the pleasure of accompanying you again?"

"Oh yes, please." She didn't care how forward that sounded. "I should be delighted."

He held her hand a moment longer. "I wish to have no confidences withheld from each other, so I shall tell you this. Wilberforce called upon me this morning and asked if I might see how you reacted to his words of last night."

"So that is why you called upon me?"

"No," Gareth replied, still holding to her hand. "But I confess I could have embraced the man for giving me such a perfect excuse."

"I see." Somewhere in Green Park a bird trilled such a high note Erica shivered in harmony. "Why do you suppose he asked you such a thing?"

"I do not know. I suppose he wanted to be certain you had not taken offense at his words."

"Please tell Mr. Wilberforce I feel—" she searched for the proper way to express herself—"I feel that I heard not merely him speak but the Master through him."

Chapter 21

Erica did not want to attend a social gathering, of course. But she could hardly refuse Lavinia, after all the kindnesses the Aldridges had bestowed upon her.

"I have been invited to a ladies' gathering which I am sure will be a dreadful bore," Lavinia had announced, "but my husband wishes me to attend. That is one reason for the governess, you see, so that I might begin making the social rounds. I know you dislike such events, possibly even more than I. But I would feel so much better were I not to face these women alone. Will you come with me?"

"Of course I will."

"I knew you would say yes. What else would a dear friend like you say?"

"But I am afraid, Lavinia, that I do not have a fitting dress for such a high occasion."

Her friend had apparently already thought of that obstacle. "Ah, but my wardrobe is chockablock with garments I will never wear again, not if I live to be a hundred and sixty. There, you see? You need a dress, and I need a friend."

She brought Erica upstairs to her bedroom, the first time Erica had entered the couple's private chamber. Erica forgot her embarrassment when she saw the dresses arrayed upon the pair of settees flanking the fireplace.

"But these are lovely!"

"They are also destined never to fit me again." If Lavinia felt any remorse over her words, her tone did not reveal it. "Bearing two children has reshaped me completely. Even my feet have grown larger." She picked up the top dress, a blue frock as pale as the first wash of color upon a dawn sky. "Mama bought this as part of my wedding trousseau." She held it up against Erica's frame. "I thought as much. It should fit you without a stitch of correction."

"But you can't possibly want me to wear this!"

"Why on earth not?"

"Because . . . because it is from your mother!"

"Who is your dear friend, is she not?"

"Yes, but . . ."

"My dear Erica, tell me something. Would you take a farthing of payment for all you have done on behalf of my husband and his work?"

"No more than you have asked for rent from me!"

"Precisely. None of us is counting anything as debt. We do what we can to help one another. You need a dress, and I need moral support to charm my way through this social obligation."

Erica smiled. "You know that I am always glad to help you."

Lavinia and Erica attended the afternoon tea. The hostess was a grand dame of London society, sired by on branch of the royal family and married to another. She was also their neighbor of a sort. The home was a newish structure just off Regent's Street, named for the king's son while still in his infancy. Now that he was the Crown's representative, there was a new style of architecture named after him as well. Regency structures were far more lavish than the square Georgian structures, which Erica adored but their hostess apparently found stodgy. This particular building was rather tall, with a facade of cream-colored stone. There were curved Venetian-style balconies, one to a floor, fronting high bow windows. The roofline was shaped like the prow of a ship and adorned with ornate curlicues and cherubs.

The interior was lavish. There were servants and liveried footmen everywhere. There could not possibly be any use in such a house for so many servants, Erica thought to herself. She counted more than twenty, some scurrying about serving the chattering throng, while others stood at rigid attention in powdered wigs and stared blankly at nothing.

On their way over, they had stopped by a house in the Westminster borough to visit the great aunt Erica's mother had told her about. Erica had received a letter the previous day from the woman. Anne Crowley was residing with relatives for a time, she had written, and hoped that they might finally meet. But the encounter had not gone well. Her great aunt bore the recent loss of her husband, the Reverend Thomas Crowley, with a gloom darker than her black clothes. Her great aunt had made an effort to express delight at meeting Nicole's only granddaughter. But every topic of conversation had eventually wound its way back to her bereavement. It was Anne who had finally admitted defeat and apologized for her inviting Erica, saying that it was simply too soon to be making such feeble efforts and that come the morrow she would pack up and return to her home in Manchester. She would write Erica when it proved possible to look beyond the void in her world. But the woman's grief was so palpable, Erica left the house wondering if such a time might ever come.

At the ladies' tea, Erica felt as though she had inherited her great aunt's sorrow. Her smile seemed to be nailed into place. She could not remember the name of their hostess. The woman wore ostrich feathers instead of a hat. Her dress was a sail of billowing velvet. She wore six strands of pearls and brayed like a donkey.

Seven days had passed since her carriage ride with Gareth. For the entire week, Erica had waited and hoped for word about her case against the banker. Finally, on Sunday morning, she had gathered her courage and asked Samuel Aldridge if he had any new information. They had been preparing to leave for another service at St. Paul's Cathedral, where the great of the land came to be seen upon a Sunday. Samuel had not been in a particularly good mood. He had no interest in attending worship in a place filled with little besides pomp and circumstance, as he repeatedly told his wife. Erica's query had only deepened the lines of his face. He had shaken his head and said merely that she must be patient. But she could see he scarcely believed the words himself.

Erica sat as her mother had taught her, back perfectly straight and chin held just so. Her hair, thankfully, remained in place this day, and her hands were steady. None of these strangers would be allowed to see how her heart was near breaking and her dreams buried before they had really ever had a chance at life.

There seemed to be an endless stream of ladies pouring into the house. In the hour since their arrival the number of visitors had doubled and the volume of talk tripled. Erica could see where Lavinia sat in the midst of an older group of ladies. She heard several mentions of the Crown and the opposition and the Tories, and she knew that she should be in the thick of such conversations also. She was here to help gather information and gossip that might aid the embassy in sorting through the complex alliances that ruled this nation.

The doorbell chimed yet again, but instead of announcing more guests, the footman approached the lady of the house and spoke to her quietly. She turned and looked at Erica with an expression of curiosity and some displeasure, or so it seemed to Erica. She nodded toward Erica, and the footman followed her direction.

"A gentleman from the Inns of Court, miss, a Mr. Richmond, is waiting for you in the entryway. The ambassador has sent him to take you to a meeting in the city."

Lavinia had been watching and quietly appeared at her side.

"You will have to go, dear. Pay your respects to our hostess on your way out."

In the entryway Erica found Mr. Richmond looking like a kettle about to boil over. He led her past the imperious footman, through the front door, and down the steps at something close to a sprint. He opened the door to a functional rig with high wheels and a single leather seat facing forward. The carriage squeaked a mild protest as he settled upon the seat beside Erica and called to the driver, "Make all haste!"

"Right, sir." The driver cracked the whip smartly, and the single horse jerked forward so hard Erica had to hold on to her hat.

"Mr. Richmond, what is this?"

"It is too early to tell." Mr. Richmond plucked his pocket watch from his vest and flipped open the face. "I hope we will arrive in time."

"In time for what?"

"I just received word two hours ago. Couldn't believe my own eyes, I don't mind telling you. Sent a note straightaway for the bank's solicitor to meet me at their premises. Perhaps I should have gone by myself, but I thought it would suit matters best if you were with me. Then when I arrived at the embassy and found you were out and had to traipse over here to find you, I feared all was lost."

Despite not understanding a word the solicitor had spoken, she felt her own heart racing. "Can you tell me what is happening in words that I can fathom?"

"A miracle is what," Mr. Richmond replied. "That is, if your good friend is to be believed."

"Mr. Powers? He wrote you?"

"Not just wrote me, my dear Miss Langston. Not just wrote. He has delivered our cause from the gaping maw of defeat!" He leaned out the side of the carriage. "I say, can't you make a bit more speed there?"

"We're caught behind a pair of coal carts."

"Then find another avenue, man! We must fly!"

"The side lanes are a right mess, sir."

"The lady will be fine. Go where you must, just get us there!"

The driver wheeled off the main thoroughfare and into a noisome alley scarcely wider than their rig. At another crack of the whip, the horse sped into a canter. The carriage jounced and sprang about with such severity Erica had to grip the roof and the side rail in order to keep from being flung out. The portly solicitor was obviously accustomed to such hasty maneuvers, for he removed his top hat and slid the brim under one leg so that it would not fly away. Erica unpinned her little gray hat and followed his example.

By the time they flew about the outer rim of Parliament Square, her hair was in utter disarray, the careful pinnings all undone. She swept the hair from her face and watched as they scarcely managed to avoid ramming a trio of workers unloading sacks of grain. The driver was shouting now, both to speed on their horse and to warn those ahead. People shouted back at them from both sides of the road, but the carriage was bouncing around so hard Erica could not make out a single word.

They arrived in front of the Bartholomew Merchant Bank in less time than she would have thought possible. Before the rig even drew to a halt, Mr. Richmond was already bounding down. "Come along! We can only hope their solicitor is still present."

"One minute." She plucked all the remaining pins from her hair, pulled it together as taut as she could manage, then whipped the silk ribbon into a knot. "Is that all right?"

"You ask my opinion about a lady's hair? I am a solicitor, trained for thirty-seven years in the laws of this land. I am sure you look fine."

"Never mind." Erica stepped down from the rig and, as before, quailed slightly at the name emblazoned above the door.

Her companion gave no mind to her nerves. Nor did he wait for the footman. He pushed open the door and ushered her inside, grumbling as he did so.

"Ah, Mr. Richmond. You are singularly ill timed." A stern-faced man in formal black approached down the center of the bank. The banker Erica had recognized during her previous visit hovered a few steps behind. "I was just leaving."

"This will not take but a moment."

"It matters not. I have waited a full hour, at your request, I might add. Since it was all an utter waste, I shall be required to bill your office for my time."

"Do what you will, but not until you hear what it is I have to report."

The banker pointed a shaking finger at Erica. "If it has anything to do with that colonial, I do not care to hear it!"

"A colonial no more, Mr. Bartholomew," Mr. Richmond replied. "As you well know."

"It is no matter." The banker's solicitor had a supercilious manner and an upper-class drawl. Every word he spoke held a slur. "My learned colleague is well aware of the plight of all war claims set before the court."

"This has nothing to do with the war, except for Mr. Bartholomew's manipulation of events to his advantage."

"Lies!" The banker retreated a half step. "You dare to insult my good name?"

"Forgive me," Mr. Richmond shot back. "Precisely what good name would you be referring to?"

"Pay no mind to this little man's rantings," the narrow-faced solicitor ordered. "He seeks to make a scene because he has no case. And even if he did, he is well aware of what happens to those who cross swords with the Crown's allies." His thin lips drew back into a sneer. "That is, he *should* know."

Erica observed a crimson flush rise from Mr. Richmond's shirt collar. "We are also not without friends, as you shall soon see."

The banker quailed, but his solicitor was made of sterner stuff. "You dare to bluff me?"

"This is no bluff. In eight days, a motion of censure will be tabled in the Houses of Parliament."

"What?" Banker and solicitor cried as one.

"A motion of censure and a demand for recompense. And a query as to whether the Crown either knew or condoned such actions as shall be described in this highly public document."

"A sham," the solicitor declared but with less certainty now.

"Eight days," Mr. Richmond repeated. "Unless, of course, your client chooses to reach an agreement and pay my client in full."

"Who will present the motion?"

"You and your minions will discover that name quite soon, and quite publicly," Mr. Richmond replied grimly. "No doubt your royal connections will be most distressed to learn they will soon be publicly sullied by these matters. Certainly you are aware of the distresses they currently face because of other accusations. I am positive they will be most displeased to learn you have embroiled them in yet another act of fraud and deceit."

"Lies," the solicitor snapped. "Unsubstantiated, unprovable."

"Are they indeed," Mr. Richmond said, turning toward the exit. "Come along, Miss Langston."

Erica did not dare trust her voice until they were back inside the carriage. "Mr. Wilberforce is going to speak on my behalf?"

"Wilberforce, is it? I should have known." Mr. Richmond called to the driver, "Back to the embassy, and take your time about it."

"Gareth did not say it was Mr. Wilberforce?"

"He chose not to, and wisely so, I might add. It is far better for no one to know who your champion is before the battle is waged. Thus the opposition is unable to array its forces against you."

"What precisely did he say?"

"Only enough for me to make this final appeal, to grant

Bartholomew's one last opportunity to see you right before their affair is brought into the public light." Mr. Richmond held to a trace of the grimness he had shown within, but there was a gleam of satisfaction in his gaze. "I must say, my dear, this is turning out much better than I had anticipated. The minister and I wracked our brains as to whom we might approach on your behalf. Neither of us considered circumventing the royal household entirely."

"Do you think this will work?"

"I dislike predictions. But yes, I must say I have hope for the first time since learning of this matter." He fiddled with the rim of his hat. "How ever did you manage to attract Wilberforce to your cause?"

"It was all Gareth's doing. Could we perhaps go by his establishment? I would like to thank him."

"I am not certain that would be wise, given his current state."

Erica turned in her seat. "What do you mean?"

"He is gravely ill."

Erica looked stricken.

"It was the only reason he did not call upon me in person, or so he wrote. He has been unable to rise from his bed for several days."

Erica gripped the solicitor's arm. "Please, Mr. Richmond. May we go to him?"

Chapter 22

Erica hurried to Gareth's small apartment in the former stables across the rear cobblestone courtyard from his printing shop. The two arms flanking the shop itself bore thatched roofs over stout stone walls. It might well have been a medieval coaching inn at one point, particularly since the courtyard's entrance was large enough to permit a full-size carriage to pass beneath the portal. The place would have been charming, save for the clutter of disused equipment.

Erica could not believe how ghastly he looked. Gareth's face had aged ten years—no, twenty. His complexion looked like gray candle wax, his eyes sunken deep into his head. "Why did you not let me know you were ill?"

"We don't know each other that well," he protested. "I didn't wish to trouble you." He wore a white shirt undone at the collar and stained with his perspiration. His dark pants were tucked hastily into the tops of his boots, clearly donned as he heard their arrival.

She was tempted to scold him further, but at that moment he began a coughing fit that left him gripping the doorjamb for support while perspiration beaded upon his forehead. He gasped for breath and wheezed, "Forgive me."

"Gareth, what has the doctor said?"

His expression told her that he had not consulted a physician.

Erica turned toward the hulking presence approaching the doorway behind Gareth. "You are Daniel, is that correct?"

The man nodded. "That's right, my lady."

For once Erica did not correct his form of address. "How could you possibly have left him alone and untended in such a state?"

"You don't know the major, my lady. I've been after him to let me bring in the doctor. He won't hear of it."

"Well, he most certainly will now." She turned to Gareth in exasperation. "Gareth, are you not the man who just a week ago lectured me about even the strongest individual needing friends?"

Gareth avoided answering by bending into another coughing spell.

"I am sending for a physician. He will attend you. I trust you will heed his words and do as he says." She did not wait for a response but turned to Daniel.

"Where does the doctor live?"

"Not half a league from here, miss."

"Hurry and fetch him, please."

Daniel did not need to be told twice. His hobnailed boots clattered across the courtyard as he raced for the portal.

Gareth's energy just drained away then. Had Erica not been there to catch him, he would have collapsed on the stones. She staggered back under his weight, for he seemed unable to offer any support at all.

In a flash Mr. Richmond and the carriage driver were there to assist her. Between the three of them they managed to cart the tall man back inside and settle him into the chair by the fire. The driver went back to the carriage, and the solicitor nodded toward the doorway to indicate that he would wait there.

Erica set a kettle on to boil and did her best to ignore the mess that almost smothered the parlor. If there were a clean cup and saucer in the place, she could not find them. Nor did she see any fresh-cooked food. She washed a cup and sliced a bit of bread and made Gareth a cup of tea.

Feverish eyes examined her. "You are so kind."

"I am a friend." She could not understand why such simple words might bring a sting to the back of her own eyes. It must be the state she had found him in, suffering there alone.

"Erica, you are right. I need help."

His voice was so hoarse that hearing him say the words hurt her own throat. "Drink your tea." As he took a dutiful sip she went on, "We will bring round some good hot food. I am certain that your church members will want to be of help. You will start building up your strength and be your old self in no time."

"You are also right to scold me." His voice sounded stronger now with the tea.

She saw the way he tried to stifle a shiver and rose from her place by his chair. "Where can I find you a blanket?" Then she spotted a wrap, brought it over, and tucked it in around him. "May I get you anything else?"

He looked up at her. "Erica, I need your help. There is to be a protest, a march, in Manchester, three days from now. There have been quite a few. But even those in London we normally hear of only after they are over. The broadsheets never report on them. So the populace is fed rumors and bits of tales. There has been very little that I could reliably print." He fortified himself with more tea. "But I have received word in advance this time."

"Manchester is quite far north of here, is it not?"

"Two days' hard ride." This came from the solicitor hovering in the doorway.

"I have tried and tried to find someone to go for me. But Parliament is in session, and there are many other urgent matters at hand." His eyes glittered both from passion and illness. "I was wondering . . ."

"Yes?"

"That is, if you could possibly . . ." The hand that raised the teacup was shaking now. "Might you know of someone at the embassy who could help me? Someone who would make a reliable source from which I could write my report?"

At the sound of footsteps racing across the courtyard, Erica rose from her crouch by the chair and gave him a reassuring smile. "Of course I do."

"Upon my word," Mr. Richmond said. "That is a most remarkable young man."

"Indeed."

"I have read his pamphlets on any number of occasions. So many of his competitors write the most utter tripe; I don't mind telling you that his have a strong basis in fact. So I have often said."

Erica's mind was so busy she scarcely heard what the solicitor was saying. She had never used the word *providential* before. But nothing else could describe the meeting earlier that same day with her great-aunt.

"Have you heard a single word I have uttered?" he continued. When she did not respond, he gave her a shrewd glance. "You will need a proper escort if you are traveling to Manchester."

Erica looked startled. "How did you know I was intent upon going myself?"

Mr. Richmond harrumphed a cough. "Miss Langston, where else might he find such a reliable witness?"

Erica blushed. "Would you mind terribly if we stopped by a house near St. James's Palace?"

"Not at all."

"I have a great-aunt who has recently lost her husband. She is down visiting from Manchester, you see, and plans to return there tomorrow."

"Sounds a perfect fit, if you ask me." He rapped the side of the rig with his cane. "I say there, Harry. Run us by St. James next, will you?"

"Right you are, sir."

Mr. Richmond gave her a shrewd gaze. "If you don't mind my saying, Miss Langston, our Mr. Powers is fortunate to have you on his side. Oh my, yes. Most fortunate indeed."

Chapter 23

They set out the next day for Manchester in Gareth's fine carriage with the top up, the hulking Daniel at Gareth's driver's side, but they were jostled about like peas in a leather-lined pod. Beyond London's outskirts the roads were in miserable condition. Long stretches had not been repaired for fifteen years, since before the outbreak of war with the French.

Yet Erica felt somehow exhilarated by the unexpected journey. She had prepared herself for the sort of objections her mother would have raised, but the Aldridges had been eager to help her out. Even Abbie had aided in the frantic packing of cases and the preparation of meals for the road.

Erica's great-aunt, Mrs. Crowley, was dressed all in black, right down to the black knit traveling gloves fastened about her wrists with black pearls and the black pins used to hold her stiff black hat and half veil in place. She was not particularly stern or forbidding, just quiet. She knitted her way over the easier portions of the road and stared silently out the window when the ruts grew too harsh.

Erica did not mind the quiet. There was so much to think about. Mr. Richmond had been rushing about, full of tense expectancy that Bartholomew's bank might indeed be convinced to make good upon Erica's claims. Mr. Aldridge was delighted both with the connection to Wilberforce and with Erica's journey. He too had heard the swirl of rumors about marches and was anxious to receive a trustworthy account. His job, as he put it to Erica in a hurried last-minute conversation, was to report upon both sides of the nation, both what the Crown wanted him to see and what the Crown wished to keep hidden.

Then of course there was the chance to do something for Gareth. Erica did not even try to pretend she was merely repaying the favor he had done for her. She did, however, attempt to keep a damper upon her occasional upsurge of desire to have remained in London where she could see after his needs.

Over dinner the first evening, at an inn on Oxford's outskirts, Erica told Mrs. Crowley about Gareth's illness and asked, "Do you think he will be all right?"

The woman inspected her across the shining waxed table. "London is a dreadful place for humors of the chest. Even in the summer, all it takes is a few days of wet weather for the air to fill with soot. You must have noticed."

"Yes, ma'am." It was impossible to go anywhere without noticing the soot. On the worst of days the rain was gray with its burden and ran in black rivulets over the cobblestone lanes.

"By all accounts your gentleman friend is young and strong. He was a former officer, did I hear that correctly?"

"A major."

"I should imagine he will be up and about by the time we return." She took a thoughtful bite. The inn's specialty was venison, and their meal was a bowl of savory stew, fresh-baked bread, and butter churned that very morning. Thick golden candles flickered and hissed merrily from every table. The light eased the strain upon Mrs. Crowley's features. "How old are you, my dear?"

"I turned twenty-one in May, ma'am." Erica steeled herself for some comment over her unmarried state.

Instead, the woman merely said, "I married young. But I lost my first husband early on. I was carrying my son at the time. The only child I was able to bear, as it turned out."

"I'm very sorry for your loss, Mrs. Crowley."

"Thank you, dear. I met my second husband while visiting England. I suppose you've heard the tale of the Harrow family's earlier turmoil."

"I'm not certain I ever quite understood it all," Erica replied delicately.

"The tales, though no doubt confusing, are indeed true. I was switched at birth with your grandmother. This saved my life. I was not a healthy child, you see, and the Acadian expulsion would have been more than I could have survived. Nicole became a sister to me after we were reunited as adults. She has been lost to us these many years, of course. As fine a woman as ever walked this earth. And her husband was remarkable. But Gordon must have passed on before you were born. Did you have occasion to know your grandmother, Nicole Harrow Goodwind?"

"We met several times, when I was still very young." Erica recalled how charmed she had been as a child by her grandmother's smile, the shining eyes, and the way every word carried a musical lilt. "And the stories of your son being made heir to a vast fortune, this was true as well?"

"It is strange to think of, I know. But my son was indeed named heir to Uncle Charles' estate. What is even more remarkable is that this took place only after your own grandmother refused the honors. But Charles lost everything through his backing of America in its battle for independence. He was such a dear and honorable man." Anne was silent for a time, then said, "Forgive me. I have quite forgotten how I came to be speaking of such matters."

"You mentioned meeting your husband," Erica supplied, touched deeply by the woman's evident grief.

"My recently departed husband, Thomas is his name, he was such a good man. My son now pastors the Manchester church where Thomas served the final years of our life together." Anne spoke in a voice as gentle as her gaze. "I suppose I should say that nearly four decades of happiness is enough for any person. But it is not true. I was not ready for this. My life . . ." She clenched her jaw so as to halt the sudden tremble to her lips. But her eyes welled over. Finally she managed, "I miss the dear man so very, very much."

They sat, joined together thus, for a time. Mrs. Crowley finally straightened in her seat and asked, "Do you have a suitor back in America pining for your return?"

"I fear not, ma'am. I did have a young man who was interested in courting me some time back. His name was Horace Cutter."

"Indeed. Was he strong and dashing?"

"He was . . . a very kind young man."

"Ah. A family arrangement, was it?"

"My mother thought a great deal of him," Erica replied.

"And approved of his family, no doubt."

"He is brother to Lavinia Aldridge."

"I see." The older woman nodded sagely. "Even so, I should imagine a striking young woman such as yourself has had no end of suitors."

"My family has been beset by problems, ma'am."

"Ah. Of course. Your mother's letter was quite circumspect, but I gathered you have experienced great trials of your own."

"Nothing like yours, I am certain."

"Pain is pain," Mrs. Crowley replied simply. "And what of this gentleman for whom you are traveling north?"

Erica retreated somewhat. "It is all rather complicated."

"Such matters often are." The gentle gaze turned keener. "A word of advice, my dear. When love comes calling, let nothing come between you and the beckoning of your heart. Not logic nor all the demands of an overfull life. Do not pretend that a better time will come, or a better man, or even that duty has any right to stand between you and destiny. For destiny it is, I assure you."

Mrs. Crowley rose up higher and spoke with the authority of long experience. "God is love; we hear that all our lives. Yet when the time comes for love to appear in the form of an earthly mate, we are likely to pretend that we can do without. What utter folly that is, my dear. You must recognize it as the divine gift that it is and take the human flaws as merely part of the mystery."

The woman turned and stared at the candle, and a yearning poured forth with the words. "For that is what love truly is. A mystery we can never divine. One that comes when we least expect and departs when we are not ready."

The morning's journey began as the night had ended, with two women who scarcely knew each other sitting comfortably in the other's presence. Erica watched avidly as they proceeded through Coventry and began their passage through the region known as Midlands. Mrs. Crowley did not speak any more than the previous day, but there was a different air to the carriage just the same. At noontime they brought out the picnic basket prepared by the innkeeper and lunched upon bread and soft-churned butter and good cheddar and fresh strawberries. That afternoon the road improved, and the carriage rocked gently. The air was filled with the songs of birds and the bleating of sheep, the creak of wheels and the regular footfalls of the horses, and the smells of summer mowing.

Erica poured them both mugs of fresh-pressed cider and confessed, "I have spent much of the morning reflecting upon what you said last night. I was wondering . . ."

"Yes?"

She sipped, lowered the mug, and fastened her gaze upon it. "I fear I would not know love if ever I chanced upon it."

The silence drew on until Erica found she could no longer keep her face turned down.

Mrs. Crowley had clearly been waiting for her to look up, for she asked, "Are you a believer, my dear?"

Again the question, once more the sense of being returned to their upstairs parlor and the last discussion Erica had had with her own mother. "All my life I have considered myself such."

"And now?"

Erica struggled to put her unfinished thoughts in some order. "God has always been a part of the natural order. He has resided in His house. I have visited Him there. Then I have left and returned to my own life."

Mrs. Crowley smiled for the first time since they had begun the journey. In a heartbeat all the seams and shadows of her face softened. She asked once more, "And now?"

"Everything is changing," Erica said, striving to use spoken words as a means of sorting through a jumble of disconnected thoughts. "I am meeting people who, well . . ."

"Who challenge you," Mrs. Crowley offered, still smiling. "Who suggest there is more to the divine friendship than visiting with God once a week."

"They have what I do not," Erica agreed.

"A moral compass," Mrs. Crowley said. "A prayer life so strong it offers them an occasional glimpse of eternity. A connection with their Maker that helps them find their way through all of life's many muddles."

"Just so." Erica leaned back in the carriage seat. How different it was to be so open with a stranger. And yet, how right it felt. When she looked back at her earlier years and the way she had insisted upon meeting every challenge alone, *that* seemed so very peculiar to her now. Why had she felt so obligated to confront every obstacle without help?

As soon as she asked the question, she knew the answer. Pride. She had wanted to prove to herself and to the world that she could. That she was good enough. That she was strong enough.

The carriage traveled through a village, past an afternoon market of some dozen or so stalls. Erica noted everything outside her window but saw little of it. The truth was, she could not meet all of life alone. Nobody was that strong. She could see this now. Did it make her a failure? Did it make her any less able?

She turned her gaze back to Mrs. Crowley, who continued to watch and wait. No, Erica decided. It only made her open.

Erica said quietly, "You are a friend."

The older woman rewarded her with yet another smile. "I have every confidence," she said, "that you will learn to hear your Father's voice more clearly. And as you do, you will also learn to hear your destiny when it calls."

Manchester was a bustling city of squat brick and stone structures and crowds as dense as London's. Smokestacks belched great plumes to a sullen sky. The city's multitude of warehouses and factories marched in lockstep to a grim future. As they left the periphery and moved toward the center, the sky darkened further still. By the time they halted before a lovely townhouse of lead-paned windows and dressed stone, a light rain was falling.

There was brief consternation among the members of the household at Mrs. Crowley's unexpected return, for there had not been time to send word. Her son and his family were off attending a conference in Scotland, although Erica soon learned there were three other people who shared the space as well: a young gentleman who served as assistant pastor in Mrs. Crowley's son's church, his wife, and an older woman who clearly did very little but had been with the family for years. There was also a young couple that looked after the house and did the cooking. The place smelled wonderful with spicy fragrances emanating from the kitchen.

Now that she was here, Erica had no idea what she was to do. Yet the customary sense of helplessness did not flood her. She unpacked her few things, sat down on the side of the bed, and closed her eyes. A quick prayer, not much of one, but quite a big step for a young lady who before had always used a prayer book to talk with God. And even then, it was not really a prayer, not in the sense of talking with a friend. Erica's eyes shot open at that thought. Never in her life had she considered a *friendship* with God. The concept seemed fairly scandalous. She found herself recalling the grand church in Washington with its huge stained-glass windows and soaring stone edifice. Then she thought of her mother and how Mildred Langston's new church possessed far less beauty but far more heart.

Erica rose from the bed feeling as close to her mother as she had since her arrival in England. She found Mrs. Crowley in the kitchen and confessed, "I have no idea what I should do."

"How refreshing. I often feel the same these days, but I scarcely ever have the courage to admit it. Would you care for a cup of tea?"

"Yes, please." She waited until the steaming cup was set before her to observe, "You are smiling a great deal more than at the beginning of our journey."

"I suppose I am."

"You must be very glad to be home."

"I dreaded making this journey back to Manchester."

"Why?"

"Because it was here that I sat helplessly and watched my beloved husband fade away." Yet there was little sorrow to the words. Mrs. Crowley looked at Erica over the rim of her cup. "You have proved a tonic, my dear."

Erica still found it very difficult to accept such compliments. She changed the subject with, "Do you have any idea how I can learn about this march?"

"As a matter of fact, I do."

Together they rose and went into the front of the house, where the other occupants of the house were gathered. Erica noticed how all three of them treated her hostess. She saw the love in their eyes, the kindness in their voices. They spoke of her deceased husband as though he had just popped out for a newspaper and would be back soon.

It was the young pastor who offered, "I have heard tell of such a march."

"When is it, do you know that?"

"Rumors swirl about all the time. You know how it is, with the troubles and all."

Shadows flitted across all the gathered faces. Mrs. Crowley said, "Let us leave that for another time or we will never be done with it. You were saying about the rumors."

"The march is planned to finish up in the main square, St. Peter's Field."

"It can't possibly," Mrs. Crowley cried.

"That's what they're saying. It's to be all peaceable-like, so as not to have trouble."

"But they must know there will be trouble," she replied, rising from her chair in distress. "The authorities can't permit such a march to take place right in the center of things."

"What I said myself, ma'am. But you know how desperate the situation is growing. And these folks, well, they aim on being heard."

"They'll be more than heard, I fear," Mrs. Crowley replied. "I fear that very much indeed."

Erica interrupted, "Please, I don't understand what you are saying."

The little group seemed reluctant to tell her anything more. Finally her aunt said, "I am a Dissenter. You are aware of what this means?"

"A little. I have attended one of your services, and I have read several articles on the issue."

"The troubles are very grave and growing worse. The enclosure laws have driven many of the small farmers off their land. Many never even knew the land they tilled for generations was in fact not theirs but belonged to the local manor. Modern farming methods require open fields and better drainage and a more careful usage of fertilizer and such. Or so they tell me. All I can tell you is the new laws favor the rich and cause the poor to suffer greatly." Mrs. Crowley twisted the handkerchief she held into a worried knot. "As we shall no doubt see Monday."

Chapter 24

Their footfalls sounded like softest rain.

That is what Erica would always remember. She and Anne Crowley had been taken to the home of Mrs. Long, a friend of Anne's and a member of her congregation. Their hostess fretted over the rumors being true. Erica probably said a few polite words about the lady's home. But the front parlor's window drew her like a magnet.

Manchester was formerly a medieval trading center, and the center of town had held both the guildhalls and the city's richest merchants. This was a very fine house, rebuilt any number of times and faced with Cotswold stone. Three tall sash windows overlooked St. Peter's Field, the city's central square. The sill where Erica leaned her arms was the color of soft butter in the dim light. It was a far cry from the squalor and dusty hovels on the outskirts of town.

Mrs. Long came and wrung her hands and fretted over the people and the riffraff and the soldiers and the state of the nation. Finally Mrs. Crowley recognized that Erica was trying hard to concentrate, to observe everything as Gareth would have wished. She took her friend by the arm and led her to the kitchen off the back hallway, where they could sit and have a nice chat in peace.

The marchers were not used to being here in the center of things. Erica was so close she could see the astonishment and hesitancy on many faces. That and the hunger. They entered the central square with rounded eyes and sunken cheeks. There was awe, especially on the children's faces. And there was desperation.

They gathered over on the far side, where a makeshift stand had been erected. Upon this stood a trio of a man and two women. They were dressed in the same severe black as the regulars at the Audley Chapel. The first man rose and began addressing the crowd through a funnel-shaped mouthpiece, no doubt meant to amplify his voice. Erica saw that he held a book in one hand stretched out over his head. Another Dissenter, she decided. Probably a pastor. She debated whether or not to go out to the square. She knew her aunt would object. Strangely enough, this had come to mean a very great deal to her. She did not want to displease her newest friend. But the question was, what would Gareth want her to do?

Erica had no way of guessing the numbers, but she would have supposed there must have been five thousand or more. Some shouted back in response to whatever it was the leader was saying, but most of them huddled together, clutching at their children and listening.

More and more people continued to join them. The square was a quarter-mile wide, and before the first man finished addressing the crowd, the square was three-quarters full. Erica decided there was little to be gained by joining them. She could not have hoped to get closer to the front, the people were so tightly packed together. And at least from this perch she could see everything.

More footsteps began approaching from one of the side streets to her right. These were joined by more from her left. The footsteps were so loud many of those closest to where she sat turned to see what was happening. She saw their eyes go round a second time. Erica did not realize she had risen to her feet until her head bumped the frame of the open window. Those were not footfalls scraping against the cobblestones. They were hoofbeats.

The sight of the first line of troops froze her blood. They were royal horse guards, and they carried the long staves of combat. Their horses' flanks were sweating in the sun. Their helmets and breastplates gleamed in the bright light. They looked menacing. Evil.

The spokesman on the makeshift stand faltered. The entire crowd was turning now as the cavalry began spreading out. Erica watched as they made a double-filed line around the back of the square, so that eight of them were almost directly below her window.

The horses stomped and pawed at the earth. The crowd began muttering and backing away. The dark-suited man upon the stand called for them to stand fast. They were unarmed; they had every right to gather.

The officer barked a command. Erica could not hear the words, but the front rank of horsemen swept back their cloaks and drew pistols. The officer barked again, and the horsemen took careful aim.

"No!"

She was not aware that she had screamed. The crowd was screaming as well now. Children were being passed back through the throng, away from the horsemen, stuffed into doorways and shunted down side lanes. People were streaming away, but the lanes were narrow, and there were so many people. Thousands of them.

"Fire!"

Erica screamed again, this time joined by the voices of Mrs. Crowley and their host. But none of them could even hear their own sounds, for the square was filled with shots and smoke and shrieks.

"Charge!"

The cavalry reslung their arms, aimed their staves, and drove straight at the crowd.

Erica's legs would no longer hold her. Mrs. Crowley pulled the weeping Mrs. Long away from the sight. Then she came back and tried to draw Erica away from the window as well.

Erica was sobbing so hard she could scarcely take in enough breath to keep from choking. She wanted to tell her aunt to leave her be, to get away from the window; there was no need for both of them to suffer through the anguish of what was unfolding down below. But she could not find enough breath to do more than weep. She could not even wipe away the tears. All she could manage was to hold on to the windowsill and keep her face pointed at the square and try her best to see through her tears.

PART
THREE

Chapter 25

When they managed to return to Anne Crowley's home, it was to discover that Daniel already had the coach ready and waiting. They did not need to ask how he knew. Each person's face was somber—a complete contrast to the bright sky overhead. Erica sent him to try and ascertain the numbers. It was hard to form the words, but again Daniel seemed to understand; he did not ask numbers of what. Erica knew that to say more than that would have broken her yet again. They packed in haste. The cook had prepared a fine meal, but Erica could not bear even to look at the food. Mrs. Crowley merely shook her head at the thought. The cook packed the food in two hampers for the return journey. As soon as Daniel returned, more grim-faced than ever, they were off.

They spent hours in silence, but now it was the quiet of two close friends, drawn ever more tightly together by the sharing of what they had just seen. It was late into the afternoon before Erica found the strength to say, "I do not see how God could permit that to happen."

Her aunt nodded.

Erica squeezed the damp handkerchief to her cheeks once more. The scenes remained branded upon her mind and heart. "I want to understand."

"I know."

"But this horror . . ."

Mrs. Crowley slipped across the carriage to settle into the seat alongside Erica. "My late husband came to the cloth late in life. Previously he was a successful solicitor. He had such a gift when speaking on the eternal truths. Such fervor, such gentle passion. We lived in Nova Scotia for a number of years; then the church here begged my husband to return. At first we intended to preside over a revival and then go back to Canada. But while here we both felt called to remain and shepherd this flock. My happiest moments have been sitting and listening to my husband preach the Gospel to these people who have become my closest friends and family."

There was no escaping grief that day. Erica's heart was leaden, as though soaked in the tears she had shed. But sitting here in the rocking carriage with this fine woman eased her pain. She could not explain why hearing of the other woman's loss calmed her so. Yet the carriage became filled with the companionship of two women sharing sorrow. She reached over and took Mrs. Crowley's hand.

The older woman looked down at Erica's fingers, but she didn't seem to see them. "He began having pains. His back, his chest, his legs. They grew worse and worse. Then one day . . ."

Erica did not speak. She felt no desire to tell her friend to stop adding to the day's darkness. Instead she sat with a patience that was most certainly not her own and listened.

"One day he could not rise from his bed." She took a ragged breath. "Through those next eight months I prayed so hard. Night and day I prayed. At times I had the strongest feeling that God had heard me and my husband's health would be restored. And life would go back to the way it was before."

When she stopped this time, Erica knew enough to offer what the woman would have found so hard to say. "Then he died."

"He left me all alone. My life was so empty. How could God have done this to me? Why was I left here when he was gone, and my heart was ashes, and my life an empty corridor with nothing ahead save dust and memories? All the assurances in the world that my dear man was with God meant nothing. I was still here, you see. And I wished to have nothing to do with a world where he was no more."

Erica found herself nodding slowly, a motion in time to the carriage's rocking. She was beginning to not only listen to the woman beside her but think in line with her. Was this the meaning of friendship, to feel without barriers?

Erica recalled something she had heard at Audley Chapel. The words had not meant anything at the time, but now they solidified into a reality so strong they shouted through her wounded heart long before she spoke them aloud. "This is not our home."

"Precisely. This is an imperfect world. We pass through here, we cling to our Maker, we seek His guidance. There is so much *wrong* here. So much we would prefer to have otherwise. But life within His embrace is still a glorious thing. I have found that even in the midst of my own darkest hour."

"Tell me how."

Her aunt slipped back so as to meet Erica's eye. "By asking the Father to give even the sorrow a purpose and a meaning."

Erica looked out at the hills. "Perhaps we should pray, then."

"You begin, my dear."

Erica took a long breath. She closed her eyes. This was not a time for distance or formality. It was a time for two new friends to turn together to their eternal Friend. One who was there for them, in the good times and the bad. One who hurt with them. One who suffered with them. One who had come to die for them.

"Dear, dear heavenly Father," Erica began and knew it was so.

The trip continued at a sad and steady pace. The minutes were paced out by creaking wheels and plodding, snorting horses. The hours were filled with recollections of what they had witnessed and with a few more tears. From time to time they prayed. They held hands and spoke in the fashion of long-time friends.

As they were preparing for bed that night, Mrs. Crowley asked Erica to call her by her first name. There was great comfort to be found in such small gifts, Erica decided as she closed her eyes upon a heavy day. She heard Anne saying her prayers from the bed across the room and wanted to listen, for she knew that this was a woman with a lifetime's experience of talking intimately with God. But Erica's eyes were too heavy, and she fell asleep instantly and did not dream.

Erica was awakened during the night by images so shocking they bolted her upright in bed. She sat there with her heart pounding, not recalling exactly what it was she had dreamed but remembering instead the previous day. Little things she had forgotten or perhaps only seen with one segment of her mind. A single small boot with a hole where the heel should have been, lying in the dust. Erica felt as though she could not find breath in the dark chamber.

Then she heard the sound of sobbing.

She tiptoed across the room and sat upon Anne's bed and gentled the woman with a touch upon the shoulder. Eventually the older woman quieted and her breathing eased into slumber. Not a word was said. Erica returned to bed, her face dry. She knew Anne had wept for both of them.

The next morning Erica awoke to the sounds of birds and a rising wind. The whole world seemed to be rushing about. She stared out the window as the sun seemed to urge the wind to push all the remaining clouds out of the way.

"Good morning," Anne said from the other bed.

"I hope I didn't disturb you."

"Not at all. What time is it?"

"Just gone seven."

"Has something happened?"

Erica looked at the other woman. "What do you mean?"

"You seem so, well, *purposeful* I suppose is the proper word."

"I don't know," Erica replied. "But I have this rather strong feeling . . ."

"Yes?"

"That something is pushing at me."

Anne wore a beribboned head covering that had slipped down over one ear. She righted it as she swung her feet to the floor. "Come over here, and let us pray about it."

Erica did as she was told. Afterward she opened her eyes and stared out the window. She could smell the sweet scents of a fresh summer day carried upon the breeze.

"Well?"

Erica looked at the older woman. "I really think we should hurry."

The feeling of haste infected them all. It seemed a matter of minutes from when Erica followed Anne down the stairs and announced their desire to leave swiftly, to the moment when Daniel was ushering them into the carriage and they were setting off for London.

The carriage rocked in time to the road and the wind. The breeze was strong from the north and west, as though designed by a great and invisible hand to press them farther and faster toward their goal. They breakfasted from one of the picnic hampers packed with food meant for the previous day. The other was topside, being devoured by the men deprived of their breakfast by the morning rush.

Erica confessed as she ate, "I am ashamed to be hungry."

Anne neither asked what she meant nor objected to the sentiment. Instead she handed Erica a slice of apple and said, "For weeks after my husband died, I ate only when ordered to. Every time I lifted a spoon to my mouth, I felt as though I was being disloyal. It made no sense, not even to me. But I could not deny my feelings merely because they were illogical."

The day was too beautiful for the burden she carried, the food she ate too splendid. The air was too perfumed by all the flavors of late summer. Through the carriage window Erica watched three families gleaning the remnants of a harvest. Life was far too rich.

She confessed, "I wish I could erase all of yesterday."

Anne formed a question by the way she cocked her head. "You wish you never made this journey?"

"Yes." She finished her bit of bread and fresh curds. "Well, that is . . ."

"Do you wish Gareth had been well and seen this himself? That is your gentleman's name, is it not?"

"Gareth, yes. But no, I wouldn't want anyone to see what we observed. I wish it had never happened."

"But it did happen. It is the situation in our land. Do you wish to blind yourself to what is?"

Erica folded her napkin about the remnants of her meal and set it on the seat. *Yes,* she wanted to say. She wanted the world to go back to how it was . . . when? Back before her father died. Back before the bankers stole from her family. Back when she was young and safe and such things as this never happened, or if they did, she had no need to learn of them.

Anne waited until she lifted her gaze to say, "You see? Life does not always grant us the goodness we would wish for. But in the midst of these harsh moments, there are gifts to be found. Friendship. Communion with our fellow believers. A greater trust in our Lord. And, if He wills, a purpose to grant the hardship meaning. A mission."

Erica mulled that over for a time before asking, "How long did it take for it to leave?"

"For what to leave?"

"You said the illogical feelings of guilt finally passed. How long did this require?"

The older woman regarded Erica in a curious fashion. "In my case, it was rather a long time. Several months, in fact."

"What happened?"

Deliberately Anne wiped her hands, then smoothed the napkin back into her lap. "I met a new friend, by the grace of our Lord. A young lady who needed me."

Chapter 26

When they arrived at London's outskirts, Erica viewed the scene through different eyes. The city was ringed by squalor and misery. "I don't know what to do about this, but I must do something."

"Good," Anne replied firmly. "That is our nation's problem, to my mind. We prefer not to see, and when we must, we seek not to feel."

"Was I a fool to drag us out of bed and hurry us back, do you think?"

"Never for a moment did that enter my mind," Anne said firmly. "Where do you think we should go first?"

They went straight to the pamphleteer's. They needed guidance, and they needed to report—though just the thought of recounting what she had seen left Erica's throat feeling swollen and raw.

But Gareth was not there to greet them. Instead, one of the other workers came out to the carriage and reported that not only was Gareth still ill, but he had been moved to William Wilberforce's house at Kensington Gore. Anne made no protest as Erica pleaded for them to make all haste.

The Wilberforce home was a large stone house set well back from the road. A grove of mulberry trees formed a stand between the house and the front gates, keeping them from glimpsing most of it until the carriage rounded the gravel drive and pulled up by the portico. Up close it was far less imposing than Erica had feared. Perhaps if the paintwork around the windows were not quite so cracked, or if the front door did not rest partially ajar, or had a trio of earnest young men not chosen that moment to spill down the stairs and hurry away, Erica might have felt more awkward about appearing at a relative stranger's front door and asking to see a houseguest.

When she alighted from the carriage, Anne decided, "I shall remain here until you see how things are."

"Very well."

"Erica." When she turned back, Anne reached over and took hold of her hand. "Might I share with you the gift I myself have gained from this journey?"

"Of course."

"When the storms beset you, you must hold on to God with steadfast determination. In time, you will know His purpose. In time."

Erica leaned forward and embraced the older woman. Then she mounted the front stairs and rang the bell. She could hear discussion from within, but no one came. A dozen people were seated upon rusting lawn chairs and blankets beneath the mulberry trees, deep in discussion. She wondered about asking them where she should go, but they paid her no mind. Erica pushed the door open and entered.

The two large parlors opening to either side of the central hall were hives of quiet activity. People moved about, talking earnestly and sorting documents. Erica moved to one, then the other. No one even looked her way. It was as though they were so accustomed to people coming and going, and the work they were involved in was so important, they simply had no time to greet every new arrival.

She knocked on the open door of one of the parlors. Eventually a young woman, perhaps her own age or a year older, came up to her. "Yes?"

"I was wondering where I might find the gentleman of the house."

Someone called from the back without looking up from his papers, "Parliament is still in session. He won't be back until quite late."

The young woman asked Erica, "Was Mr. Wilberforce expecting you?"

"No. No, it's just . . . Well, actually . . ."

The woman gave her an inquisitive look.

"I was told Gareth Powers was residing here."

"That is correct."

"Is he well?"

"Far from it. But he is mending, or so the doctor tells us."

Erica caught the faint glimmer in the young woman's eye. *She fancies him,* Erica realized. And why not? Gareth was a most handsome man. She found her chest squeezed by an icy hand.

The young woman said, "Might I ask your name?"

"Erica Langston."

The entire room was caught in a sudden silence. Every eye turned her way. A man set down his pile of briefs and rushed over. "You would not be the lady Gareth sent north?"

"Yes, I am."

"Forgive me, I expected someone older."

"Might I speak with Gareth?"

The young lady replied, "He is sleeping."

Erica could not halt the freezing jealousy. She wanted to demand how this woman knew that. She wanted to know how Gareth felt about *her.* It was utterly illogical. She knew that. But nonetheless she found herself unable to form a single coherent thought.

The young man moved up alongside his co-worker and asked, "Did the march take place?"

The question jarred Erica back to vivid clarity. She swallowed. "It did."

"Did you witness it?"

"I fear so."

She could hear others moving in close from behind, just as those in this chamber approached. The gentleman said, "We have heard the most terrible rumors."

"Please, I feel I really must report first to Gareth. After all, he was the one . . ."

"Of course." The gentleman slipped by the young woman, who was now studying Erica with less-than-friendly intent. "Follow me."

The young lady attempted one more protest. "The doctor was with him just minutes ago."

But the gentleman paid her no mind. Wordlessly he led Erica across the foyer and up the central staircase.

The upstairs rooms were fitted out much like those above the embassy, private quarters set above a very public arena downstairs. A servant led them up yet another set of stairs to the attic rooms. As it happened, the doctor was departing just as they arrived. When Erica asked how Gareth was doing, he blew out his cheeks in exasperation.

"He's young, he's fit as a racehorse, and he works himself far too hard. I know this type. He does the labor of ten men and frets when his body complains as it is doing now. How is he faring? As well as any man can who has worn himself down to a nub."

"But he will become well again," Erica pleaded.

The doctor examined her keenly. "You are this gentleman's friend?"

"I would like to think so, yes."

"Then as soon as he is up and about, have him go to the seaside for a quiet fortnight. Walks along the shore, good wholesome fare, clean country air, that's what the fellow needs." The doctor jammed his hat down hard on his head. "That and rest, rest, and more rest."

When she rounded the doorway and saw Gareth in the plain little room, Erica could not quite stifle a moan. His complexion held the pallor of lingering illness.

He spoke in a voice that was scarcely more than a croak. "Tell me it was not as bad as they say."

"Oh, Gareth."

"Tell me the horsemen did not charge into the crowd with their staves at the ready. Tell me the women and children . . ." He was halted by a coughing fit that seemed to tear at him.

"I don't think I should tell you anything until you are better."

"Erica—"

"And you will only grow better with rest. That is what the doctor said."

The gentleman in the doorway offered, "Mr. Wilberforce went by his printing shop the day before yesterday and found him operating the press himself."

"There is so much to be told," Gareth protested weakly. "And all my fellows are run off their feet."

"Mr. Wilberforce realized that the only way he would ever rest was if someone watched over him day and night," the young man continued. There was a note of reluctant respect in the gentleman's words.

"I will tell you nothing," Erica repeated. "Not now. First you must rest."

She halted further argument by rising and addressing the butler hovering in the background. "Is there an empty chamber where I might remain for a time?"

"Nothing that befits a lady, miss." Somewhat ashamedly he led her to a room at the hall's opposite end. "These upstairs rooms are seldom used."

The chamber held to a monastic severity. There was a narrow bed, a desk, a single chair, a candlestick, a simple cross upon the wall. Yet as soon as she saw the little table set beneath the window, Erica knew this was where she had been drawn. The sense of pressure she had felt all day became even more concentrated.

She spoke in a low voice to the gentleman. "Please, would you be so kind as to bring me pen and paper and ink?"

"Immediately, Miss Langston."

"My friend awaits me in the carriage downstairs. Her name is Anne Crowley." Erica turned back to the window and the little table. "Ask her to join me, please."

On one level Erica was aware of everything that went on around her. On another she was completely apart. Anne came in and spoke to her, several times in fact. On one occasion she and Anne actually prayed together. Erica refused to turn away from the table but bowed her head over the partially formed words. She prayed because she had to. She did not know the first thing about writing, and she had no idea how difficult the process truly was. She wrote and then she tore up the page. She started over and crumpled up that page as well. Over and over this went, until she was surrounded by tattered little bundles of half-finished thoughts.

Anne did not say a word when Erica rose from the table and walked down the long hallway and opened the door to observe the slumbering Gareth. Erica knew the only thing that might hold Gareth to the bed was knowing his goal was being reached.

Anne came over to stand alongside her. In the silence Erica could hear the rough edge to his breathing. Each intake of breath seemed to tear his chest within. Erica did not object when Anne walked her to the door and back down the long hallway to the little desk. The empty page stared up at her like an accusing hand.

"I do not know if I can do this," Erica quietly confessed.

"Of course you can."

"It is so difficult."

"Many of the important things in life are." Anne patted her on the shoulder. "Let me go downstairs and brew you a fresh cup of tea."

Erica sat unmoving and listened to Anne's descent. At that moment, Gareth seemed far closer than a distant chamber down an unadorned hallway. Erica stared down at the blank sheet of paper and felt the same gentle pressure as before. She knew she should be writing. But how ever could she shape the proper words?

She bowed her head down so far her forehead rested upon the paper. *Show me, Father. If this is indeed your will, make it clear to me how I should proceed. Amen.*

She opened her eyes and raised her head. She stared out the window. But it was not the rather unkempt back garden that she saw. Instead she witnessed anew the horror from St. Peter's Field.

Then she realized the mistake she had been making. She had sought to embellish what was already too strong. She had sought to add her own feelings. But why should she? What was the importance of one person's emotions here? Gareth had not sent her north so she would *feel*. He had asked that she go so that she would witness and report.

Erica picked up the quill. She inspected the tip, then dipped it into the inkwell. She knew what must be done. She would not write for herself. She would not write so that the page revealed her at all. She would simply write as a clerk reporting accounts. She would set the barest of facts down on the page. That was the task at hand. Let the words speak for themselves, just as numbers should. Her mission was to give the information a proper structure. She would arrange the events in a careful way so that all could read and understand. Then they would feel for themselves.

Erica paused for a moment, long enough to realize the thought that had just taken form. She nodded to the window and the scene that remained planted before her mind. This was indeed her mission, she realized. This was her responsibility. She had been sent because she could do this. And do it well.

Several times people came by and asked if she was all right. Around sunset a little man approached so closely that he cast a shadow upon the table. She frowned mightily, and he stepped back. He said something to her. She must have answered satisfactorily because he left and did not return. Only when she paused long enough to down a cup of tea and a slice of toast did she realize it must have been Mr. Wilberforce himself. For an instant she wanted to rush and find him and thank him for taking in Gareth, and for his kind offer of assistance with her family's own crisis, and for the use of this room, and for the words he spoke to her the other evening, and so much else. But she stood over the half-finished page with her cup still in her hand, and she saw the next word that was required. And the word that should follow. And then she was seated once more, and the quill was bearing down upon the page, and the words continued to form, almost as though they were taking shape by themselves.

The pen scratched and then dipped and scratched some more. Her hand became a single dull ink-colored ache. She had ink on her blouse from where a stray lock had fallen upon the wet words and she could not be bothered just then to do more than sweep the hair back over her shoulder. Her neck was sore, and her shoulders.

The light was too meager, really. The thought fashioned itself several times, but Erica could not halt long enough to rise and search out someone and make a request. Then other hands came and set more candles around the table's edge. By the time the next paragraph had been formed and she could halt for an instant, the hands were gone. Erica stared in confusion at the new candles. Beside them were a new quill and a sharpening knife. Had she actually asked for more light? She could not recall. She so wanted to rise and stretch and ease the ache in her fingers. She dared not look at the narrow bed against the opposite wall. Then her eye chanced upon the unfinished line. She sighed. The next word was already fashioning itself upon the page, as though merely waiting for her to set the ink in place. Which was a very good thing, as her mind was becoming somewhat fuzzy around the edges. Erica began a new line. Each thought seemed to rise from the fog of weariness unbidden. And suddenly the page was done, and she was dusting it to help the words dry evenly and starting a new page.

Twilight came, lingered a time, and departed.

She would write just this one more line. That thought carried her through an intensifying series of aches and pains. The soreness of her hand now extended all the way up past her elbow. Her fingers were cramping so the words looked scrawled by an elderly hand. Just this one more line, perhaps finish this paragraph. Then she would rest. Her free hand rested constantly upon her neck and shoulders now, massaging wherever the ache was worse. Now and then she wished the words would stop flowing across the scroll of her mind. She so wanted to lie down and close her eyes. But the next word appeared, and she knew she must write it while it was there. Why, precisely, she could no longer recall. But she knew it was necessary.

She finished the page. She dusted it. She set it atop the last one. She dipped the quill into the ink. And she waited.

Nothing came.

Erica stared blankly at the empty page. She was so tired the realization could not take shape within her addled mind.

Then she was weeping. It was not the bone-deep aching of her body. Nor was it because she had to pluck the quill from her fingers with her other hand and massage the writing hand out into proper shape. Nor did she cry because the work was done. No.

She cried from a loss that was now hers.

Anne Crowley appeared in the doorway. One glance was enough to spur the older woman forward. She spoke, but Erica was unable to fashion the sounds into coherent meaning. Anne pulled her up from the chair, guided her over, and settled her down into the bed. Erica looked up at her and wanted to explain. How by writing these words upon the page, she had made herself a part of the tragedy. How it felt now as though it had been her own children trampled beneath the horses. How she ached from wounds that were hers now. How the meaning had been given to the day, and the meaning was a wound that left her clutching her chest and weeping with the sorrow of bereavement.

Anne settled a quilt about her shoulders and spoke with

such caring and love that the sobs simply lifted. The shivering breaths continued until Erica found herself drifting away. Not into sleep. It seemed as though she was so tired she might never sleep again. She simply went away.

Chapter 27

When she awoke, Erica lay and listened to a world so quiet she could hear people talking in the garden two floors below. She had no idea what time it was or even what day. She knew that she must rise. But it felt so good just to lie and relax. It seemed years since she had lain abed with no pressing urgency, or another journey, or more words to write. She sighed aloud.

Anne Crowley must have been listening for just such a sound, for there came a gentle knock upon the door.

"Come in."

"How are you, my dear?"

Even finding a response to this simple question seemed to take ages. "Hungry."

The older woman chuckled, the first time Erica had heard her make that sound. "I am hardly surprised."

"What time is it?"

"First you must tell me how you feel."

Again Erica applied herself to what should have been a simple query. She decided, "I feel very good, thank you."

Anne's smile broadened. "I am pleased to hear it."

Erica probed her heart as she would a tooth that had formerly been aching badly. She said, "The pain is still there. And the memories."

Anne nodded. "They will remain a part of us both, I should think."

"And yet . . ."

"You are ready now to go on with life."

"Yes, that is it exactly." Erica stared up at the woman, content to lie abed with a relative stranger looking down upon her. Such an attitude of seeming weakness would never have been comfortable before. "What do you think has happened?"

"I believe we both have found a divine purpose to our sorrow." Anne motioned to the table. "You with your writing."

"And you?"

She replied calmly, "As I've said before, I have discovered that there are others who need me to care for them."

The emotions were still very close to the surface, Erica discovered, for the quietly spoken words were enough to bring tears back to her eyes. She rose to a seated position and said to the floor by her feet, "Yes, there most certainly are."

"It does not make the situation perfect. Nor does it cause me to miss my husband any less. But there is an order to the universe. Forgive me, I find the entire concept of looking into the future so novel I am unable to express myself well."

"No," Erica said quietly. "You have said it very well indeed."

The first thing she saw when she lifted her eyes caused a little tremor of alarm, for the table was bare. But before her protest could be fully formed, it was stifled by an overwhelming sense of trust. If her words had been shared with anyone else, it would have been done for proper reasons. Of that Erica was certain.

Anne must have followed her gaze, because she spoke up at once. "You wrote with such urgency, I was certain this was something that they needed as quickly as possible."

Who were *they*, Erica wondered and felt another tremor. But all she said was, "Yes."

"When Gareth woke earlier this afternoon, it was the first thing he asked about. Not for food, not who I was, nor anything else. First he wanted to know where you were, then had you completed the writing. When he woke in the night I told him what you were about, you see. I thought it would calm him, knowing that you were seeing to his needs in this way. And I was right."

"What did he say?"

"Nothing, really. But he smiled. It was a good thing to see, from a man so ill, that smile. He ate a little and then went back to sleep." She examined Erica. "I would say he cares for you very much."

Erica looked out the window once more. It registered then what Anne had said, how Gareth had woken earlier in the afternoon. Erica rose to her feet in alarm. "What time is it?"

"Just gone five."

"It can't be!"

"But it is."

"I have to go—"

"You must do nothing."

"But the Aldridges will—"

"They have been informed. Everything is taken care of, my dear, save your need for some sustenance." She motioned to a frock hanging from a hook on the wall. "I have even taken the liberty of drawing a fresh dress from your valise and hanging it so the wrinkles would fall out."

"You are too good to me."

Anne rose to her feet. "I will just check on Gareth while you ready yourself."

When Erica emerged, Anne led her to the hall's opposite end. Gareth was sitting up in bed with a half-dozen cushions behind his back.

"How are you feeling?" Erica asked.

"Better by the minute. Far too good to be lying here while the world spins so frantically."

"You are only better because you have rested."

But he did look much better. The dreadful pallor had eased somewhat, and the light in his eyes was not so feverish. He had managed to shave and change into fresh bedclothes and robe. He looked altogether improved from the previous day. Erica could still hear the rustle in his chest when he breathed, however. "You must do as the doctor says and remain where you are until your health is fully restored."

He did not object. Instead he gazed at her and said calmly, "What you have done is truly a thing of magnificence."

The color rose in her cheeks, and she started to protest.

Gareth paid her no mind. "I wept as I read your words. As have many others."

"Someone else has read it?"

Again he did not respond to her. "Erica, I wish I knew precisely what to say. I felt so dreadful when I heard what had happened, knowing you had witnessed such horror. But when I read your words, the sparse manner of your descriptions, the careful way you avoided . . ." He stopped and looked at the wall by the end of his bed. His jaw muscles worked hard for a moment. "Forgive me."

Erica stood in the doorway, unable to respond.

Finally he turned back to her. "I am quite certain that there was a higher purpose to your visit that day."

"There was. At least you are resting and on the mend."

"Please, I beg you, do not deflect what I am about here. You know I am speaking about your words upon those pages. I and my fellows in this struggle are indeed grateful."

"It is so little, Gareth. When I think of what happened there . . ." Her throat closed up once more.

"We cannot change that. The world goes in a direction not of our choosing and most certainly not as our Lord would have it. Our task is to do what He in His divine wisdom sets before us. And to rely upon Him and our friends in Christ when our own strength is not sufficient."

She thought that was all and started to depart, but he stopped her with an upraised hand. "Miss Langston . . . Erica . . ."

She felt her heart rate soar. She thought her own voice sounded somewhat strangled as she said, "Yes?"

Anne Crowley looked from one young face to the other.

She gave a little smile and said, "I shall await you just down by the stairwell."

When the older woman had retreated, Gareth continued, "I have lain here and thought of little besides you." He coughed, but it was not the wrenching sound of yesterday. Instead, it held almost a nervous quality, as though he had caught a bit of her own tension. "I do not wish to sound forward. And goodness knows you have every reason to turn away just now."

"Gareth—"

"Hear me out, I beseech you. My words are clumsy, and I am far too weak to offer them properly. I am dressed shoddily and my demeanor is sickly. But it is in this weak state that I have come to realize something, and I must say it, and now."

The air felt tightly compressed around her. "What is it, Gareth?"

"I admire you more than I can say and find myself harboring the deepest affections for you." He coughed throatily. "There, I have said it, and in the most wretched form imaginable. But it is the truth, Erica. I find myself comforted by your strength and wisdom." He looked at her, his dark eyes sparkling with far more than mere fever. "Do you think these might be sentiments you could share?"

She wanted to sink down to the floor. She wanted to laugh out loud. She wanted to list all the reasons this was impossible. Impractical. Out of the question.

She wanted to lean forward and wrap her arms around this good and honorable man.

"Erica?"

"I think they are indeed sentiments I could share," she whispered.

Nothing could have prepared Erica for what she found upon arriving downstairs. All she wanted was a quiet bite to eat and perhaps a nice word with their host, then off they would go before it became too late and she would awaken the entire

Aldridge household. But it was not to be. Anne led her into the kitchen, where it seemed that a smiling young cook tended several pots that were kept constantly filled. She set half a small loaf before Erica, asked if she knew a dish called Welsh stockpot, and ladled out a steaming bowl of delicious-smelling chicken stew.

"Sit, my dear," Anne urged quietly. "Take up the spoon and nourish yourself."

But Erica sat frozen to the spot. For there in the middle of the kitchen table was the latest pamphlet. Gareth's masthead glimmered, obviously still slightly wet from the presses. Beneath it ran the title, "Tragic Occurrences in Manchester." And below that were the words that held her fast: "Eyewitness Account by Miss Erica Langston."

She looked up to meet Anne's eyes.

"Yes, I know. It shocked me as well when I saw it. Gareth was uncertain whether Daniel and the others would be up to the task of printing without him there to supervise. But his men knew just what to do. Gareth has found but two errors in the entire six pages—which is less than he discovers within his own work. He was very pleased."

Yet another realization halted the spoon's progress. "This means . . . The pamphlets, they are out there? Being sold, I mean."

Anne had a manner of showing humor with little save a heightened sparkle in her gaze. "Gareth's men have spread out far and wide."

Erica felt dizzy. First the declaration upstairs, now this; the day could scarcely hold another thing.

Or so she thought.

"Ah, there you are." The little man with the unkempt clouds of white hair came into the kitchen. "No, don't you dare rise. Hasn't our cook outdone herself with that lovely stew?"

"The master scarcely eats enough to keep a bird alive," the chef protested.

William Wilberforce gave his gentle smile. "Perhaps this is why they call me the Sparrow of Parliament."

The young woman who had met Erica in the front parlor the previous day entered the kitchen. "It is the Nightingale of Parliament that they call you, as you know full well."

"Is it? I don't recall." He kept his gentle gaze upon Erica. "Did you rest well?"

"Indeed, sir. I cannot thank you enough for your kind hospitality."

"This house is open to you at any and all times. But enough about that. I wished merely to congratulate you on your most remarkable work."

She could not bring herself to look over at the pamphlets. "I wish it were better."

"Of course you do. We all wish the same thing. For our efforts are so vague and our thoughts so fretful."

Anne chided softly, "You must finish your meal, my dear, before it grows stone cold."

Wilberforce's gaze had the power to calm, so that Erica could return to her meal in peace. "It is just as you say, sir."

"Gareth approached me after our first meeting and said that he was convinced you would become a worthy addition to our cause. I am very pleased to see how right he was."

"I did not do this in hopes—"

"Of course not. You did this to help a friend. And in so doing you found yourself confronted with the horrors of a world living outside God's divine will."

Erica managed to say, "Just so."

Wilberforce pulled out a chair and settled himself down beside her. "Shall I tell you something I discovered many years ago? By leaning upon God's will, we are granted new and remarkable freedoms. The outside world sees us as chained. We go where they choose not, we see what they prefer to ignore, we dress in a manner they call severe. They hold up to us the so-called freedoms of this world and declare themselves happier for it. They live in blindness, both to the pains of others and the remorse and strife within their own souls."

Erica set down her spoon. "Your words are a great comfort, sir. And a greater challenge."

He was silent a moment, then said, "There is a passage from Proverbs, one I sometimes feel God has said to me and me alone. And yet I desire to share it with you, one friend to another."

Erica felt a faint tremor race through her. Friend.

"The passage reads, 'There are many devices in a man's heart; nevertheless the counsel of the Lord, that shall stand.' Do those words speak to you, my dear?"

She did not trust her voice, so made do with a nod.

"There, you see? I was right to trust you with this confidence. The prophet Hosea says, 'Sow to yourselves in righteousness, reap in mercy; break up your fallow ground: for it is time to seek the Lord, till he come and rain righteousness upon you.'"

William Wilberforce rose to his feet. "I shall look forward with great anticipation to our next meeting, my dear. Thank you for the service you have rendered to our cause."

Chapter 28

Erica's eyes were stinging when the carriage pulled into the embassy forecourt. By this time of evening the official ground floor should be empty and all the stern men with their pressing affairs gone. Now it was a home, and a welcome one at that. Jacob Harwell was stepping down the front stairs and adjusting his hat. "A very good evening to you, Miss Erica. The family is very happy to hear you are returning."

"Hello, Jacob. Are you the last to leave tonight?"

"The ambassador asked me to complete a matter for him."

"I am certain you did an excellent job of it." She held a hand up to assist Anne from the carriage. "Might I introduce someone it is my honor to call a friend? Anne Crowley, this is the deputy minister plenipotentiary's most trusted aide, Jacob Harwell."

"An honor, ma'am."

"I feel quite the same, sir. My dear, are you certain it is proper for me to accompany you upstairs?"

"I insist that they meet you."

"They are looking forward to it, ma'am," Jacob added. "Word has come that you were the one who assisted Miss Erica in Manchester."

His meaning sank in. "Do you mean that they have heard about the pamphlet?"

"All of London talks of little else."

"Jacob, please, I am unsettled enough already. You mustn't jest about this."

"Jest? Miss Erica, do you not know?"

Her hand flew to her throat. "Know what?"

"Crowds gathered before Parliament this afternoon. No one knows who called them together, but they came in the thousands. All of them waving your pamphlet over their heads and crying for justice."

She said weakly, "This can't be."

"I must tell you, I was forced to halt my own reading on three different occasions when the words blurred before my eyes." He cleared his throat. "Even now I cannot think of those poor women and children without feeling a true agony in my heart."

Her reply was halted by a high-pitched cry from inside the front hallway. "Must I wait upstairs *forever*?"

"Of course not, dear," her mother replied. "Go on now and greet her."

A little figure raced through the front door and flung herself at Erica. "You have been gone so long!"

"Abbie." She never thought the greeting of a child could bring her such joy. "I have missed you so much."

The little girl refused to let her go. "You can't go home and leave me here forever. You can't."

Lavinia stepped up next to her daughter and said, "Don't forget, you yourself will be going back to America as well one day."

"Yes, but that won't be for years and years."

The pressure of her mother's hand upon her shoulder pried Abbie away. "Should Erica remain here for you, just to have you go and leave her alone?"

Abbie's little hands rose to brush at her cheeks. "But I missed her."

"And now she is home with you once more. So we must be happy for this blessing." Lavinia embraced Erica. "It is good to see you again."

Abbie turned to the dark-clad stranger and gave a proper curtsy. "Hello. Are you Erica's friend too?"

"I am indeed and count it as a great blessing." Anne Crowley smiled at the child. "You are Abbie, and you must call me Miss Anne."

"How do you do." She curtsied a second time. "Please, Miss Anne, why are you all in black?"

Her mother rolled her eyes. "Abbie, please."

"But she is, Mama. Look, she even has shiny buttons on her gloves, and they are black as well."

"They are pearls, actually. Would you like to unhook them?" Anne bent over and allowed Abbie to unbutton and pull off a glove. "I lost my husband, you see."

"And you miss him still?"

"So very much."

The second glove's button proved much harder to undo. "Do black clothes cry for you so you mustn't weep all the time?"

Abbie must have sensed the sudden tension in the air, for she jerked her head around, fearful she had said the wrong thing. Before her mother could chide her, however, Anne replied in an easy manner, "That's part of it, I suppose. But it is also a sign to all the world that I am in mourning."

"But it's almost nighttime."

"Indeed it is, what an observant child you are. But no, this is a different word that sounds the same as the dawn hours. This particular word means, well, means I am learning to live with loss." She helped Abbie pull off the second glove. "Would you like to put them on your own hands?"

"Oh, please, may I?"

Lavinia moved up alongside Erica. The two of them stood in companionable silence and watched as Abbie's open-hearted curiosity charmed yet another person. It was good to be back in a place of calm and welcome.

Abbie asked, "How long must you wear black?"

"Polite society says a year."

"That seems like ever so long a time."

"Yes, it does, doesn't it," Anne agreed thoughtfully.

"I know," Abbie said brightly. "Perhaps you could wear pretty clothes when no one else can see you. Or when you are just with friends who won't ever tell."

"What a novel thought."

Lavinia sighed but said nothing.

Even so, Abbie caught the sound and added hastily, "Not that your clothes aren't lovely, Miss Anne. I meant only that they are so . . ."

"So very black. I could not agree more." The older woman reached forward and stroked the young cheek.

Abbie turned around so as to show off her black-clad hands. "Look, Mama! Aren't they lovely?"

"May you never have need of such for years and years." Lavinia turned to Anne. "Might I invite you upstairs for tea?"

"Thank you, but my own family is expecting me." Anne's smile shone in the sky that was just beginning to darken. "Perhaps you will permit me to accept the invitation some other day?"

"You are most welcome any time you wish."

Abbie peeled off the oversized gloves and handed them back. "Does this mean we are to be friends?"

"Do you know," Anne replied solemnly, "I could think of nothing that would please me more." She said her good-byes to Erica and Lavinia and turned back toward the carriage.

Erica collected her things and watched the unloading of her two valises. She stood with one arm around Lavinia and the other upon Abbie's shoulder and smiled a farewell as the carriage pulled through the embassy's front gates. Although she was emotionally spent and physically exhausted from the past few days, though her heart still ached from all she had witnessed, still she felt as rich and complete as she ever had in her life.

She raised her gaze to the moon that had appeared in the still-blue sky overhead. *Thank you, Father,* she prayed, *for this place of welcome and people who accept me as family. Thank you for giving meaning to even the darkest moments of my life. Thank you for showing me how to speak with you like this, in comfort and in love.*

Lavinia picked up one of the valises and ushered Abbie toward the front door. "Welcome home, my dear."

Erica hefted her remaining case and turned her back on Piccadilly and the trundling traffic and all the outside world.

Friends.

Chapter 29

By the middle of the following week, Erica's life had entered into a new routine. Mornings she spent working through the embassy's accounts and helping Lavinia about the home. Lunchtimes were given over to hearing Abbie report on her latest lessons. Then precisely at two, Daniel appeared in Gareth's carriage to escort her to the manor of William Wilberforce.

There was a new bounce to her step these days, a new smile upon her lips. Even the weather was with her, for the days were bathed in a brilliant summer light. And most important of all, Gareth was making steady progress toward full recovery. He was always dressed and seated upon the front portico to greet her. Anne Crowley was often there as well, for her great-aunt was increasingly active in work related to new Manchester projects. Anne always greeted Erica with genuine warmth, then left her with Gareth to stroll the unkempt gardens and talk.

Erica remained amazed at how much she had to say to Gareth. She was startled by her own openness and yet thrilled by all they were sharing. She awoke in the middle of the night, full of new ideas, recalling matters she had meant to speak of the previous day that had been swept away in a tide of ideas and thoughts and passions. There was so much goodness and wisdom to this man, so many hidden facets to delight in. She increasingly found their parting each afternoon to be a genuine trial.

Then three letters arrived from home—two from her mother and a lovely note from her brother. After she had shared them with Gareth, he had hesitantly drawn a page of his own from his pocket and read to her the first words he had penned since becoming ill. Her heart felt so full, hearing Gareth read and then seeing how avidly he sought her response. She could not stop a single tear from escaping. The day was just too full.

Late that afternoon Erica walked to Grosvenor Square to survey the building site. Normally Abbie accompanied her on these outings, but today the little girl was busy with her governess. Erica missed her company; Abbie had the ability to brighten the most mundane of activities, such as counting the workers on the almost-finished house.

Normally Erica would go and speak a few kind words to the bricklayer or a nearby apprentice, exchange formal greetings with the master builder, and be on her way. Today, however, the robust carpenter doffed his hat and stepped away from the worksite.

"I'd be grateful for a word with you, miss."

"Is there a problem, Master Dobbins?"

"Not with the work, miss. We'll be done and gone in a month, two at the most."

She watched the way he twisted his cap in his heavy hands. "I have been most careful to pay everything on time—"

"You've treated me better than most, miss." The cap went through another dusty revolution. "Better than I deserve."

"You have done excellent work, I am sure, sir."

"Aye, we've tried to deliver as promised." He heaved a sigh. Dust from the bricklayers' work liberally coated his features. His eyes looked remarkably blue, framed as they were by his dirty face. "You never made mention of the early times, miss."

"I never saw any need, Master Dobbins."

"Aye, but others might've used this against me. . . ." He

fumbled with his words as he did his cap. "There's been strangers about here."

"I beg your pardon?"

"Strangers," he repeated. "Up to no good, I warrant. Dark, they were. Dark in their souls. Asking the wrong sort of questions."

Erica's hand rose nervously to clutch at her dress collar. "I'm certain I don't understand you, Master Dobbins."

"Questions," he repeated. "Asking questions about you."

"But whatever for?"

"Couldn't say, miss. But they were here. And when I shooed them off the site, they made like they was offering money to my apprentices. Wanting to know when you came. How often. What time of day."

"But . . ." Erica could not explain why such news would frighten her so. "But that makes no sense whatsoever."

"Aye, unless they were out to do you harm."

"Master Dobbins, I assure you—"

"It's none of my business what you're about, miss. I know I'm building a house for folks at the embassy, and I know when to leave well enough alone." He started to turn away.

"Just a moment. Please." Erica did her best to gather her scattered thoughts. "Can you tell me anything else about them?"

"Bad people." Now that he had delivered his message, the builder was eager to return to the work and the world he knew. Master Dobbins replaced his dusty cap and touched the rim. "If I was you, miss, I'd be watching my back."

"Thank you, sir," Erica said to the departing master builder. "I am indeed most grateful."

She took her customary route down Audley Street. The clouds had thickened, becoming far more foreboding than on the outward journey. She found herself recalling what Lavinia had told her in the carriage on that first outing they had taken together. How diplomacy could reap the most unexpected benefits, forging alliances where none could logically exist.

How true those words had proven, no matter how difficult the lesson!

She turned onto Piccadilly. The open expanse with the leafy park opposite her seemed somehow ominous. Even the birds seemed to be communicating a warning. All her senses were on alert.

Which was how she noticed the danger in time.

A long line of carriages was making its way back from Hyde Park's Rotten Row, just as they did every afternoon about this time. Occasionally Erica would study the people, their dress, and their haughty manner. Today, however, she searched the passing faces for any hint of threat.

Then a young man driving a carriage half rose from his seat, his eyes wide with alarm. He pointed with his whip and shouted words Erica did not take time to fathom.

In that same instant, she heard the pounding hooves.

She jerked about and saw the horse. A broken bridle dangled from its froth-flecked mouth. A trace jounced and jangled about its right foreleg. There was a wild look to its eyes.

The horse bounded down the empty walk. Heading straight toward her.

Erica leaped sideways. One heel became trapped in her hem, and she almost went down. The horse would have pounded straight across her had she not caught the metal post of the fence lining the walk. With almost inhuman strength she pulled herself up onto the crossrail and flattened herself tight against the iron rods. Even so, the horse's flank punched her hard into the fence, bruising her knees where they collided with the rail.

Up and down Piccadilly, carriages halted and drivers shouted warnings to pedestrians further along the lane. Erica heard shrieks and neighing and the crack of whips.

She remained precisely where she was. Now that the danger was past, she could not manage to release her hold upon the railing.

"Miss Erica!" The embassy porter scurried down the lane. "Miss, are you all right?"

She wanted to speak but could not. Her breath came in terrified little gasps.

"Here, miss, let me help you down. Ease up on the grip there . . . that's it. All right, I've got you. Steady on, miss. Can you stand?"

She looked down the now-empty walk and leaned heavily upon the older man. "Where did it come from?" she cried.

"No idea, miss. All I know, one moment I spotted you walking back from the square like always. The next, this great beast was bearing down on you like death itself." The porter was sweating profusely from the closeness of the call. "How you managed to leap out of the way is beyond me."

She pushed herself upright. "I'm all right now."

"Aye, that you are, miss." The porter studied her with open admiration. "Never seen anybody move that fast in all my born days."

Chapter 30

Erica woke the next morning and lay listening to the birds and the wind. It was fresh for late summer, and the breeze blew straight from the north. She could feel a slight chill through her narrow window, which she had left ajar all night. The room faced the back of the house, and she could hear a handyman out back making a racket with some job or another. She snuggled deeper under the covers. From the sunlight's strength she knew she had overslept. But there had been very few moments of such deep rest. She lay with her eyes wide open, her covers tucked up under her chin, and luxuriated in this stolen moment. Outside her window a mockingbird trilled its way through every melody known to nature.

Her thoughts were interrupted by a very soft knock on the door. Assuming it was Abbie, she said good morning.

But it was Lavinia who opened the door. "And a very good morning to you. How did you rest?"

"Fine, thank you." Something in the woman's tone suggested this was not a casual interruption. "Is something the matter?"

"I would not have disturbed you for all the world."

"I was already awake."

"It is just that the rather large gentleman who traveled with you—forgive me, I have quite forgotten his name . . ."

"Daniel." Erica swung her feet to the floor. "He is Gareth's right-hand man."

"He is downstairs."

"In the embassy?" Erica was on her feet now and scrambling for her clothes. "Whatever for?"

"He would not say. Only that it was urgent, and he must discuss it with you alone."

Gareth. It had to be something about Gareth. Something terrible.

"I am so sorry to wake you like this, after everything—"

"That doesn't matter now. Where is my other shoe?"

"Right here under the bed. Erica, be calm. Whatever it is that has brought Daniel can wait for you to wash your face. Abbie?"

"Here, Mama. Good morning, Erica. I've brought you your tea."

"I can't—"

"Isn't Abbie a dear to help us out like this? Darling, run and dampen a towel in the kitchen basin. Make sure the water is clean, and add a bit of hot water from the kettle."

"Yes, Mama."

"Here, hand me the brush," Lavinia said. "You take a sip of tea; it will do you a world of good."

Erica did as she was told while Lavinia began to brush her hair.

"I should be doing that, Lavinia."

"Drink your tea. I can do this twice as fast; haven't I been up with the baby since before dawn?"

Abbie scampered back with the towel in hand. "He has been crying so terribly much."

"That's enough, child. Hand Erica the towel. Rub your face hard. It will add as good a blush as any powder to your cheeks. What I would give to have your lovely skin and features."

"She doesn't like her nose," Abbie announced.

"Doesn't she? Why not?" Lavinia tied a ribbon in Erica's

hair. "Have you finished your tea?"

"Yes, and now I really must go."

"Almost done. All right, stand up. Let's have a look at you." Lavinia fiddled with Erica's collar, swept her hair back behind her head, and said carefully, "You remember our discussion about diplomacy?"

"Yes, but . . ."

"Now is the time to apply this lesson with diligence. Your writings have placed you firmly in the public eye. When you go downstairs all the world will be watching."

Erica's heart had continued to accelerate until she felt a need to scream just to let out a bit of the pressure. "But Gareth—"

"You cannot help him by showing panic. Take your time. Be the lady. Let them see you as calm and collected."

"I don't know if I can do that."

"Then walk Daniel outside before you let him speak." Lavinia took a very firm grip upon both of Erica's upper arms. "Remember where you are."

Erica took a deep breath. "Yes. All right."

Lavinia released her. "Off you go. We will be praying for you, won't we, Abbie?"

"Very hard," the child solemnly agreed.

Erica managed to walk down the embassy stairs only because she was in truth not entirely there. Instead, she seemed to float above herself, watching this young lady in a borrowed dress of lavender and cream stroll down the stairs with a calm that was most certainly not her own. Just as Lavinia had said, every eye was upon her. The foyer and side chambers were filled with the normal crush of dark-suited men, their pipe smoke filling the air overhead. A number of them doffed their hats and murmured greetings as she passed. Erica held onto her half smile by mentally freezing it into place.

"Daniel." She offered her hand palm down, as she had seen her mother do on a countless number of formal moments. "How nice of you to come."

Daniel remembered enough of his military days to come to full attention and bow stiffly over the hand. "Forgive the intrusion, my lady."

The honorific helped steady her nerves. "Nonsense. You are always welcome. Don't you find the air a trifle close? The morning is so lovely; let us walk outside."

Daniel was dressed in what undoubtedly was his best—a hastily brushed topcoat and frilled shirt washed and starched so that it billowed out before him. His cheeks were clean shaven and his hair held back in a ribbon almost the same color as her own. Though Erica wanted to grab his arm and shriek for news, she did precisely as Lavinia had instructed. She walked through the front door and down the front steps, only to realize the outer way was lined with yet more men wishing a moment of the ambassador's time. "Have you ever seen our back garden?"

"No, my lady, that is . . ."

"Follow me."

Only when they had passed behind the house did she recall the workers whose racket had awakened her. Two men were busy pounding a long strip of metal into some unrecognizable form. At this range the din was astonishing. Erica walked over to them and said, "Please be silent."

The leering response was halted by a massive shadow falling over the three of them. The men set down their hammers. "The master said we was to have this done by nightfall, miss."

"We will not hold you up overlong." Erica turned her back on the men. She could not wait another moment. "Tell me now. Is it Gareth?"

"No, miss. That is, he is doing passably well. Somewhat better than yesterday, if you ask me."

The steel grip of fear eased its painful hold upon her chest. "What is it, then?"

"You know about our regiment, how we were disbanded and left to rot when the wars were done."

"Yes. Gareth has told me. But whatever—"

"I ask on account of how you need to know there's some questions I can't answer."

"Oh. Very well."

"There's men who lost all hope of ever rejoining the human race, men who've gone all bad. But they still hold a debt to the major."

Erica studied him a moment. "I see. You have news from a source within the underworld. But I am not to inquire who that person is or how the information came to you."

Daniel's massive features shone with admiration. "Everyone says you're the sharpest of them all, miss."

"So tell me, what is the news?"

His grave manner returned. "There's been a price put on your head."

The shock drove her back a step. "What?"

Daniel closed the distance so as to keep his voice low. "Someone wants you done away with."

"But why?"

"There's two fellows who came with the news. The major and I know them. They'd not come up with something like this on their own. They claim they don't know who's behind it, which is as good as saying we may never learn the answer." Daniel fumbled with his top hat. "The major wanted to come tell you himself. But the master of the house wouldn't hear of it."

"No, no, of course not. He must remain in bed." Her thoughts should have been swirling. Instead, they seemed to be moving with the slowness of molasses. "Did Gareth suggest why this might have happened?"

"The major doubts it's on account of the writings. He says to do you harm now would only add fuel to the fire and point all sorts of fingers at people in high places. The major wants to know if you can think of anyone else who might want to do you harm."

The answer was there before her instantly. "Mr. Bartholomew, the banker." Strange how identifying the source of this threat did not jolt any harder. "He feels the pressure to repay my father's gold and has responded in this vile manner."

"So the major and Mr. Wilberforce thought as well," Daniel agreed.

"Mr. Wilberforce is informed of this matter?"

"He is as distressed as the major himself." Daniel fumbled in his jacket and withdrew two sealed notes. "This one is from the major. Mr. Wilberforce penned the other himself."

The words from Gareth caused her to blush, such was the strength of his caring concern. "He is such a fine, dear man."

"Aye, miss. As good as they come. He thinks the world of you as well, the major does."

The note from Wilberforce was penned in characteristic haste.

> *My dear Miss Erica,*
>
> *Would that I might take this new burden from you. Know that I stand ready to assist in any way possible, just as you have done for us and our cause. Might I share one thought with you? I would imagine your recent experiences, the journey to Manchester, penning the magnificent pamphlet, and now the growing bond with Mr. Powers leave you feeling a new intimacy with the Almighty. You have moved into the procession of servants acting out His will. And now this. Perhaps there is a sense of stepping back, of retreating from this intimate glory and returning to the mundane.*

Erica looked askance at the hulking former soldier. "He has such keen insight."

Daniel did not need to ask what she meant. "The major claims Wilberforce is like no other man he's ever met."

"He has voiced thoughts I have not even managed to shape for myself."

Erica returned her eyes to the page. It seemed as though she could hear Wilberforce's own voice speak as she read.

> *Living in this far-from-perfect world often means drawing back from the heights. Remember our earlier discussion, I urge*

you. Seek to relieve your family's dire financial straits. This sum is rightfully yours. Christians should indeed stand up for justice, even their own. Only beware the lure of vengeance and the burden of rage, and take on neither. And know I stand to aid you wherever possible.

Yours ever in Christ,
William Wilberforce

Erica spent a long moment lost in thought. Daniel waited alongside her, as patient as the sun overhead. Gradually her thoughts coalesced into a clear plan.

"Would you happen to know where Mr. Wilberforce is to be working today?"

Evidently her question had been anticipated. "He said to tell you he has meetings running the day through, and they'll keep him pinned to home base."

She started for the front walk. "Come with me, please."

"As I had planned, miss. The major says I'm to act as your guard."

Erica felt some measure of comfort knowing this big man would accompany her. So long as she was to remain at the embassy, she would be safe. But mobility was required. Strange she could form such thoughts now. Yet her mind retained an astonishing clarity. For how long, she did not know. "We must hurry."

Erica held herself with decorum as she moved back through the crowd. Many of the men tipped their hats to her, and she responded with a brief nod. Inside the minister's outer chamber, she found Jacob surrounded by a bevy of somber-faced men. She offered what she hoped was a brilliant smile. "Mr. Harwell, might I trouble you for a moment?"

He came instantly to his feet. "Of course, miss. Might I say, your article is causing quite a stir—"

"Mr. Harwell, forgive me, a matter of rather pressing urgency has come to my attention. Might I have a private word?"

"Certainly. Gentlemen, if you would excuse us?"

"But the minister—"

"—will be with you momentarily. Thank you, gentlemen." When the outer doors closed, Jacob said, "What is it?"

"Might I make use of your pen and paper?"

"Of course."

Erica slipped into his chair and said to Daniel, "Tell him what you can."

While the two men spoke, Erica wrote a hasty note. By the time she finished, Jacob was almost dancing in alarm. "Mr. Aldridge must be told."

"And he most certainly shall be. But Daniel is here to protect me now, and we are all safe in the house. I need you to go with all haste to Mr. Gareth Powers."

"He is the pamphleteer, is he not?"

"Just so. You will find him at the residence of Mr. William Wilberforce in Kensington Gore. Will you do that for me?"

"Anything."

"You are indeed a friend. Please bring your response to me at . . ." Where should she go first? Erica pondered on this a long moment, streaming together all the fragments that were taking shape in her head.

"Erica?"

"You will find me awaiting your response outside the Bartholomew Merchant Bank."

"Where the embassy has its accounts." Jacob looked extremely concerned. "Is that quite safe?"

"Daniel will be with me. I shall require the carriage; can you make your own way?"

"I would be much faster on horseback."

"Speed is everything, Jacob."

But he was already reaching for his hat and coat.

Erica remained seated where she was. First she would tell Lavinia and ask her to inform her husband. Then . . . Oh yes, she knew precisely what she must do next. But only if Gareth agreed.

She bowed her head. No matter that a half-dozen faces

peered through the now-open doorway. No matter that talk and smoke swirled about the downstairs chambers. This was too vital a matter to enter into without guidance.

When she lifted her eyes, she found Daniel waiting with the stolid calm of a mountain. She rose to her feet. "Let us begin."

Chapter 31

Erica was amazed by her own reaction to the day. If anyone had described it to her in advance, relating all the events leading up to this moment and what she intended to do in response, she would have imagined herself collapsing from the strain. Instead, here she sat in the carriage, as collected as if she were popping out to the market for a loaf of bread. She felt a faint flutter of nerves, but they brooded off beyond the horizon somewhere, like a thundercloud that rumbled occasionally yet never approached. Even this awareness was calming in a strange sort of way, because she knew it had nothing to do with her. She was at peace because she was not alone.

Mr. Richmond sat on the carriage's leather seat beside her with an arm's breadth between them. The solicitor's pudgy middle bulged against a waistcoat sewn with brilliant gold thread. He fiddled with his watch chain, drew out his pocket watch, and flipped open the cover. "How long must we wait here, do you reckon?"

"Two things must happen before we can enter," she replied, as calm as ever she pleased.

"And they are?"

Erica didn't answer. Instead she bowed her head and closed out the world. *Guide me, Father,* she prayed for the dozenth time that day. There was little else to be said, so she made the request a second time. Then she merely sat and waited, for in truth she had not lowered her face in order to speak more words. She had shut her eyes to draw closer to what she now felt, which was the presence of the most remarkable peace.

Were she to describe herself to a stranger, one word that most certainly would not come readily to mind was *calm*. Yet here she sat, beset by cares and pressures from all sides, content to reside in this realm of peace. It had been with her the entire day. And she knew it did not come from herself. It spoke to her more clearly than words and visions ever could, particularly upon a day such as this. It was more than a gift. It was a sign that God was near and that she was doing as she should.

Mr. Richmond said, "Here comes their solicitor."

Erica opened her eyes. She was assailed by a flutter of fear as the stern and angular gentleman hurried from his carriage and entered the bank. That was one of the actions she had needed to see happen. "I am very glad your note worked."

"I planted every seed of alarm I possibly could," he said with evident satisfaction. "Though precisely what it is we are so concerned over, I am still waiting to hear."

Erica had not planned on telling him anything. Not because she did not trust his confidentiality, but rather because he might attempt to alter her course of action. And though she was sure she was taking the right steps, she did not want to lose her forward impetus by having to defend herself against this solicitor's professional doubt.

Yet all this changed by the way he fretted just then. What *we* are concerned about, he had said. She looked at him and said, "Thank you, Mr. Richmond."

"Whatever for?"

"For being there in my hour of need."

"My dear young lady, that is my professional duty."

"But it is more than that," she said, certain enough to correct him.

He started to object, then caught himself with a smile. "That very first time I saw you in my front hall, do you know what I thought of you?"

"I know you were cross."

"Ah, but that was before I heard you out." His smile was broader now. "After you departed, I was filled with a most sincere regret. I liked you tremendously, you see. And I feared that would be the last occasion I would have to meet you. I decided my world would be poorer for the lack."

"You are too kind."

"I am nothing of the sort. I am a professional solicitor, which means I am paid to be contentious." But he was still smiling as he said it.

"I shall tell you what is the matter," Erica said. "But only if you promise not to ask too many questions. There is not time to answer everything . . . and I fear I might lose both my edge and my nerve."

"Very well." He laced his hands over his ample belly. "I am eager to hear."

His alarm grew steadily as she recounted the recent events. "But this is terrible!"

"I could not agree more."

"And you think the bankers are behind this threat?"

"Gareth seems positive it is not the result of the pamphlet."

Mr. Richmond pondered on this deeply for a moment, his lower lip protruding in a most unattractive pout. "I agree with his assessment. The Crown would be severely damaged by even the slightest hint that they took this sort of revenge. Particularly with your being connected to the embassy. No, they would wait long enough to ensure that blame would be attached elsewhere."

"And these bankers are people who have attacked before under the guise of other conflicts."

"Eh? What is this?"

Erica recounted the attack upon the Langston warehouse yet again and Gareth's inquiries that cleared his own men of any wrongdoing.

Mr. Richmond regarded her with something akin to admiration. "A most remarkable deduction."

"Do you disagree?"

"Not in the slightest." He tapped his fingers upon the windowsill. "Though I find myself regretting the promise not to ask questions of you."

Erica's need to respond was cut off by the pounding of hooves. A cry came from behind them. "Miss Erica?"

"Jacob! In here!"

The instant between her response and the young man's perspiring face appearing in the carriage window seemed to last forever. He took a deep breath and said, "Gareth Powers and Mr. Wilberforce both wish you every possible success."

She felt the faint grip of nerves. *Do not distance yourself now, O Lord.* "They approve?"

"More than that. Mr. Powers says to tell you that your intention is brilliant. Mr. Wilberforce agrees and says that he will be praying fervently for your success."

"Then it is time to begin," she said, wishing she could hold the tremor from her voice and her limbs. "Mr. Richmond, if you would be so good?"

"Certainly, miss." He opened the carriage door, stepped down, and offered her his hand.

"Jacob, I really should not ask you for anything more, but ask I must."

"Name it," the man said with alacrity.

"I would be immensely grateful if you would enter with us and offer the embassy's official presence. You need say nothing, of course."

"I should be honored to offer a friend in need whatever help I can."

She reached for his hand and gripped it firmly. "Mr. Richmond, may I have the honor of presenting Jacob Harwell."

"We have met at the embassy."

"Indeed so. Your servant, sir."

Erica said, "I would consider it a great boon if you might become friends, as you both are to me. Good, dear, and trusted friends."

The solicitor said, "I have always considered the quality of friends a good measure of one's worth."

"My own father has often said the very same thing," Jacob agreed.

Erica took a breath, steadied by the strength that surrounded her on every side. "Let us do this thing while I still have power in my heart and limbs."

There was a most satisfactory expression of shock upon the banker's narrow features as they entered. Mr. Bartholomew and his solicitor stood in the back corner, behind the waist-high wooden partition. It was his throne room, in a sense, the point from which he could survey his kingdom and all that transpired. But it also put him at a disadvantage, at least in this moment. For he had no way of hiding his alarm at Erica's arrival.

Was this how a diplomat would gauge the moment? Erica wondered. Being able to observe the opponent's response, measure how it affected plans, and so forth. She had no idea. All she knew for certain was that she wished the entire affair were over. Even more than that, she wished it had never begun.

But life did not unfold according to her wishes—that was one truth on which she could rely. Perhaps part of maturity was coming to recognize this fact. Instead of crying over how things might be different and better, there was the need to accept, to pray, to strive, and to search for a meaning greater than the moment's trial.

Her thoughts came with the same deliberate steadiness as her tread. She crossed the bank's main chamber with a calmness she both felt and knew was contradicted by her racing heart. *Do not fail me now, O Lord.*

A senior clerk, dressed in formal topcoat and striped trousers, inserted himself between Erica and the banker. "Might I be of service, miss?"

"I wish to have a word with Mr. Bartholomew."

"Your name?"

"He knows my name."

"I am sorry, what—"

"Show the lady in," the banker snapped. "Although I must warn you, miss, I have little time to waste upon nonsensical matters this day."

"This will only take a moment of your most valuable time." Erica waited for Jacob to pry open the swinging gate. She ignored the banker's solicitor entirely. "I came merely to report that our ally in Parliament has agreed to postpone his public question for one further week."

The two men sneered in unison. It was the solicitor who responded. "Undoubtedly he saw the futility of such an act."

"You misunderstand me," Erica said. She kept her voice calm. Her eyes rested unwaveringly upon the banker. "I requested the delay."

"You—"

"Perhaps you have had an occasion to read the pamphlet I recently wrote. The one that has caused some minor stir of public attention."

"Mere froth and fantasy," the solicitor scorned. "Here today, forgotten tomorrow."

"No doubt," she agreed equably. "Even so, the publicity has been somewhat distressing in some quarters, or so I hear."

"And that is of concern to us?"

"I cannot say. What I can speak of with some certainty, however, is that a second pamphlet might be of some concern to your good selves." She let that sink in before adding, "One that is dedicated solely to asking questions about matters related to the recent conflict in America."

The solicitor exploded, "Libel of the worst sort!"

Mr. Richmond spoke for the first time, as calmly as Erica. "There is no libel in asking questions."

"Which is all I shall do," Erica confirmed. "The same questions that will then be presented before Parliament."

Mr. Richmond now had the bit between his teeth. "Certainly whatever the young lady chooses to write next will receive a most remarkable amount of attention. The sort of notice that would undoubtedly have a most unfortunate impact upon your business."

"It's Wilberforce, isn't it," the solicitor snarled. "That popinjay is your ally."

"This you shall learn," Mr. Richmond replied, "on the day your actions are made most horribly public."

The banker's solicitor shouted loudly enough to silence the entire bank. "I shall invoke an action in court to halt this defamation!"

"And I will fight you tooth and nail," Mr. Richmond countered. "And you will lose, as you most certainly know."

Erica motioned to where Jacob stood. "Allow me to introduce Mr. Harwell, personal aide at the United States Embassy. My writings will be lodged with his office, as well as with Mr. Richmond. Were anything to happen to me, I am certain these good gentlemen will ensure that my word still is printed and my case preserved."

"Not only that," Jacob added, "but I will ensure that the ambassador's own voice is added to any resulting outcry. Of that you can be most certain."

The banker's face turned a most satisfactory shade of puce. "I will destroy you."

"Ah, now that *is* worthy of court action," Mr. Richmond said.

At the same time, the other solicitor snapped at Mr. Bartholomew, "Be silent, else you obliterate any chance we have remaining!"

"One week," Erica repeated. "You will deliver my father's gold to Mr. Richmond's office within seven days. Else all the world will know what you have done to my family."

She turned and left the office and exited the bank, followed by Jacob and Mr. Richmond.

Daniel was there, waiting for her to emerge through the front doors. "All right, miss?"

"Nothing is right. Nothing at all."

"Best we get you back to the embassy and safety."

Erica sank gratefully into the carriage.

Mr. Richmond piled in behind her. "My dear, I am speechless."

"You were splendid," Jacob agreed through the carriage door.

"You are a born diplomat," Mr. Richmond enthused.

"I am afraid I am nothing of the sort." Now that it was over, she felt so weak she could scarcely form the words. "I am just a young woman who has no choice but to pretend to be more than I am."

The two men studied her. Mr. Richmond said, "Miss Erica, I have observed countless men of substance and power. And I can tell you truthfully that what you did in there was nothing short of astounding."

She leaned back in the carriage seat. "Would you mind terribly if we just went home?"

Chapter 32

The week did not proceed in a rush, as Erica might have expected. Instead the days flowed by in a steady current of work and friends. Mornings began with a walk shared with Abbie over to the building site. Jacob Harwell insisted upon walking with them, and Mr. Aldridge agreed. Erica doubted very seriously that anything untoward would happen now, especially since Gareth's secret contact informed him that the order to harm Erica had been rescinded. Still, everyone insisted upon caution, and Erica felt no need to contradict.

Work on the new residence moved forward at a pace that everyone called astonishing, now that she and Jacob checked their progress daily. Erica then returned home and tended the embassy's books. Now that matters had been entered in an orderly fashion, her work scarcely required an hour each day. Occasionally Jacob would join her so that someone else became familiar with the work. Once, Samuel Aldridge sat through an explanation, though Erica had the distinct impression the man did so merely to show how much he valued her services. She early on had discovered Samuel Aldridge truly had no head whatsoever for figures.

Their midday meal became a delight. The baby knew Erica now and loved nothing more than to be bounced upon her knee while Lavinia prepared the baby's plate. Abbie pretended not to care that Erica gave precious time to her brother. Once the infant was being fed, however, Abbie would recount her lessons of the morning and bombard them all with questions. Erica found her heart expanding on a daily basis, just to make sufficient room for the affection she held for this family.

Sunday they went back to the Audley Street Chapel. Erica knew a number of the parishioners now. And even more knew about her writing the pamphlet. There were almost as many greetings cast her way as to Mr. Aldridge.

Afternoons Daniel arrived and accompanied her back to the Wilberforce residence at Kensington Gore. Gareth was making steady progress, enough such that he was seated most days at a downstairs table, working on his next pamphlet. Most of Erica's own time was given over to what she did best, which was making sense of a vastly complex set of books. A second hospital was being erected south of the river, where no one would ever be turned away for lack of funds. What was more, a new project had been started in Manchester, one designed to aid both the families who had suffered in the demonstration and the larger body of poor as well. Subscriptions were being taken from friends and allies all over the nation. Erica's help was desperately needed. Anne Crowley proved a great help in drawing the required information from a wide variety of sources.

But her most cherished moments were those spent with Gareth. For hours they wandered isolated wooded paths behind the manor, times so precious she could not bring herself to mention them to anyone, not even Lavinia.

Erica wrote her mother three separate letters, each a day apart. The first one was by far the hardest, for it was necessary to recount all that had transpired with Gareth, all that she had withheld speaking of before now, all that Gareth had come to mean. The letter ran to seven pages and took until well after midnight to complete. The second and third were far easier, the words almost flowing of their own accord. For she was now free to describe the man she had come to care so deeply for with no reservation. She did not allow herself to think further than that, for the uncertainties of the future held far more questions than answers. One letter was given over to describing her work on the pamphlets and the lessons of faith Gareth had inspired, and through him the connections to William Wilberforce. The other was about Gareth the man. She was flushed and breathless by the time she finished penning these words, and surprised at her own frankness. But the letter had to be written.

She was in the process of helping Gareth into his coat for just such an afternoon stroll when the messenger arrived. She heard a voice call from the front foyer, "I seek Miss Erica Langston!"

"It's all right." Erica recognized the gentleman as a clerk in Mr. Richmond's office. Which could mean only one thing. Her hands clasped firmly together of their own accord. "Yes, please, what is it you wish?"

"Mr. Richmond's compliments, miss. He regrets that an urgent matter at court keeps him from delivering the news himself."

Gareth moved up beside her. "Out with it, my man!" he directed.

But the clerk was not to be hurried. "He sends you his most sincere compliments, miss. And specifically instructed me to say that he counts your performance of the other day to be one of his fondest professional memories. He asked that I stress that word, Miss Langston. *Professional*."

"Please thank the good gentleman," she said, holding to an outward calm. "I remain most grateful for his support, then and now."

The clerk gave a stiff little bow and delivered news that caused his features to flush with pleasure. "Mr. Richmond instructs me to inform you, miss, that payment from Bartholomew's Bank has been received."

Erica felt Gareth's hand supporting her arm. "What—what are you saying?"

"Paid in full," the clerk announced, obviously trying to hold back a smile.

Strangely enough, it was Gareth who she heard draw in a deep breath and who reached for the wall. "You're certain of this? There can be no mistake?"

"None whatsoever, sir."

Erica managed a swallow. "Paid in full, did you say?"

"And in gold," the clerk said. "Mr. Richmond thought you would want to know immediately."

"Mr. Richmond is most kind." Erica looked up at Gareth, then back to the messenger. "Please, excuse me. I—I must have some time—"

"Yes, most certainly, miss."

"You will thank Mr. Richmond for me?"

The clerk was grinning broadly now. "He was most distressed not to be able to tell you himself, my lady. I am ordered to return and give him the fullest possible report."

"Off with you, then, my good man," Gareth answered for her. "And add my own thanks to those of Miss Langston. Come along, my dear. Let us take a turn through the garden."

Erica and Gareth walked twice around the garden. Erica could feel that he had something he wished to say. But she was grateful for his silence. She had some difficulty fitting her mind around what had just occurred, much less making room for anything else.

How long had she been after this moment? How long had she dreamed and struggled and worked? The answer was simple. Ever since her father died and the family responsibilities, complex as they were, had fallen on her. Her sorrow, her frustration, her anger at the injustice of it all, and her long journey to this point flashed through her mind in a moment. Now here it was. And what did she feel? Exultation? Vindication? Relief? The answer was clear. She felt nothing at all.

"Gareth," she began slowly, her voice sounding almost foreign to her own ears.

"Yes, Erica?"

"I would like to give one-tenth of the sum to Mr. Wilberforce's new project in Manchester."

He slowed their pace and turned to look into her face. "Are you quite sure?"

"I feel an urge to begin with this gesture, this tithe if you will. It is nothing, really. All of this is God's doing, and I'm sure He will direct the Langston family in the use of the money." She stopped to return his gaze, looking steadily into his eyes. "But this payment is only a small part of our Lord's guidance, I am thinking. My coming to England, our meeting, the important people and work to which you have introduced me—these are pieces in a painting I have not yet seen in its entirety."

"Yes, I too am coming to realize that. But—"

"I know my mother would be in full agreement in making this contribution. I know it."

Tears filled her eyes, and she looked away.

"What is the matter, my dearest?"

"Nothing. Everything." She was overcome with a sudden sense of longing for her family. Yet at the same time there was nowhere else she wished to be than here beside this man. She took a deep breath. "Gareth, I have never properly thanked you."

"There is no need."

"What I am feeling goes beyond mere gratitude," Erica continued as though he had not spoken. "I have come to hold you in the deepest affection."

Her voice was so low Gareth bent toward her to hear the words. His grip upon her arm strengthened. "My dear, sweet Erica."

"You are without question the finest man I have ever met." Her lips trembled with the strength of her emotions. "I spend my mornings awaiting the moment I can come and be here with you. The thought of being away from you for a day, a week, it tears at me. And yet, and yet . . ."

Gareth did not respond for a moment, then said gently,

"You must go home to America. You must deliver this news and these funds in person and see how your family fares."

"Why must there be such heartache at this time when what I came for . . . ?" She could not finish the question as she looked through tear-blurred eyes into his face.

"I also have a question which presses at my heart." Gently he touched her wet cheek. "Why have I waited so long to tell you how my heart is filled with love for you?"

"Love," she repeated softly.

"Yes, love. Love and more love. Such a simple word and so hard to say. I love you. It is said."

Erica's heart was so full she could not speak for a moment.

"Oh, Gareth. Your words give me such joy—and such pain. You have your work here, your calling. And I must return home. What else can either of us do?"

Chapter 33

Erica began the journey back to America in a routine almost identical to her first voyage. Almost, but not quite.

Daybreak was a soft velvet sheen painted upon the rolling waves. The land birds that had followed them up to the previous evening were gone now. The ship was making good time, cleaving great troughs in the frothy sea. A freshening wind snapped the sails taut and caused the halyards to hum with anticipation. The ship's captain roared a command from his quarterdeck, sending the crewmen aloft. Erica kept her back to the ship's frantic activity. Beyond the rail stretched an endless shifting vista of dawn-flecked sea. She could almost shut out the ship's clamor entirely and give herself over to a whirl of thoughts within.

Today being Sunday, those crew members not tending the sails were on their hands and knees holystoning the deck. Soon enough the Sabbath routine, the first of this voyage, would ensue. A sail would be rigged as temporary cover over the middle deck. Benches and chairs would be arrayed. Most of the passengers belonged to three Dissenter congregations off to begin new lives in America. The senior pastor, Mr. Wainwright, would lead the service. There would be singing. And a fine sense of communion.

All this would be followed by the week's best meal. Since they had just set off from England, there were still fresh vegetables and a capon already set to stew. She remembered that in a few weeks they would be down to salted beef with a new barrel opened each Sunday, and hardtack for bread, and for dessert tiny apples tasting of the brine in which they had been stored. This time, Erica was the experienced traveler. So much had changed since her voyage to England. Including her own cabin topside, which she deeply appreciated.

She cherished these quiet dawn moments, watching for that glorious moment when the sun's intense glow first appeared on the horizon between sea and sky.

Gradually the daylight strengthened. The ship's din increased behind her. Still Erica remained as she was, reluctant to give in and let the new day take over her time and attention.

"Erica?" Mrs. Wainwright, the senior pastor's wife, inserted herself into Erica's reverie. Mrs. Wainwright was friends with members of the Audley Street community and had been introduced to Erica by mutual friends before the ship sailed. Erica was relieved to have found a chaperone for the voyage on short notice. Despite the fact that Mrs. Wainwright had never set foot on a ship before, she had decided Erica needed even more than a chaperone. "Child, you have missed breakfast entirely."

"Good day, ma'am. Thank you, but I was not hungry."

"Stuff and nonsense. Whatever would your good mother think of me if I let you waste away on your journey home?"

"She would offer her heartfelt thanks for being such a friend and companion. As do I."

Mrs. Wainwright came to stand at the rail beside Erica. "Never in a hundred lifetimes did I ever expect to be making such a journey."

"Yes, I'm sure it seems daunting. But you are up to the challenges. Of that I have no doubt."

"It's not me I'm worried about." Mrs. Wainwright was a plumpish woman whose black dress was rimmed at neck and wrists with starched white lace. "But my grandchildren need a godly home. And the other young ones of our flock who are immigrating to the New World."

"Of course you are right."

"Now, you stay put while I see if I can rustle you up a bowl of porridge." Mrs. Wainwright patted Erica's hand.

"It's really not necessary, ma'am."

"None of that, child. They've cleaned things up in the hold to make room for Sabbath preparations. But I'm sure the cook can find us a last bit of gruel to keep body and soul together."

"You are so very kind, Mrs. Wainwright."

"Well, now, I'm usually thought of as more nosy than kind. But let me go see if there's any—"

"All the porridge is gone, I'm afraid, Mrs. Wainwright. The children have spooned out the last straight from the pot."

To Erica's ear, it was the most welcome voice in the world, belonging to the finest man. As she turned she felt an inner shiver go through her just like the halyards in the wind. "Good morning, Gareth."

"I brought you the last of the tea and persuaded Cook to part with some of the bread meant for our supper." He gave her a warm smile. "How long have you been up on deck?"

"Hours and hours, I'm sure," Mrs. Wainwright offered. "Her face has gone quite rosy in this wind."

The older woman must have realized neither of them was paying her any mind at all. She gave a slight cough to hide her chuckle and said, "I'll just go make sure the grandchildren are scrubbed up proper for the morning service and . . . Yes, well, until later, then."

"You look most delightful this morning, Erica."

She turned to face him with an answering smile, desiring with all her heart to tell him what their hurried farewells had suppressed. All their preparations for departure had been compressed into just three short days; a ship bound for the Chesapeake had been berthed at London's Thameside port, and berths had still been available.

How Gareth came to be standing there at all remained something Erica could scarcely comprehend. Her mind went back to that momentous day, back when Mr. Wilberforce had ushered them into his study. With his keen insight, the gentleman had clearly seen how their hearts twisted in bittersweet anguish over a love acknowledged but an ocean that soon would separate them.

Yet still he had greeted them with great good cheer. Then he had ordered them to make this journey together.

"This is without a doubt a divinely fortuitous event," he had announced to their utter astonishment. "The Americans are fighting their own struggle against the evils of slavery. I see the both of you greatly aiding our American brethren in this valiant quest."

Wilberforce had pointed out that Gareth had an able staff who had already shown themselves capable of carrying on without his direct supervision. Besides which, a sea voyage would do Gareth wonders, forcing him to rest further and recover his full health. He could travel with his portable writing desk and work through a multitude of ideas. And that was that, said the gentleman who had become spiritual mentor to them both.

William Wilberforce had then joined the two of them on their knees. He committed them and their journey to the Father's care and commissioned them for this new mission.

"And of course I am not expecting to give you up permanently," he had said in parting, embracing them each in turn. "The Lord may indeed have more for both of you to accomplish here in England, somewhere down the road."

Erica was now smiling at Gareth over the rim of her mug. "Thank you very much for this. It warms my heart and my hands."

He wrapped his hands over hers as they circled the mug.

"How did you rest?" she asked.

"Well enough, for being crammed into a too-small bunk

with neighbors who brayed like donkeys all night." His smile captured the rising sun.

She finished the bread, drank the last of her tea, and set the mug aside. "I've been thinking."

"Aye, I've seen you at the railing for hours on end."

They both turned once more to gaze out over the unending expanse of waves. "Do you miss your men?" she wondered.

"I suppose I do. They're the closest thing to a family I have."

"Are you glad you are here?"

He looked down at her, his smile gone and a most serious expression on his face. "Absolutely, Erica. I have no doubt. Not in the slightest."

"Thank you, dearest. Thank you." She then looked up at him with a playful smile. "This must mean you are glad I have accepted your proposal of marriage."

He quickly looked around the deck, then gathered her into his arms. His "Yes" was in his kiss.

As though in divine blessing, the ship's bell rang out and the pastor's voice wafted up to them in a voice as clear as the day itself. "Let us all gather and give glory to God!"

Book Two/HEIRS OF ACADIA
THE INNOCENT LIBERTINE
She vowed to be a voice for the oppressed,
but some are seeking her silence. . . .

Abbie Aldridge has grown from a precocious girl into an impulsive young woman. The swirl of political and social life at the American Embassy in London has exposed her to everything from the splendor of royal courts to the squalor of working-class hovels. The more she sees, the more outraged she becomes over the chasm between her Christian ideals and the plight of the poor.

Abbie's passion tends to move her from first impression to instant action, often without reflection. And so it is that a well-intentioned afternoon of Bible study with the actresses at the Drury Lane theatre ends in disaster. Court officials, under pressure from moral reformers, choose that day to stage a raid on the premises. In the sweep of arrests of gamblers and swindlers and harlots and panderers, Abbie finds herself in jail, branded a libertine.

The scandal echoes through diplomatic circles and her family's Christian community. Of course, her parents trust Abbie's explanation. But when a dowager countess offers to escort Abbie to America for a period of respite, they readily agree. Perhaps then the worst of the rumors would ease, and Abbie could restore her reputation and her marriageable status.

Abbie embarks on the journey, looking forward to a reunion with Erica and her husband, Gareth. Abbie has long admired their work toward the abolition of slavery and hopes she can be of some help. She is also drawn to stories about spiritual revival on the American frontier. But no one suspects the true motivations of the countess, and the twists and turns of coming months reveal a struggle between the darker powers and God's providence. The broad expanse of the American landscape—and an encounter with a brilliant young scholar—opens Abbie's heart to a new understanding of her strengths, her failings, and her divine purpose.

Watch for this next story
on your book retailers' shelves
next September!